REST IN PIECES

BARBIE THE VAMPIRE HUNTER BOOK ONE

LUCINDA DARK

Cover Design by Covers by Christian

Bottom line is, even if you see 'em coming, you're not ready for the big moments. No one asks for their life to change, not really. But it does. So what are we, helpless? Puppets? No. The big moments are gonna come. You can't help that. It's what you do afterwards that counts. That's when you find out who you are.

JOSS WHEDON

ACKNOWLEDGMENTS

As always, I want to take a moment to show my appreciation for all of the people who worked with me on this new series. A lot of people might think that a book's creation belongs to its author, but it doesn't. I'm not the only one who has worked hard to turn this story into something beautiful, wild, and enticing.

So, without further ado, I'd like to give praise where praise is due. Thank you so much to Heather Long and Kristen Breanne, two of the most amazing editors I've ever had the pleasure of working with. You ladies light a fire under my ass and always make me strive to be better. Thank you to Ellen, my wonderful proofreader. To the betas—Angela, Anna, Sue, and Sam—who were so wonderful and willing to give Barbie a chance.

Special thanks and appreciation goes to Jenna Lee, who has supported Barbie from the very beginning. You've been a wonderful friend to me, and I cannot thank you enough. Thank you to the real Beth and Jon, two very good friends of mine. Thank you to my friends,

Desireé, Caitlyn, and Ashley. Without my friends, I don't know where I'd be. Probably typing away on a plastic keyboard in an insane asylum somewhere.

Finally, a last thanks. Thank you to everyone who has supported me thus far, both for this new project and for past ones. Thank you to everyone who has shown such excitement for this book and who has believed in me. I hope Barbie lives up to your hopes and dreams.

DEDICATION

To all the Barbie Girls out there. To the girls who are feisty and the ones that are not. To the girls who are strong and the ones that are vulnerable. To the girls who love black and the ones that love pink. The girls who talk and the ones that don't. No matter our preferences, we're all beautiful.
This one's for you.

ONE

BARBIE

LIFE'S A BITCH AND THEN YOU DIE.

I crumpled the remains of the surprisingly accurate fortune and popped the rest of the broken Chinese cookie into my mouth, chewing slowly as I stepped back and looked up at the massive side of Broadhaven's Church of Christ.

My fingers were already aching, and I hadn't even started yet. Stuffing the stupid slip of paper into the back pocket of my jeans, I sighed. None of the doors had been unlocked and while I was willing to do a lot of things in the name of my cause, breaking down the door of a church was not one of them. I was also pretty sure the thirteen-year-old pickpocket rooming with me at the Youth Home for the last three weeks was behind my missing lock picking set.

I reached up, stretching on my toes as my fingers closed over a brick and began the climb. As I scaled the side of the building, tightening my fingers around the uneven edges of the stone bricks jutting from the wall's

1

surface, I thought—not for the first time that night—how fucked up my life had become. Rather ironically, Ginger, the same thirteen-year-old pickpocket, had mockingly asked me to think *what would Jesus do* before I had snuck out of our cramped shoebox sized shared bedroom.

Never in my seventeen years on this Earth had I ever actually considered the question: *What would Jesus do?* Whatever choices He'd make, though, I was pretty sure it wasn't this. I reached the edge of the windowsill, my fingers clamping down as I strained up—my pointed toes barely making contact with the small ledge I teetered on.

Please don't be locked. Please don't be locked. I repeated the silent mantra in my head as I reached for the edge of the window, and somehow, His Holy Grace must've been looking down on me with favor because the damn thing was not only unlocked—it had been left slightly ajar. Wedging my finger between the window screen and the pane, I shoved upward and gained a few inches.

Muscles straining and sweat coating my upper lip, I shoved again, earning a nearly inaudible squeak as it slid the rest of the way up. No matter how quiet the sound had been, however, I paused and glanced inside just to make sure I hadn't been discovered. No one appeared to be in the main hall of the cathedral. I sighed in relief and gripped the window as I leveraged myself up and inside, turning so that my legs dropped down first before the rest of my body.

I released the window and let my body fall, my feet smacking the cold hardwood floor behind a pillar. This wasn't the first time I had been in a church, but it certainly was the first time I had broken into one. The soft scent of smoke lingered in the air. At the altar, a row of candles was displayed for visiting members who might appear for a late night prayer. Though, how they'd enter when the doors had all been locked, I didn't know. Only two of the candles were still lit. A third had been mysteriously blown out—the tendrils of smoke curling above its still warm surface where the wax hadn't yet dried.

"I don't think you're supposed to be in here."

My heart nearly leapt out of my chest as I whirled in the direction of the unfamiliar voice, my hand going to the inside of my leather jacket and clamping around the handle of the dagger I kept there. I blinked. A short boy, not much younger than me, with a curly crop of carrot colored hair, stared at me with a perturbed frown. My fingers itched to withdraw the small dagger in my grasp, but I knew this boy wasn't a likely threat. The creatures I hunted couldn't enter a church. I slowly released the dagger and withdrew my hand from inside of my jacket.

"Who are you?" I demanded.

His frown deepened. "I'm Mitchell Callahan. Who are *you*?"

"A figment of your imagination," I replied.

His eyelashes fluttered. The frown remained. "I'm going to get Father Gabriel."

"Why?" I asked, straightening and taking a step back. "It probably wouldn't do to have him find out that you're seeing people that aren't really there."

3

His lips pursed. "Your voice echoes, you're here," he replied.

I turned towards the altar with a sigh. I just needed what I came for and then I could be gone as if I really were a figment of his imagination. "No, I'm not," I said.

When in doubt: deny, deny, deny.

"Yes, you are," he pressed, his voice growing thick with irritation.

I pulled out the empty bottles I stored in my jacket as I strode up the steps of the dais where the priest would have given his sermon had he been there and had the church actually been open. "Nope." I reached the basin of water in the center of the dais and paused for a moment, looking back. "Has this water been blessed by your priest?" I asked.

"Of course," he replied. "Why?"

"Because I need it," I said with a shrug and began to load up. As soon as one was full, I recapped it and started on the others.

"Why would a figment of my imagination need holy water?" the boy asked.

I flashed him a glance over my shoulder and asked another question, rather than answer his. "What are you doing in a church so late at night?"

He narrowed his caramel colored eyes at me. "I was helping Father Gabriel clear out the basement for a food drive. Why are *you*?"

In lieu of lying to him, I once again ignored the question. "Why only you?"

"It's not only me," the boy informed me, making my spine stiffen. "My whole family is here. They're downstairs with him. They sent me up to get something out of the car." He waited a moment as I recapped the second bottle. The weight of holy water in my jacket made me feel marginally better—like I'd wrapped myself in a security blanket. "Your turn," he said matter of factly.

I chuckled, turning towards him. I looked at him and then the front door. "You going to let me leave the easy way if I tell you?" I asked, spotting the key that dangled from a lanyard in his fist.

"Maybe," he replied, "if you don't steal anything."

"Only thing I'm stealing is the water," I said, lifting my hands in mock surrender as I descended the dais.

He rolled his eyes and with a huff turned and strode towards the door. "You can't steal holy water," he snapped over his shoulder. "It's just water. We give it away for free."

"Then no, I won't steal anything," I promised as I trailed after him—my gaze bouncing around, looking for shadows and things beyond them.

"You going to tell me why you want the water?" he asked as he stopped in front of the door and inserted the key.

I moved up behind him, my head canting down slightly. The top of his head barely came to my shoulder. *Had my brother ever been that small?* I wondered. Brandon had always seemed like a giant to me.

I reached past him and turned the key when he didn't make a move to do it himself, making the boy's back stiffen as I fingered the handle of the door. Leaning down, I gave him his wish. I gave him the truth.

"I'm hunting vampires and you shouldn't go out at night all by yourself."

Gripping the door handle, I opened the door and slid around the astonished boy. I disappeared into the darkening shadows of the church's parking lot. Sure enough, the kid probably thought I was some crazy lady who had broken in to steal free water. But maybe—just maybe—he might heed my words and his family wouldn't end up like mine.

Dead as doornails.

TWO

BARBIE

"Okay, I'm calling it," my social worker said with a sigh of frustration. "I think we're lost."

"Wow, genius. Took you a whole hour to figure that out. Must've set a record." I rolled my eyes and laid my head against the passenger side window as she shot me a dirty look.

Six months, I had lived just fine in the group home. The roommates had been crap. There had been absolutely no privacy, but there had also been no connections. Why my social worker thought it was necessary to stick me with some supposed godparents I had never met was beyond me.

"Can you at least try to be polite?" she asked.

"I could try," I offered, "but why be polite when I could be an asshole?"

"Of course," she griped. "You do it so well, after all."

"So proud you noticed," I deadpanned.

Terra Rhodes was at the threshold of middle age

and that meant she had a lot of internally suppressed rage—probably directed at her biological clock or the way society no longer considered her as young and beautiful as she once was. Add to the fact that she had to deal with 'grumpy' teenagers like me, as she liked to say, and she was a scant step or so away from unleashing all of that feminine fury at any given moment. Yet, I still couldn't help myself from provoking her, wondering what kind of cat-like ferocity she might release.

"This thing hates me," she complained, her fingers jamming at random buttons on the screen of her GPS. I eyed her from the side as she huffed and glared at the piece of technology as if it had greatly offended her.

"Could try charting the stars," I commented lightly. "Or maybe, go inside and *ask for directions*. Seriously? I thought only men hated asking for directions."

"We don't need directions," she insisted. "We've got this." Terra gestured to the ancient GPS.

I yawned and scooted down further in my seat. "Suit yourself then. If we make it there before I turn eighteen, wake me up and I'll get out."

"That's great. Very helpful, Barb."

My eyes shot open and I growled at her. "I hate that name."

"Oh, do you?" She hummed dryly. "Well, it's your name. I would've thought you'd be used to it by now. Seventeen years with it and all."

"Barbie. I like Barbie. Not Barb. Not Barbara. Not Berry. *Barbie.*"

She wrinkled her nose in distaste, but I didn't

comment. "Right, it must have slipped my mind. I'll remember next time," she said.

Maybe I would tattoo it on her forehead while she was sleeping, I silently considered. *Something to remember me by…*

"I think I've got it this time," Terra said as she clicked a button on the GPS and it recalculated our location. "Oh, it says we're right around the block."

Terra cranked the engine of her sedan and backed out of the convenience store parking lot she'd pulled into in order to let me run to the restroom. I hadn't needed to go to the bathroom. She just couldn't admit that she was a fucking techno-idiot, aka someone who couldn't properly work even the easiest of technology.

But this time, she was right. We were only a few streets away from the location she was taking me to. I was almost relieved when she pulled up to a white three-story house with four pillars lining the front porch. Those weren't marble, were they? I thought only rich people lived in houses made of marble.

"Um … Terra." I didn't want to sound weak or anything. I mean, hand me a gun and tell me to point and shoot, fine. Let me take a few blows to the head, all right. Roundhouse kick me in the gut? I could take it and come back swinging. But this … this was a whole world of difference. These people looked like they had money. Not pocket change kind of money, but like … someone might be related to royalty kind of money.

Terra shut off the car and turned to me, putting her serious face in place. I leaned back. "Okay, let's get this straight, Barbie," she started, using my name correctly. "It took a lot of tracking down to find your godparents.

We spoke with them over the phone and they agreed to take you in temporarily. Do you understand how important this is?"

I nodded slowly. I knew that these people were gonna give me a roof over my head for another year or so until I aged out of the system and had to hack it on my own. That was about it.

She must have sensed that and known that it wasn't enough—at least, not for her—because she sighed and reached for my hand. I pulled back before she could touch me and she froze. "Sorry," she mumbled, "habit."

I shrugged but tucked my hand under my thigh just in case she got the urge to reach for it again.

"Anyway," she began again, "it's important because they agreed to a *temporary* set up." She stressed that word. I still didn't get it. Yeah. I knew it was only temporary. A year or so was all I got. "They're giving you a chance—one that not a lot of kids in the system get."

I narrowed my eyes on her. "Not a kid," I snapped.

She waved my comment away. "If you mess this up, you could be sent back to me, do you want that?"

"Wait. What?" It was like she had slapped me with an ice cold bucket of water.

She nodded. "This isn't permanent," she repeated. "If something happens or they aren't sure if they can handle another…" She eyed me and I knew she was about to say something like 'child' or 'kid' again. I squeezed my other hand into a fist until my nails dug into the crevices of my palm. She coughed awkwardly. "They can send you back to social services. They're not adopting you, not yet. They're your godparents, but they haven't been in contact with your parents for a long time. Their existence is more of a technicality. They signed legal papers agreeing to be your guardians for the time being. We're lucky they're even giving you a chance, so don't mess this up. They do have a choice on whether or not they take you in. Just … try hard to get them to like you, Barbie," she finally said. "Things would go a lot easier if they did."

"For who?" I asked. "You or me?"

"Both of us, Barbie. For both of us."

We got out of Terra's crappy, gray sedan and met the couple that had walked out and now waited for us on the front porch. The woman was tall and slender with a series of freckles that ran down the bridge of her nose and spilled out onto her cheeks. From the way her hair was done to perfection—highlights in all the right places and not a strand out of place—I would have thought she'd find her freckles to be a flaw and try to hide them. But other than her hair, she seemed to be makeup free and comfortable. She wore loose silky looking pants and a floral blouse, while her husband—at least, I assumed he was her husband since he looked to be about the same age—was dressed in khakis and a blue polo.

"It's a pleasure to meet you, Mr. and Mrs. McKnight. I'm Terra, we spoke on the phone." Terra shook their hands before turning to me. "And this is Barbara Steele."

I shot her a nasty look.

"Hi, Barbara, it's lovely to meet you. My name's Elizabeth and this is my husband, Jonathan. It's been a long time since we've seen you." The woman stuck out her hand.

I stiffened and looked down at it. "Barbie," I said. I forced my arm to lift. I took the hand she offered, shook it once, and as soon as the tremors hit and my palm grew slick with sweat, I dropped it and backed away. "Nice to meet you, too," I muttered, forcing an uncomfortable smile.

If Mrs. McKnight noticed my aversion or the way I'd snatched my hand back as fast as I could, she didn't comment. Instead, she gestured towards the front door as she said, "Why don't we go inside and get acquainted?"

"I think that's a lovely idea," Terra said, nodding for me to go ahead.

With slow movements, I edged past them and entered the house. It was just as big on the inside as it was on the outside. The walls were a cream color, lined in ivory at the base and top. The floors were a dark mahogany hardwood. This house was already far nicer than anything I'd lived in, even when my parents had been alive. A minister and a historian couldn't afford something like this. I wondered how my godparents had even known my family much less been close enough to be there for my birth.

A wide staircase led up to the second floor. I tilted my head as Mrs. McKnight stopped at my side and directed her gaze towards the top of it. Twin orbs of burning autumn brown reflected cool disinterest. My lips parted as I took in the man at the edge of the top step. Tall, tan, with his hair shorn close to his scalp all around. He looked every inch a bad boy, except instead of the black t-shirt and shitkickers I expected a bad boy to wear, he was dressed in a football uniform of white and navy blue.

Suburbia. Where even the bad boys come with money and a football fetish.

"Maverick, why don't you come and meet Barbie?" Though she phrased it as a question, it was clear that she meant it as something else. An order.

Nonetheless, the guy descended the stairs, scowling my way as he skirted past us. "Can't," he barked over his shoulder as he moved towards the entryway, "I'm late for practice." I didn't miss the look that Mrs. McKnight shot her husband as the front door slammed behind him. Mr. McKnight shook his head.

"Sorry about him," Mrs. McKnight said, drawing Terra's and my attention. "He's been under a lot of pressure this year to bring home the championship. It's only a few weeks away now."

"No worries," Terra replied cheerfully. "Besides, I know how teenagers are." As if she couldn't help herself, her eyes flicked toward me and I mimicked the same scowl the guy had given me. Her lips twitched in amusement.

"Shall we head into the living room?" Mrs. McKnight asked.

"Lead the way," Terra replied. I followed as Mrs. McKnight led us into a lavish living room complete with an overstuffed couch and a matching chair and loveseat.

Popping my ass on a single chair so I wouldn't have to sit next to anyone else, I turned my face to the side and made a slow examination of the rest of the house. An older woman with olive toned skin and graying hair bustled through the open doorway, across the room, and into the kitchen.

Terra and the McKnights began discussing things like weather and the drive. It was just small talk. Assessing talk. Questions that should have already been answered—that probably had already been answered by tests, interviewers, other social workers, emails, and papers that the McKnights likely had to fill out before they had me shipped here. But small talk made them comfortable as they eased into what they were about to do—accept some strange girl into their home.

I sighed, zoning out as I propped an elbow up on the edge of the cushioned seat and let my chin drop to rest in my hand. Exhaustion pulled at my nerves, and somehow, it was even more tiring not letting it show. That little side trip to the church the night before had been worth it, but man was I beat.

My gaze drifted back to the group as Mrs. McKnight reached for the coffee table in front of her and flipped open a book. "—college roommates and you wouldn't believe the trouble we got into." My eyes widened as I realized how much of the conversation I'd missed because somehow the subject had turned from nonessential irritating small talk to talking about my parents. And they had pictures.

All of the warmth in the room disappeared and ice cold stones fell straight into my stomach as I caught a glimpse of the picture Mrs. McKnight turned Terra's way. It was my mom. A much younger version of my mom than I'd last seen, but I'd recognize her white-blonde hair anywhere. It was the same as my own.

"Oh, she's lovely," Terra said, sounding intrigued. "She looks just like—" Terra's face lifted and she paused. Something in my expression must have given me away because in the next breath she handed the photo back and changed the subject. "Thank you for showing me these." Her tone shifted, moving from conversational to all business, and I resisted the urge to thank her as she directed the McKnights' attention away from my parents. The one subject I couldn't stand anymore.

"I've already contacted the principal at Mav's school," Mrs. McKnight replied, shooting me a quick smile. One that I couldn't find the strength to return. Not when she was still holding the photo of my mom as she slipped it back into the album in her lap. "St. Marion Academy is one of the best schools in the state. They have advanced courses, beta clubs, great sports programs."

Terra nodded. "That sounds wonderful. I'm sure Barbie will fit right in, won't you, Barbie?" All eyes fell to me with the question.

I shrugged my response. "I guess so." *St. Marion Academy*, I thought. *Sounds like a school for rich pricks.* "Is it a Catholic school or something?"

"Oh, well no…" Mrs. McKnight trailed off, biting her lip. "It used to be a religious based private school, I think, back in the sixties. It's no longer like that now. St. Marion focuses primarily on education. It's got all of the resources a blossoming student might need." Mrs.

15

McKnight flashed me another mega-watt smile. "New schools always seem scary, but don't worry, I can take you for your first day. They give you a tour and everything. It's your junior year, right?"

"Sort of," I hedged, shifting uncomfortably.

When she frowned, Terra jumped in with an explanation. "It seems that Barbie's education was primarily … er, what I mean to say is that she was homeschooled. We've had her in the school system while she was at the group home—mostly self study. She hasn't been in a classroom yet. It took a while to determine where she is developmentally—but…" Terra looked back to me.

I sighed. "They had to put me through a bunch of stupid tests to figure out if I'm dumb or smart. Surprise, I'm smart." I paused. "Enough anyway. I've pretty much tested out of most of the upper level classes."

Terra shot me a look for my tone, but Mrs. McKnight didn't seem particularly offended. "That's right, I forgot Delvina went on to become a history professor. She probably had you doing a whole slew of academic work at home. So, would you be considered a senior then? You'll be in the same grade as Mav."

I ignored my mother's name as best I could. "Yeah, technically…" I replied.

"What else did you learn while you were home-schooled?" Mr. McKnight asked, speaking to me for the first time.

I met his soft brown eyes, similar to his son's. "My dad liked to work out and he taught me and Brandon how to shoot and box," I said, my tone stilted. "And with boxing, we practiced different martial arts."

It had been just fun for Brandon and me. Neither of us had ever thought we'd need that training, despite what our parents had claimed. We'd never seen the monsters they had warned us against and for most of our lives, they had been nothing more than shadows in the dark. That was … until those shadows had come into the light. Just for one night. And when they left again, my whole world had been painted in red.

Mr. McKnight's lips lifted into a smirk as his wife gasped, drawing me away from my morbid memories and grief stricken thoughts. "Your father gave you a gun?" She sounded absolutely horrified. I wondered what she would do if she knew why he gave me that gun. A gun that now sat somewhere under the burned rubble of my old house.

I shrugged again. "It's not a big deal."

Mrs. McKnight obviously didn't know what to say to that, but from the pallor of her face and the way she kept shaking her head in disbelief, I knew it wouldn't be likely she'd agree to take me gun shopping. Even though me having a gun would probably have made the both of us safer.

THREE

BARBIE

"Oh dear, is that the time?" Terra stood abruptly. "I'm so sorry, Mr. and Mrs. McKnight—"

"Please," Mrs. McKnight waved away her concern, "call me Beth."

"Well, thank you so much for having me, Beth," Terra said, "but I really must be going. I have to return the rental and catch my flight to—oh geez, has my watch stopped working?" Terra stopped and tapped against the screen of her techno-watch. It flickered for a moment before the screen went black. Her eyes widened.

I smirked. As much as it pained me to even silently admit it—her issues with technology were not always entirely her fault. In fact, I wouldn't have been surprised to find out she'd been cursed. Nothing ever seemed to work right for her.

"What time is it?" Terra whirled around and when she spotted a grandfather clock against the far back wall, her gasp choked in her throat. "I'm going to miss the flight!" Terra cried.

In almost no time at all, Terra had bustled towards the front door, her keys in hand as Mr. McKnight followed her out. I trailed after them absently and he helped me unload my bags—a worn backpack one of the older kids in my group home had given me and a black trash bag for the rest. It was only when I had the bag in my grasp that it truly hit me. I almost didn't realize what was happening until it was too late.

A tight feeling settled in my chest. Terra had been my one constant since my parents had died. Everyone else's faces had passed in and out, some staying days, some weeks, some even months, but none of them were as familiar as she was. And now she was leaving me on the doorstep of virtual strangers. I peeked up at Mr. McKnight as he walked back up the path with me. He was an average sized man, quiet, with soft brown eyes and a scruffy beard. He grunted as he reached for my backpack, but I held onto it. I didn't want to risk him finding the things I had in there.

Our gazes met and he nodded once, as if to tell me it was alright. I shook my head and with a sigh, he released it and continued into the house as his wife came out onto the porch. Mrs. McKnight put an arm around my back as she waved to Terra. My social worker paused, lifting her eyes to meet mine through the windshield. Something passed between us then. An understanding. I had her card in my backpack. I had her contact information and before we'd even gotten in the car to come here, she had told me that, no matter what, I was always welcome to call her if I was in trouble.

I nodded, letting her know I was going to be okay. If it was a lie or not, I wasn't sure. But it was the hope for now.

Terra Rhodes reversed out of the McKnight's driveway, and I winced when she nearly clipped their mailbox. But, thankfully, she swerved and avoided it at the last minute. I snorted. I'd bet anything in the world that she was cursing an embarrassed blue streak right about now. The sun began to set in the distance as the red glow of her taillights faded down the road.

It was always the plan for her to leave me behind, but for some reason, my chest ached with hollowness as if I were merely an empty trash bag blowing in the wind. Lost and bereft. I didn't want to admit that I was scared. That I hated the idea of being left here with these strangers. Alone. The truth was, whether I was left there or put in another group home somewhere else, I would always be alone. No one else knew what I knew and it was probably a hell of a lot better that way. If they knew, the world might literally turn into a bloodbath.

"Hey," Mrs. McKnight's voice filtered into my mind and I turned, glancing up at her pretty, smiling face as I stuffed my emotions down into a dark hole and covered them up with a placid smile. "Dinner should be ready soon. I think we're having Chicken Cordon Bleu tonight. It's one of Jon's favorites. I hope you like it."

I knew she was trying to be nice, but I honestly

didn't know what else to say except the truth. "I don't know," I said. "I've never had it."

"Oh, well, trying something new is always nice." She tried to sound enthusiastic, but I could sense the awkwardness by the strained, tightness of her voice. She reached for the front door and pushed it open further.

"Yeah," I lied, following her back into the house. She stepped to the side and let me enter. Something new wasn't always nice. Sometimes, something new was the result of losing something precious. But I didn't say that.

Mrs. McKnight took me up to the second floor, which was just as expansive as the first. It was bigger on the inside than what it had appeared from the front. As we walked, Mrs. McKnight prattled on, informing me that there were two separate home offices, a game room, and a formal dining room.

"We mostly just eat at the breakfast nook, though," Mrs. McKnight said as she passed through the hallway at the top of the stairs, stopping every so often to gesture and tell me which rooms were what. "That's the library," she said, causing my eyes to bulge.

They had a fucking library in their house? I thought. *What was this? Beauty and the Beast?* Then I recalled their son. I was no princess, but I suppose he was pretty beastly.

"Bathroom number two. The first is on the first floor," she announced. "This is mine and Jon's room." She popped the door open. It was as big as it was neat— as if someone had gone over it with a fine-toothed comb, looking for any hint of clutter or dust and removed it immediately. "We also keep a couple of guest bedrooms." She gestured to a pair of closed doors. "For when family comes to visit, or for when Mav has friends stay the night. Jon and I go into the city every other weekend for some *us* time." She sent me a bashful smile. "Keeps our marriage fresh, you know?" She paused, a pretty pink blush rising to her cheeks. "Anyway..." she continued on.

Even as I tried to memorize the path we took, the twists and turns and stairs and doors transformed the unfamiliar house into a labyrinth for an outsider like myself. I visually sought out any possible emergency exits, filing them away for the unfortunate—and hopefully unlikely—chance that I might need them. Doors leading into unknown rooms. Windows in the hallways —all possibilities.

We turned down another side hallway and stopped before two doors, each across from the other. One door was closed and the second hung open. It was that second one that caught my attention as I stepped into the doorway. Despite the fact that I could feel Mrs. McKnight's gaze on my face, I gaped. I knew she was assessing my reaction. It was ... pink. A whole lotta pink.

"What do you think?" she asked hesitantly.

"It's ... pretty," I said—for lack of a better word. I hated to admit it. It was better than my room at my parents' had been, and I frowned when I spotted my black trash bag full of shit on the bed. "So, I guess this is where I'll be bunking down." It wasn't a question, but she nodded as if it had been.

"Yes, it is. I thought you'd like the view from this one," she said, gesturing to the windows covered in gauzy curtains on either side of the bed. The big, queen sized bed with a pink coverlet and a white metal base and headboard.

I hesitated, but my curiosity was too much to contain. I moved into the room, dropping my backpack next to the trash bag as I stood in front of one of the windows and slid the curtains to the side.

The window looked out over their perfectly average backyard. There was an in-ground pool next to a stone patio, crisp green grass, and a shed set further back and half hidden by a few overgrown bushes. I knew that wasn't the view she was talking about though. It was the sight far beyond the yard that made my breath catch in my chest. There were sparse trees to disrupt the image. Instead, they seemed to frame the visage of the valley beyond. An actual motherfucking valley.

The house, I hadn't realized, was built into a hill— more like a veritable mountain, it seemed. Below, I could make out several more homes and my eyes widened. If I thought the McKnight's home was lavish, the homes in the valley appeared to be ten times as opulent. They weren't houses at all. They were mansions.

"I think you can see the school from here," Mrs. McKnight said as she stepped up to my back. I stiffened at the feel of her reaching past to take the curtain from my grasp with one hand as she pointed with the other. "There it is."

Forcing myself to relax, I followed the direction of her finger. The building she pointed to didn't look like much of a school. It looked like a miniature castle. At least three stories high, with rows of windows that spanned each level, the red brick building looked like it belonged in Victorian England. There was even a clock tower.

"Can you see the stadium behind it?" Mrs. McKnight shifted her finger. "It's newer," she explained. "They only built it in the last thirty years or so."

I could vaguely make out what looked to be stadium lights not far beyond the monstrosity that was the school. Her hand dropped away and I couldn't help the sigh of relief I let out when she took a step back. I turned to face her, coming to a halt at the soft sheen of unshed tears in her eyes.

I took a step back and bumped into the windowpane without even thinking, grimacing when she smiled at me and shook her head. "I'm not going to hug you, don't worry," she said quietly.

"Sorry," I said, "but yeah, no hugging is probably good. I'm not a touchy-feely kind of girl."

"When Terra and I spoke on the phone, she said you don't like being touched. I hope you don't mind me asking, but is it because of..." She trailed off, her features tightening. She wanted to ask, but she didn't want to finish the question herself.

Was it because of my parents' deaths?

I shrugged. Getting touched just made me feel like stabbing someone. There was nothing more to it.

She sighed, clasping her hands tightly in front of her. The movement made me frown. She seemed nervous, but what did she have to be nervous about? I was the stranger here. One phone call and she could send me packing. She had all the authority, while I had … I glanced to my backpack where it lay on the bed. I had whatever power I could scrounge up and hide away.

"Listen," she continued, "I really want you to like it here. I'm sure things are hard after … everything that's happened, but Delvina and I were close once. We fell out of contact and that's my fault, but I think she and your father and your brother would want you to be happy. Jon and I, we don't want you to be afraid to come to us about anything. We've always wanted more children, but it never happened." She cupped her clasped hands over her stomach, a sorrow in her tone that hurt my ears. "I hope you don't mind if we think of you as our own now, too, Barbie. We want this to be your home if you'll let it."

I bit down on my tongue, tasting copper in my mouth as I jerked my head in another nod. She looked like she wanted to say more but then thought better of it. She backed up, stopping in the doorway. "I'll have someone come let you know when dinner's ready," she said. "But don't feel like you have to come down. I know this is a lot to take in. You can stay up here and get unpacked if you want, and I can bring something up later. I'll drive you to school tomorrow to get your schedule and for the tour. You can ride with Mav until we get something else figured out. Fair warning, though, he goes in early for morning football practices."

"Thanks." I forced the word out and she shot me a grateful smile that I didn't understand. *Why would she feel grateful?* I didn't get the chance to ask, though, because she turned and left the room.

I waited a moment before deflating and sagging onto the mattress. The McKnights were as normal as a family could be. Mrs. McKnight was kind and caring. Her husband was quiet but no less attentive. I looked to my trash bag of clothes. *Man, this sucked balls,* I thought. The nicer they were, the more I might come to care for them, and really, that just wasn't going to work for me. I almost wished they had been shitty, terrible people. At least, then I wouldn't feel bad for what I had to do.

A sudden rush of memories assaulted me. Blood on the floor. Blood on my hands. A sword. Holy water. My mother's unseeing eyes staring up at me from where she lay next to the couch, her throat torn open.

I squeezed my eyes closed and pressed my palms against my sockets until it hurt. It would be a horrible shame if anything were to ever happen to the McKnights. I couldn't let my first mistake repeat itself. I had to protect them. And if that meant leaving when I turned eighteen, then it didn't matter what they wanted —even if they wanted to keep me and love me as if I were their own—I would do what needed doing. I would protect them from the monsters in the shadows and more than that, I would protect them from me. Because there was no doubt in my mind, those monsters that had ruined my life hadn't done so on a mere whim.

Someone had ordered the hit on my family, and I wouldn't rest until I found out exactly who the vampire named Arrius was.

FOUR

BARBIE

Mrs. McKnight—Beth, as she asked me to call her—drove me to St. Marion Academy the next day. I stood in the front office, staring at the white walls and checkered couches, trying to feel something other than bored. I'd never been to an actual school before, but somehow it wasn't as awe-inducing as I thought it would've been. The front office looked like the seating area for an expensive retail store. The couches and chairs were overstuffed. The paintings were in the strange unusually bland taste that showed up in all the professional offices, except these had been granted elaborate faux golden frames as if that somehow made them less boring.

While Beth stood at the counter talking with the secretary about the details she had already given her, I perused the reading collection on one of the side tables. Business magazines and Ivy League college pamphlets. I would just bet that all of the students here had bright futures. College. Boyfriends and girlfriends. Careers.

Marriages. It must have been nice to have your whole life ahead of you and no dark secrets to weigh you down.

My fist tightened and I pulled away without picking up one of the glossy booklets.

"Barbie?" Beth's voice drew me from my thoughts, and I stood abruptly as she gestured for me to step forward. "This is Pam Costella, Principal Miller's secretary. Pam, this is my goddaughter, Barbie."

"Hmmmm." The older woman tilted her glasses down and observed me, scanning me up and down with hawk-like scrutiny and frowned when I could tell she found me lacking. She looked from my scuffed sneakers to my ripped jeans straight out of a second hand store to the white t-shirt turned gray from age that sagged against my stomach. "I see." The woman turned her attention back to Beth. "And you're sure you want to put her in the advanced senior courses?"

I snorted, but Beth ignored it as she smiled back, either uncaring or unaware of the obvious doubt in the woman's voice. "Of course," she said. "Barbie's very smart. Her mother was a professor. She was taught by one of the brightest stars in my own college courses."

I shot her a look, but she was fixated on the secretary. Pam pursed her lips and switched her narrowed eyes to me once more before sighing and then returning her focus to the computer. Her slightly gnarled fingers flew across the keyboard at lightning speed. "I'll have her placed in advanced British Literature, Calculus Two, advanced World History, and advanced Chemistry," she said as if that was a big concession. I didn't quite care. It wasn't like I'd need anything this school could teach me. "That still leaves her with two open slots."

"What about study hall?" Beth suggested, looking to me for confirmation.

I shrugged. "Doesn't matter to me," I said.

"Hmmmmm." My gaze shot to the secretary once more.

"Something in your throat?" I asked pleasantly.

She narrowed her eyes on me, but before she could reply, Beth cut in. "What about one of the physical education classes?" Beth asked.

Pam nodded. "Yes, that'll do." She typed in the last class and then the whirring of the printer at her back started up. Ripping the paper from the machine as it spat it out, the secretary turned and slapped it on the countertop just as the door behind us opened. "Good," Pam said, nodding to whoever it was. I turned as a thin brunette with wide set eyes and slim cheeks stopped before the counter. "Mrs. McKnight, this is Janessa Bales, she's one of our student ambassadors. I've called her here to give the two of you a tour—"

"Oh, I won't need a tour," Beth said, interrupting the woman. "I've been all over this school for Mav's football games." She laughed, turning to me. "But you go on ahead with her, dear. I'll be in the car making some phone calls. Come out when you're done, and we'll go school clothes shopping."

"I don't need—" I started, but she wasn't listening to me.

"Thanks again, Pam!" she called back as she waved goodbye to the secretary and sailed out of the office.

I huffed out a breath. "Don't worry, I don't bite," the girl at my side said, sending me a polite smile.

"I should hope not," I replied. Because if she did, then I'd have to stake her.

She sent me an odd look but moved back to the door that Beth had exited. "So, where are you coming in from?" she asked as she led me down the front hallway.

"Nowhere special," I hedged.

"Are you Mrs. McKnight's niece or something?" she asked.

"Or something," I said with a tight smile as she gestured down a hallway.

She frowned and shook her head. "That's the freshman wing," she said, striding forward. "So, if you're not her niece, what are you?"

I lifted a brow and eyed her. "Does it matter?"

Her lips firmed and she turned away. It was clear, though, that I'd made my point. I didn't want to talk about myself and she didn't ask anymore throughout the tour.

I slowed to a stop as we passed by a wall of glass windows on the second floor. It looked like it led into the largest library I'd ever seen, even bigger than the ones I'd been to as a kid. "Do you want to take a look inside?" Janessa asked. I shrugged, but she went for the door anyway, holding it open for me. I passed through and glanced up, stopping between the book detectors when a shadow fell over me. I paused and so did the man trying to leave. Behind me, I heard Janessa squeak. "Oh, hi, Torin," she said, sighing.

I arched one brow as Janessa lifted a hand to her

hair and twirled a strand of it around one finger as she peeked up through her lashes. Turning back to the man she was obviously attracted to, I eyed him up and down. Wide shoulders, the scraped shadow of beard growth, and eyes the color of green electricity—almost neon in their brightness. His lips twitched into a smirk. Yeah, he was attractive. And that fact only made me frown harder.

"Hi, Jan, who's this?"

"Oh, this is Barbie." Janessa waved her hand at me. "She's new."

"Giving her the tour?" he asked.

"Yeah, would you like to join us?" She sounded breathless. I shot her an irritated glance.

Torin shook his head, but that smirk only lifted a bit more when he noticed my scowl. "Nah, I gotta head back to class. It was good seeing you though. Do you mind if I get through?"

"Oh, of course no—"

"Why don't you back up and let us through and then you can get out?" I asked.

"Barbie!" Janessa gasped.

I turned back. "What?"

Whatever she had been about to say, however, was cut off by Torin's dark chuckle. "Sure thing, *Barbie*."

I whipped my head around again and narrowed my eyes. He seemed amused as he stepped back and gestured grandly for us to come forward. I strode past, avoiding him when I stepped to the side and Janessa hurried up to my side, nearly plowing into me in her bid to get out of Torin's way as fast as she could.

"Sorry, Torin," she said, blushing.

"It's no problem." He shook his head.

Janessa giggled apprehensively and stayed nearby, suggesting that there was something else she wanted to ask and not a moment later, she proved my assumption correct. "Are you still having that party this Friday?"

It wasn't the question so much as his immediate physical response that confused me. Torin's lips pressed together sharply before he schooled his features into a polite facade. "Yeah, after the game. Are you coming?"

Whatever noise that escaped her lips must have given him the answer he needed—though I didn't know how he could have interpreted the high pitched sigh-gasp-squeak hybrid that escaped her—because he nodded. "Cool. I'll … ah … see you there." He started for the door again. As he went, our gazes met. A bolt of heat hit my nerve endings and sent boiling warmth down my spine. I tensed, waiting to see what he would do, wanting to know if he had felt the same.

But he did nothing. He didn't even pause as he strode out of the library and down the hallway without looking back. I stared after him, focusing hard and watching as the ripple of sunlight moved over his uncovered face and arms. Seeing that, I relaxed and turned away.

"Okay, so, first thing you definitely need to know," Janessa announced. "That guy—that's Torin Priest. And if you ever run into him again, you can't talk to him like that."

I tilted my head to the side, trying to figure out if she

was serious or not. From the set of her shoulders and the hands on her hips, she seemed perfectly resolute.

"Why not?"

Her mouth opened, but no words came out and she blinked a few times before shaking her head. "Because you just can't."

"If you don't give me a reason, then I'm just going to treat him like I would anyone else," I pointed out.

"He's not just 'anyone else,'" she said, lifting her fingers to emphasize her air quotes as she glared at me. "Torin Priest is richer than God. Well, his family is. And his sister is kind of scary. But he's like … The King of St. Marion. You don't want to get on his bad side."

"Why?" I asked again.

"Because he could ruin you," she snapped. "Just do yourself a favor and avoid him."

"You don't seem too keen on avoiding him," I said with a raised brow. In fact, she had looked ready to prostrate herself before him and kiss the tops of his worn boots. It was odd, he hadn't dressed like he was richer than God. He'd been dressed like an average person.

"Yeah, well, I'm smart enough to know how to handle someone like him," she replied, flipping her hair.

I bit back a laugh as she turned and started through the library. "Smart," I muttered. "Yeah, that's what that was."

If she heard me or didn't, she never replied and we finished up the rest of the tour rather quickly. Janessa led me back to the first floor of the building, pointed to a door that would lead me out into the parking lot where

Beth would be waiting, and then headed off to her next class with another flip of her hair.

Shaking my head, I pushed against the doors and headed out into the slightly chilled late autumn air. Beth was waiting in her white Range Rover just like she said she would be with a phone pressed to her ear and a tablet in her lap.

"Yes, I'll get that sent to the office later. Gotta go, my girl's back. I'll talk to you later, Joan. Thanks for taking care of that for me. Bye."

I hopped in and buckled my seatbelt as Beth reached forward and started the car. "How was it?" she asked.

I shrugged. "Fine. It's a school," I said absently.

"I thought we could go over to the outlet mall. They've got some good shops." She put the car in reverse.

I rested my head back against the car seat. "I don't need clothes. I have enough."

After a moment, I noticed she hadn't backed up and I flicked a glance her way and widened my eyes. Beth had her fingers locked so tightly on the steering wheel that the skin over her knuckles was white. Her eyes flashed in desperate pain. "Barbie..." she started, swallowing around a thick throat. I stared at her in horror. Beth's eyes were misty as if she were on the verge of tears. I didn't know what I would do if she started crying.

"What?" I asked, hoping she'd take my fast reply as a signal to hold the tears at bay.

"I know," she said, "about what happened to your stuff." A buzz jackknifed through my spine. "Even if you were in foster care, the group home, for the last six months, they should've still given you as much time as you needed to gather your clothes before you left your home." I avoided her searching gaze, flipping my focus to the windshield. "But there was nothing left."

"Fine, we can go clothes shopping," I said, hoping against hope that she'd drop the subject. If she started crying, she'd have to lock me in the car to keep me there.

"A lot of people grow attached to their things. The clothes they wear. Their journals. Their books and games. There's so much you don't have now, and I want to give you a chance to find new things. Things that you can grow attached to again."

I closed my eyes with a grimace, but it only made the memories that much worse. They assaulted me from every angle. Flashes of a gas can in my hand, lighting the match that had burned down the only home I'd ever known along with the bodies of the three people who had loved me unconditionally—Mom, Dad, and Brandon.

"It's just stuff," I said uncomfortably.

"Jon told me I should wait," Beth admitted quietly, "but I can't. Barbie, it's okay if you want to see someone about everything you've endured. I know you're short with me because you're uncomfortable. I know you're scared, but there's no reason for you to be."

"I'm not scared." It wasn't a lie. I really wasn't scared. In fact, I doubted anything would ever scare me again. I'd faced my greatest fear—losing my family— and come out on the other side. And though I wouldn't call what I did *living*, I had to admit that my heart was still beating and blood still pumped through my veins. That night had been the worst of my life and perhaps it might have destroyed me had it not also given me a purpose to continue on.

I let my eyes glide open once more. "I'm really fine, Beth," I replied, my voice odd to my own ears. It was as though the words were spoken by someone else. I couldn't feel any emotion on my face, but my voice sounded content and gratified when I knew I was anything but. "I appreciate all that you're doing for me, and I'm happy to go clothes shopping. I'm just not used to the attention anymore."

"Oh, honey." Beth's hands left the steering wheel and I didn't move when she leaned over and wrapped me in an awkward hug. She buried her face against my shoulder and sniffled. "It's going to be okay now, Barbie. Jon and I are here for you. No matter what."

Lifting a hand, I awkwardly patted her back, wishing I was anywhere else but there. In fact, I wished vampires could walk around in the daylight. I might have given anything to be attacked by one just then.

I took a breath. "It's over," I heard myself say. "The past is the past."

And yeah, I'd been the one to set it aflame.

FIVE

BARBIE

Six months earlier...

I crept up the sidewalk along the front of the tan bungalow my parents had owned since I was a child, waving as my neighbor's boyfriend pulled away from the curb. I was grateful to Hannah; without her, I'd never get to leave the house and go do normal teenage stuff, and her having a boyfriend with a car certainly made things easier—things like going to a party and meeting Travis.

I sighed. Travis was hotter than any guy I'd seen on TV. He'd probably be right at home in a superhero movie. His shoulders were wide enough. I couldn't wait to get inside and reminisce about how wonderful tonight had been. Even if Travis hadn't kissed me, I'd spent all night hanging out with him and his friend, Kent.

"Hey."

The jarring masculine voice startled me so badly as I strode up the front walkway towards my front door that my shoe caught on the edge of an uneven stone and I nearly went down. Righting myself at the last moment, I swallowed the scream that nearly erupted from my throat and whirled around. "Oh, my God!" I snapped, gasping as I pressed a hand to my chest before blinking into the darkness of night. "Travis?" Think about him and the man appeared. I gaped at him in bewilderment, but there he stood with one hand raised and the other tucked into the front pocket of his jeans. "What are you doing here?"

He smirked, one corner of his mouth lifting and accentuating the hard firmness of his jaw as he dropped his arm. I bit my lip and straightened fully. God, I hoped he hadn't seen me stumble like that, but knowing my luck he probably had. "I just wanted to make sure you got home alright," he said.

"You didn't have to do that." I grinned anyway. "I'm perfectly capable of getting home on my own."

He laughed lightly. "Oh, believe me, it wasn't completely altruistic," he replied, shaking his head as he moved closer. He looked down at me, eyes sharpening. They were the clearest blue I'd ever seen in my life. "One of the guys told me you lived next to Hannah; I got your address from her. I hope that's okay. I never got your phone number."

"I-I don't have a cell phone," I admitted, embarrassed. My parents would never let me and Brandon out after dark unless we snuck out, there was no way in hell they'd let us have cell phones.

"That's too bad," he replied, "because I think you'd be a lot of fun to play with."

I blinked. Had his eyes changed colors? They were swirling, beautiful gemstones turning from the light sapphire that they usually were to an illuminating ruby. I was transfixed by them. I couldn't look away. The longer I stared at them, the more relaxed I felt. As if all my cares in the world were drifting away.

"Why don't you invite me in?" he asked, reaching up to brush my hair back over my shoulder, exposing my throat to his view. His smile widened, his canine incisors peeking out over his bottom lip.

"I—my parents don't let anyone come over after dark," I said absently. For the life of me, though, I couldn't remember why.

"It'll be alright," he insisted. "I just want to meet them."

They wouldn't want that. I understood that logically, but Travis' voice was so entrancing, it lulled me into a soft cushion of security. Why wouldn't my parents want to meet Travis? He was beautiful, kind, and he had come all this way just to make sure I was safe.

I turned towards the front door, reaching for my keys and pulling them out of my dress pocket. I knew if my parents found out that I had snuck out to go to a party, they'd be furious. I'd be grounded for an eternity, but it was as though my movements were no longer my own. I slid the key into the lock and turned it. Lights flickered on inside.

"They're awake," I said. I should've been concerned about their impending wrath, I should have been panicking, but I was completely calm. It was as if I was walking through a dense fog in my mind. My movements were slow and sluggish.

Travis' hands touched my shoulders, clamping down hard until I knew from the pressure that it would bruise. And yet it didn't hurt. In fact, I couldn't feel anything anymore except the strange urge to do whatever he asked of me. His chest brushed my back as he leaned forward. His breath over the top of my ear. He never got the chance to say anything.

The door jerked open, and I looked up in a daze. My mother stood there, her wide-eyed fury turning to terror at the sight of Travis standing at my back—his red eyes glowing in the darkness. "Invite me in," Travis whispered the order and in the next breath, despite my mother already reaching for me, shaking her head and mouthing 'no' before the word could escape her lips, I did.

Travis' fingers left my arms as I was dropped unceremoniously—shoved aside into the foyer of my own house. A dark shape whipped past me. My keys dangled in the lock, forgotten. My ears popped and sound rushed in, nearly making me cry out in pain. Cupping my hands over the sides of my head, I looked up and froze.

"M-mom?"

Her eyes were glassy, tears streaking her cheeks, as she whimpered under the ministrations of the man over her. Travis leaned down, his mouth sealed to her throat and beneath that, blood ran in rivulets over her chest, drenching the soft floral t-shirt she had worn to bed earlier that night. The stain spread even as the blood dripped down further, slipping from the skin of her neck to land against the pale cream carpet of the living room floor.

"Vina?" I looked up as my Dad came down the stairs. He met my gaze. "Barbie, what are you doing…" His question drifted off as he turned his head and locked on Mom's trapped form. "Delvina!"

I had never seen my dad move so quickly, not even in training. He bolted over the stairwell railing, landing in a crouch before Travis and my mom. I whimpered. The sound ricocheted through my skull, making the pain that much worse. Dad lashed out, striking at Travis, who dropped my mom and backed away with a wicked grin, his lips smeared with her blood.

Brandon appeared at the top of the stairs in his pajamas wiping the sleep from his eyes and my dad barked at him. "Brandon, get Barbie out of here!" he snapped, diving out of the way as Travis picked up the coffee table with one hand and swung it.

I gaped as Dad rounded, his fists drawn in. He took the stance of a warrior—long-honed in battle. I knew he was strong, talented—after all, he'd been the one to continually train Brandon and me, but never before had I seen him with the true intent to kill. My gaze flicked back to my mom. Her eyes had closed, and she'd gone unnaturally still. I took a step towards her. "Now!" Dad bellowed, jerking Brandon into action.

Brandon rushed down the stairs, yanking me up from the floor as he tried to shove me out the front door.

"But Mom," I said, pushing back, stumbling over my own two feet. "She's—"

"No, we've got to—" Brandon jerked to a halt and then whirled me around, shoving me behind him, halfway back through the doorway. Though he was only a year older, he was a full head taller than me and he blocked whoever it was that had startled him. I leaned around his side and spotted one of the guys that had been hanging out with Travis at the party, the one I'd spent the last several hours talking to along with Travis.

"Kent?" I stared at him as he offered me a wide, toothy grin. "What are you doing here?" I narrowed my eyes on his mouth. Something was wrong with his teeth. They looked sharper, his canines were extended just like Travis'.

"Just helping a friend out with a little task," Kent replied.

"Barbie..." Brandon took a step back, bumping into me doing the same.

"Brandon?" I sucked in a breath. "What's going on?"

"You should invite me in, Barbie," Kent suggested. And I don't know why, but that suddenly seemed like a good idea. I nodded my head like a puppet dancing on a string—mechanically and absently.

"No—" Brandon started.

Kent switched to him and focused his attention on my brother. "Would you like to do it then?" Kent tilted his head and grinned a toothy smile. "I think you do."

"You ... I ... no! I don't." Brandon sounded as though he were fighting something unseen. But it was no use. Just as I had wanted to invite Kent inside the house the very moment he had made the suggestion, so, too, did Brandon and after several seconds of Kent's invasive glare and Brandon's wavering words, he finally caved, each word painstakingly dragged out of him. "Please … come … in."

Kent's intensity lessened. "There now, that wasn't so hard, was it?" he asked.

My dad's agonized scream ripped me from the mist of confusion that clouded my thoughts, and I whirled back towards the front door. "Run, little rabbits. Maybe you'll actually get away," Kent said with a laugh, but I ignored him—I had no clue what he meant, anyway—as I dashed back into the house. I stumbled over something and went down hard, my knees smacking the floor so hard that my teeth clanked together. I tasted copper in my mouth.

Blood slicked across my palms as I slid into a puddle of blood on my hands and knees. My eyes lifted and caught. "Mom?" I reached up. Her throat was savaged, torn open. The blood loss had gotten worse. Her eyes were clouded over, no longer glassy but completely devoid of life. I could hear my breath in my own ears, pumping—overly loud. Was I really breathing that hard? Someone nearby laughed. The sound splintered in my head, coming from all sides and ricocheting back at me. I pressed my hands against her throat. I had to stop the bleeding. I had to or she'd die.

"Barbie, get out of here!"

I gasped as I was kicked back, my hands falling away from her. I landed on my side, tears ruining my vision as agony flared to life. My ribs … I pressed a wet hand to the sore area, leaving a bloody handprint against the fabric.

Someone jerked me up by my hair and my hands went immediately to the offending limbs as they yanked out several strands. I tried to ease the ache, acquiescing to the pulling tugs of Kent as he dragged me to the center of the living room.

"Bar ... bie ... run ... you have to ... run..."

I followed Brandon's voice and gasped at the sight. He was hunched over on his side, the burn of pain tight on his face as he tried to crawl towards me through the front door.

"Do be a good fellow there, Kent," Travis said with a dark chuckle. "Let our guest in and close the door. I wouldn't want any of their neighbors to catch wind of this. We've only been authorized to have fun with the one family tonight."

Kent dropped me against the floor by the couch and headed back for Brandon. I watched as he kicked my brother onto his side and further into the foyer before closing the door and locking it for good measure.

I panted against the pain in my side, flipping my attention to Travis. The moment I did, vomit rushed up my throat. I opened my mouth, but instead of regurgitated food, a scream ripped through the air. It was my scream. I was the one making all that noise. Travis winced and nearly dropped my dad.

"Shut her up!" he yelled over me.

Kent returned and grabbed me up, once more by my hair, before backhanding me so hard the skin of my cheek split. His eyes lit on the trickle of red liquid that escaped, sliding down to my chin. He licked his lips. My scream was abruptly cut off. I didn't even have the energy to reach for my throbbing face.

"Dad?" I cried. "Daddy?"

Travis laughed again and shook my Dad back and forth. "Is this who you're trying to talk to, Barbie?" he asked. "Shall I wake him up for you?" He slapped my dad once, twice, three times, but it did no good. I sobbed. His head was detached from his body. There was no waking him. I couldn't suck in enough air. There was blood everywhere. It soaked into the carpet—stained the couch fabric.

"Why?" My whisper was a barely audible croak as I wrapped my arms around my shoulders and cried.

"Arrius really thought he needed more for the Steeles?" Travis sounded befuddled and rather irritated. "This was easier than any of the others."

"The others didn't have brats," Kent said, shaking me as if that would stop my tears. I'd stopped feeling the pain from his grip on my hair as I stared at my father's unseeing eyes. "It's like they haven't even been trained."

Vampires … the blood. The beauty. The savagery. Everything clicked. All of the stories my parents had told me and Brandon. We never took them seriously. They weren't real. They were nightmares. Phantoms in the dark. But here they were. Far more real than either of us had imagined. They had been let into our home —*I* had let them in—and they had defiled everything we'd ever loved.

Beside my father's discarded body lay his prized scimitar. The curve of the blade peeking out on the other side of his chest and abdomen. That must have been what Travis used to behead him. I wept harder. It was his favorite weapon. He'd kept it displayed above the fireplace at Travis' back. Dad had only let me touch it once when he taught me what he deemed the most important lesson about wielding a weapon.

Never pick up a weapon you have no intention of using, Barbie. If you fight, you fight to protect, you fight to kill, or you don't fight at all.

His words returned to me, mocking my weakness as I stared, emptied of everything but dark, bone-wearying agony, into the macabre sight of my once peaceful living room. The walls were coated in my parents' blood—the blood of my family. My head wobbled back and forth and I realized it was because I was being shaken.

I didn't feel it at all.

Kent's face appeared before me and he scowled, flashing those white fangs of his. I couldn't even work up the energy to blink. All of those times my parents had warned me about going out after dark. All of those hours at the shooting range. The sword training. The martial arts. It had made me fit. It had given me an outlet for my frustrations with my parents.

They had never let us do anything we wanted. No parties. No friends. No school, even. Mom had promised that it was all overrated and that everything they did was to prepare and protect us. I had scoffed. Brandon had scoffed. Neither of us had believed a word they said. Every time they had told us no to things other people our age took for granted we had merely worked harder. Pushed all of our anger and frustrations into their stupid training—if only to keep from hating them—until our bodies were aching and sore.

I wished I had taken them seriously. *Why, oh why hadn't I ever taken them seriously? This couldn't be real. This couldn't actually be happening.*

"She's broken," Kent said, tossing me aside.

"Really?" Travis sounded put out. "That's too bad. I wanted some fun with her before we ended things. At least we still have the boy."

"Barbie!" Brandon's voice echoed in my head as I watched Travis toss aside my father's head. It fell with a hard thud and rolled across the carpet until it smacked against my legs. My cheeks were soaked in salt and grief. "Barbie, you have to get out. Please!"

Kent reached for Brandon and dragged him into my line of sight. "What should we start with?" he asked, excitement coloring his tone.

"Hmmmm." Travis easily pinned my struggling brother.

Why is this happening? I thought to myself. *Why me? Why us? Why was I letting it happen?*

"Barbie, get—ahhhh!" Brandon screamed as Travis took two of his fingers in his grip and bent them back until they cracked, leaving them set at an angle that was far from natural.

My gaze locked on the scimitar. I focused on it, willing my legs to move.

"Hungry?" Travis asked, looking to Kent.

"I thought you'd never ask." Kent struck, falling upon Brandon's throat like a beast of a lion upon a wounded gazelle.

Travis laughed, standing up and giving his friend room before turning his full attention to me. "Please," I whispered the plea through dry, cracked lips. "Stop this."

He tilted his head to the side and gestured for me to move closer. I shook my head and shrank back against the foot of the couch. Lifting a brow, he strode across the room and reached for me. I recoiled as his hands brushed against my skin. "Why don't we watch?" he asked, pressing a kiss to my cheek. I turned my head away from him and away from the scene before me. "No, no, no, dear. I said *watch*."

Travis' fingers locked onto my chin and forced my gaze to return to the sight before me. I whimpered. Brandon's struggles against Kent lessened. He couldn't even keep his eyes open anymore. They were mere slits, the light in them growing more and more dim as time crawled by. I thrust back against Travis, trying to throw him off of me, but he merely squeezed me tighter, pinning my arms to my sides until my chest felt like it might cave in, until I knew any tighter and he'd break my jaw.

"Why are you doing this?" I asked.

"Because"—I shuddered as his tongue licked up the side of my throat—"we're vampires and because we can, little bird."

Because they could. The thought echoed in my skull. Because they were stronger. Because they had the power to. Because they *were* vampires. Because vampires did whatever they wanted. Because no one had stopped them. Someone needed to stop them.

But there's no one else here … only me…

"This is so touching, isn't it?" Travis let out a forced sniffle. "The family that hunts together, dies together and all that, right?"

"I've never hunted before," I said. My cheeks were stiff with the drying tears, but somehow, no more fell from my eyes. It was as if I had cried myself out. There was no more weeping, no more sobbing. I'd had enough. I had none left to give.

"What's that?" Travis bellowed a laugh. "Did you hear that, Kent? She said she's never hunted before. That explains so much." His hand fell away from my face. But there wasn't much more to see. Brandon's eyes were closed and his breaths had slowed to barely a trickle, his chest rising and falling impossibly slow. "Did they not tell you about vampires?" Travis asked.

I shook my head. "They did," I answered. "We didn't believe them."

"Well…" He shoved me forward and I stumbled over my father's body, landing on my bruised ribs. A wince escaped as the fall sent a dull imitation of pain through me. "That is a *travis*-ty." He chuckled.

Kent lifted his head from Brandon's neck and groaned. "Seriously? I'm feeding here."

Enough. I've had enough. No more. I'd do anything to make it stop. To make it all stop.

My fingers brushed cool metal, and without thinking, I reacted, clasping tight around the scimitar's handle.

Never pick up a weapon you have no intention of using. If you fight, you fight to kill.

The words were my mantra as I swung the blade up and brought it down. The blade slipped right through the center of Kent's neck but stopped short. I could hear him spluttering, feeling the squelching around the sharp end of my sword. He reached up, trying to claw at the other end poking through his trachea. Rage filled me.

No, I thought. *He doesn't get to live. He doesn't* deserve *to live.*

Of all the things my parents had taught me, they had focused on the methods with which to kill a vampire the most. As a child, I'd relished in the idea of beating up make believe monsters. As a teenager, I'd grown annoyed by their adamant urgings. I channeled all of my guilt at never believing them into my current task. Bearing down, I gritted my teeth and turned the scimitar, forcing it the rest of the way through one half. His body flopped against the carpet. All of the blood he'd just drunk from Brandon spilling out onto the floor. I felt numb inside. The blood didn't scare me—not anymore.

Travis stared at me, dumbstruck. That much damage might wound a vampire, but it wouldn't kill a vampire, I knew. Dad had always said that to kill a vampire, you had to remove the head or stake the heart. But just running this creature through with my father's prized blade wouldn't do the trick either. It needed to be doused in holy water. I glanced to the side. The kitchen. Dad always kept vials of holy water there.

Before I could move, though, Travis was across the room, his hand snapping out, gripping my throat and throwing me against the wall, pinning me there like a butterfly under glass. Spots of black and white danced in front of my eyes before I managed to calm myself enough to focus.

"I guess you're not completely broken, are you?" His lips stretched into a sinister grin.

Growling, I thrust the curved blade through his stomach. I don't know what I had expected. Perhaps shock, a cry of pain. Something. *Anything.* But neither happened. Travis merely glanced down where the sword was lodged in his abdomen and then returned my gaze with a lifted brow. "Really?" He tsked. "Tell me that's not the best you can do."

I swung my legs up and kicked until the sword sank to the hilt and reached up, raking my hands down the skin of his arm. Travis didn't even blink. I was starting to find it difficult to breathe. It wasn't until a hand grasped at his ankle that he looked away.

Kent had half crawled, with his open wound bleeding all over the place, and now clutched at the bottom of Travis' leg, his pupils blown wide, the red irises huge. Bloodlust, I realized. Everything my parents had taught me, though I hadn't taken any of it seriously, was suddenly coming back to me. A vampire in need of blood would do almost anything to attain it. The pain so great and unbearable, it made them literally lose their minds until they quenched the thirst. Kent sank his teeth into Travis' leg and Travis grunted a curse, dropping me. I grabbed the blade and tore it out of his abdomen as I went down.

A rain of blood gushed from his side, spraying Kent's face and making him shake back and forth, tearing at the bite wound he'd already inflicted. I rolled away and leapt to my feet, bolting for the kitchen. There —right out in the open, sitting on the counter—were the holy water vials. I grabbed a handful, stuffed them in my pockets before uncorking one and dumping it on the end of my reddened blade.

The blood from both Kent and Travis immediately dried up and turned to ash.

"Wow…" I guess the legends were true.

"Fuck! Get off me, bastard!" Travis' shout had me working faster. I needed to end this quickly. Mom and Dad couldn't be helped, but Brandon … if he was still alive, I might be able to get him to a hospital.

Uncorking another vial, I dumped the new water on the scimitar. Now cleansed, I readied my resolve and hurried back to the living room. Travis had Kent up on his feet, holding him by the throat as the other man snarled and fought. Catapulting him back, I jumped forward and stabbed the sword through his chest. Right where his cold, dead, unfeeling heart would be.

On a choked sound, Kent's body dissolved and ash drifted down. I grimaced, tasting it in my mouth as it coated my whole body.

"Oh, you've definitely got some fight left in you," Travis growled, crouching as he held his hands out. I watched, transfixed as his nails lengthened. "Well then, little girl? Do you want to play a game?"

Sucking in a breath, I nodded. "Bring it on, asshole."

My father's teachings flowed through my limbs until my movements became second nature. I moved with a speed I didn't even know I possessed. I dodged. I struck.

Lopping off first one limb and relishing in the agonized scream Travis released as his arm fell, disintegrating into ash before it ever hit the floor. My anger pushed me further and further, taking over until I could have sworn it wasn't blood pumping through my veins, but white-hot fury.

The sight of my parents—like slaughtered lambs—lying limp and dead drove me to the darkest of places. I didn't care if Travis killed me. When he caught me against the wall, I shoved forward, not even blinking when my shoulder popped out of joint. It should have hurt. It *did* hurt. But it didn't matter. The only thing that mattered was killing him.

Vengeance. Revenge. Recompense.

Hatred. Loathing. A bitter dust on my tongue.

I struck, sending Travis' remaining arm flying somewhere else in the room. In the next breath, I took his left leg. Then his right. Until he was lying prone on the floor, unable to move. I stood over him, lifting my leg and bringing my foot down on one of his many open wounds.

"The man that put you up to this," I said. "What is his name?" I demanded.

Travis laughed, though instead of enticing as it had been at the party earlier, it now sounded cold. "Why do you want to know?"

I saw no reason to lie. "Because after I kill you, I'm going to find him and I'm going to kill him too."

Travis' chest shook beneath my foot. "That'll never happen. No one can kill Arrius, much less a child like you."

"Yet, I was able to kill you," I replied.

"You haven't killed me yet."

I didn't think. I didn't hesitate. I drove the end of my sword down until it cut through his chest, straight to his heart. His face froze for a split second before the pallor of his skin turned gray and his body began to sink in on itself as he became the perfect outline of a man that had once been, a pile of ash and a memory of destruction left in his wake.

"Yes," I whispered to the quiet room, "I have."

I took a step back, leaving the sword where it had struck the floor. It held there, sunk through the carpet to the hard floorboards underneath.

"Bar ... bie?"

I jolted, turning to gape as Brandon's eyelids cracked open. I nearly fell over as I rushed towards him. When I got to him, I did fall. I grabbed his hand and stared at his dull eyes. Shadows were cast beneath them. I tried to avoid looking at the horrid wound at his throat.

"Brandon? It's going to be okay," I said quickly. I needed to call an ambulance. I needed...

"Barbie, you have to run," he whispered.

"What?" I shook my head, but he didn't follow the movement. His eyes were open but he couldn't see. "No, Brandon. I have to call an ambulance. You're going to be okay. I'll be right back, I have to go get the phone."

"It's too late, Barbie. I'm ... sorry." His hand went limp in mine. I paused. But his eyes were still open. He was awake. He had to be. I shook him.

"Brandon?" His eyes stared up at the ceiling. "Brandon, you have to stay awake. Help is on the way. I just have to——" I cut myself off and scrambled back reaching for the house phone where it had fallen from its cradle during the fighting. I held it in my fist, the first two numbers punched in before I even realized the futility of it.

I sunk back against the wall, the phone clasped in my fist against my chest. He was right. It was too late. They were dead. All of them.

And it was my fault...

I couldn't remember how long I'd sat there, staring at their remains. The bodies that had once housed my family were nothing more than carcasses now. Empty shells. When I finally did manage to move, I stumbled up the stairs to my childhood bedroom.

I removed my soiled clothes, the holy water vials clinking as I dropped the party dress I'd been so excited to wear hours ago on the floor at the foot of my bed. I changed and grabbed a backpack. I filled it with the bare minimum of necessities, rummaging through the house like a thief in the night. I took holy water vials. I took daggers. I took a couple changes of clothes. I tucked them all neatly inside, along with pictures taken from my mom's photo albums and then I went to the garage.

I didn't know what I was looking for until I found it. A full can of gasoline in the back of my parents' black sedan. I took it out and walked back into the house.

It hurt. I couldn't take anything else with me. How would I explain that? There would be social workers after this, I realized. People. Questions. I'd wanted freedom from my family, the choice to go out after dark, to meet people, go to school, have friends.

In a twisted way, my wish had been granted.

I poured the gasoline over their bodies. Over the ash. Over the couch. Up the hall. Through the foyer. I stood at the front door and dropped the can to the side. My hands shook as I held up the matches I'd found in Dad's workbench. Where he'd spent hours sharpening his blades. Blades that I couldn't take with me.

Still, there were no more tears.

I didn't shed a single one as I lit the match, dropped it, and walked away.

The flames roared to life, eating away all of the evidence, but nothing could burn hot enough to ever wash away my sins. Nothing could ever erase the fact that had I followed my parents' orders, they might not have died. Brandon might not have died. Their blood was on my hands.

That had been the night I'd first killed a vampire, but it certainly wouldn't be the last.

SIX

BARBIE

I yanked my hair back and tied it up as I descended the stairs of the McKnight mansion. A yawn stretched my mouth the second I hit the ground floor. Seven was far too early for any sane person. My eyes burned from the long hours I'd spent devouring the articles and research information on the laptop Beth and Jon had given me. Unfortunately, all I'd managed to uncover was the location of a couple local churches where I could restock my holy water supply when it ran out. Nothing on where to get more untraceable weapons and once again, nothing on the mysterious Arrius.

"Oh good, you're up." I looked up, bleary eyed as Beth headed towards me—or rather, towards the front door that I stood in front of—with a travel mug of coffee in hand. "I've got to head to the office early," she said. "Mav'll be taking you to school until we can get you a car of your own."

"A car of my own?"

"He's leaving in the next fifteen minutes, though, and he's not a morning person. So, you might want to get a move on. I've asked him to wait for you, but really, he's quite grumpy in the mornings," she continued, hurrying to collect her coat and purse. "I'll be at the office until late too. Mav can give you a ride back after his football practice. First strings have both morning and afternoon practices." She paused and flipped her wrist to check her watch. "Oh, damn. I really do need to go. I'll see you tonight, Barbie!"

I blinked as she rushed through the front door and let it swing closed behind her. I took one look down at my pajamas and groaned. Maverick already didn't like me. I highly doubted he'd wait around for me to grab breakfast before it was time to go. I turned and rushed back up the stairs. His door opened as I headed for my bedroom.

"I'm about to—" he began, a grumpy growl in his tone.

"Your mom told me," I interrupted, sliding past.

The moment my bedroom door was closed, I flung off my pajamas and grabbed a pair of ripped jeans Beth had forced me to get yesterday and a v-necked t-shirt. I shoved the scant school supplies I had into my backpack over the dagger and one of the bottles of holy water. A few minutes later, I was back out the door and heading down to the kitchen once again.

Maverick was already there and fully dressed. He scowled at me as I entered. "Let's go," he snapped, carrying his own travel mug of coffee as he left the room. I looked to the now empty pot and held back a whimper. It was official. Maverick McKnight was a bastard.

In the car—which turned out to be a practically brand new souped up black truck with four doors and a step that I certainly needed just to get into the front seat —we both sat in tense silence. I dared not even reach for the radio just to have some sort of noise other than the sound of his grinding teeth and my slow, quiet breaths. The tension was palpable. I didn't know what his problem was, but I hoped he got it off his chest sooner rather than later.

When we pulled into the St. Marion Academy student parking lot, I was already unbuckling before he had even put the car in park. But as my hand gripped the door handle, Maverick hit the locks and gave me what I'd wished for. I froze. A new kind of tension crept up the back of my neck as I slowly turned back around and lifted a brow.

"If you're not quite sure how locks on cars work, I'm not sure about this arrangement with you driving me to school," I said when he still hadn't said anything. "The switch goes up to unlock and down to lock."

Maverick clenched his fists on the steering wheel, his jaw tight and his eyes boring holes into me. "I don't like you," he said.

"Really?" My lifted eyebrow remained right where it was. "Color me shocked." When he didn't say anything more, I sighed and dropped the eyebrow, choosing, instead, to purse my lips as I granted him my full attention. "Is there a reason you don't like me or is it just my mere existence that has so spoiled your obviously sterling personality?"

"Up until a few months ago, you didn't even exist," he snapped, releasing the steering wheel as he unclicked his seatbelt and rotated to face me fully.

"Uh, I beg to differ," I stated with a shake of my head. "I can assure you, I did, in fact, exist before a few months ago. In fact, I've existed for seventeen years. Just because you don't see something, doesn't mean it isn't there." *Wasn't that the damn truth?* I silently added. Oh, if only this muscle bound high school idiot knew the things I knew. "So, if that's your reason for dislike, I'm sorry to have to burst your entitled bubble of bullshit, but you need to find a new one. That isn't gonna cut it."

"Listen, I don't know who you are or what you're planning, but my parents have never mentioned a goddaughter. They never even mentioned your parents' names up until 'social services' called." I narrowed my eyes as he lifted his hands and air-quoted the 'social services' part. "My parents have money, and they're well meaning people too. I know what kind of snakes money attracts."

"Your mom has pictures of my parents," I said blandly. "From when they were in college. I don't know what you think—"

"I think you're scheming," he cut in. "But even if you're not, I don't know you and I don't trust you. I know what I've heard about foster kids."

I hid the wince easily enough, but it still stung. The

slight opened up a cavern of irritation that I hadn't known I felt until that moment. I let a calm mask descend over my expression as I let him have his say.

"And what, pray tell, have you heard?" I asked quietly.

"They lie, cheat, and steal. If you think you're going to worm your way into my parents' hearts just because they're fucking nice, don't think I'll let you get away with it."

"Awww, are you scared they'll love me more than you?" I couldn't help the dig, though I knew it was cruel. He was an asshole.

Maverick pointed his finger right in my face. "I'm watching you, *Barbie*," he spat my name like a curse. "If you try to steal from them, you'll be out the door so goddamn fast, you'll have burns on your ass from being kicked to the curb."

"For your information, *Maverick*," I said, using the same tone he'd used with my name, "I'm not here to find a new fucking family. I'm here because the government *put* me here. *Comprende*, dumbass? As a minor, I don't have much of a fucking choice."

"Choice or not." He shook his head and fixed me with an outright glare. "You will not fuck with me. You will not fuck with my parents. You will stay the hell out of my way and out of my fucking business. Do you *comprende*?"

"Duly noted," I replied dryly. "And since we're on the topic of discussion, let's make a deal—you and I." Before he could agree or not on any sort of deal, I continued. "You stay out of my fucking way and I won't kick your ass. And trust me, pretty boy, I may look smaller than you, but I would have you begging in a matter of seconds. If you don't like me now, wait until I unleash my inner bitch. Therefore, if you wish to remain breathing, I suggest you *back off*," I growled. "And in case you can't understand that, understand this"—I stopped and leaned forward, moving into his space until I could smell a hint of his spicy cologne —"thou shalt not try me. Do so at your own peril." He eyed me with no small amount of cold-blooded hatred. I didn't give much of a shit. I moved back once more and jerked the door handle. "Now unlock the fucking door, Deputy Maverick, or you'll see just what my inner bitch can do."

Watching me, Maverick reached behind him and unlocked the car. As he did so, he released a breath. "I think you're mistaken," he said. "Your bitch certainly isn't inside. She's right out there for everyone to see." The door was open and my feet were on the cold hard pavement in less than a second. I slammed the door behind me and turned towards the school.

I didn't give a shit what he thought, I decided. He could think whatever the hell he wanted. I wasn't here to play family. I wasn't here to steal his parents' affections or money—though considering how much money Beth had been able to spend on me the day before and not even bat an eyelash, it was obvious they were loaded … so, perhaps, he had some reason to be worried about them. They did seem the type of people to be willing to help out complete strangers. Hell, they took me in.

I resettled my backpack on my shoulder and headed into the school via the side entrance. It didn't matter if Maverick might have been an ass out of some unnecessary fear that I was using his family. He was still an ass and I wouldn't be around for long.

SEVEN

BARBIE

Between my lack of coffee and my rough morning with Maverick's sterling conversationalism, I decided that avoiding the general school populace—at least as much as I could for the day—was preferable as I holed myself up in the one place I knew well enough. The library.

Even though it was impossibly early to be in the school building, the librarian didn't bat an eyelash as I pushed through the doors. In fact, she didn't even concern herself enough to lift her head from her computer as she typed rapidly across her keyboard, her attention glued to the screen.

I ignored her presence as well as she ignored mine, snatching a book from one of the historical shelves and falling onto one of the lounge couches. I slid my backpack to the floor and cracked open the volume in my hands—an illustrated biography about Alexander the Great—as I tried to delve my mind into something other than my circumstances.

I tried, and I failed. Miserably.

Within minutes, I scoffed in disgust as I set the volume down on the end table. *Wasted rubbish,* I thought. My mom would have been appalled that the book had even been published much less that it was in a high school library. There were, to count, at least five inaccuracies within the first couple of chapters. No doubt there would have been more had I cared to continue reading.

I closed my eyes against the harsh fluorescent lighting of the room. Sleep was something I desperately needed, but even I knew well enough not to sleep out in the open. Not where I could be vulnerable. Sometimes, I missed the innocent days where I hadn't truly believed my parents' claims. I missed sleeping well at night. I missed closing my eyes and not seeing their faces staring back at me. As soon as that thought crept up, however, the image appeared.

With a scowl, my eyes popped open to dispel it and I nearly leapt from the couch when twin orbs of moss green hovered above me. "Can I help you?" I snapped, jerking up from the couch and whirling around.

How the hell had he snuck up on me? I thought, casting a glance to where the librarian had been minutes before. She was gone now, but I could still see her shadow move beyond the wall of windows just behind the counter where I suspected her office was.

Torin Priest stood just on the other side of the couch, a small wry grin on his lips as his eyes traveled the length of me, coming back to my face as his mouth stretched even wider. My scowl deepened. "You looked tired," he said, "but I didn't think you'd appreciate being caught sleeping here by Mrs. Bates. She doesn't take kindly to students who fall asleep on the library furniture. I was going to wake you up." He rounded the side of the couch, coming closer.

I shook my head, narrowing my glare on him. "Mrs. Who?"

Torin tipped his head back, gesturing lazily to the where the librarian moved about behind the shades that separated her from us. "Mrs. Bates," he repeated.

The intensity of my focus lessened as my brows furrowed. "I wasn't sleeping," I clarified. He leaned back on his heels with his hands stuffed, nonchalantly, into his front jeans pockets. I eyed him speculatively. When he didn't respond, I spoke again, unable to help myself from poking the proverbial bear. I didn't care what that girl, Janessa, had said. "Do you usually make a habit of watching people so closely?" I asked, waving a hand to the couch between us where—just moments before—I had been sitting.

He shrugs. "Not usually."

"Oh, so I'm special then?" I pursed my lips.

He chuckled and the sound rooted me to the spot. It was low and masculine, sliding over my ears like audible chocolate. My scowl returned full force even as he said, "Everyone's special in their own way. But no, it wasn't particularly because you were"—he eyed me with interest—"special," he finished.

Bending down, I retrieved my backpack and slung it over my shoulders. "Right." I took a step to the side, as far from him as I could get between the couch and the table. "Well, perhaps I should take my not-particularly-special ass elsewhere." I scooted by, our chests nearly touching. That same shock of electricity I felt near him before hit me square in the gut, bouncing around like a ball of energy beneath my skin until I clasped a hand over my abdomen, hoping to quell it. The scent of cool spice radiated off his skin, making my knuckles tighten on my bag strap as I peeked up at him.

My mouth went dry at the intensity of his gaze. Complete and utter focus. His eyes were sharper than any I'd ever seen. That look made me feel stripped bare —it made me want to strip *him* bare. I quickly hurried to get away. "Don't leave on my account," he called after me, making me pause. "Not-particularly-special girls are welcome in the library any time they want."

"Remember that time when I asked for your opinion?" I threw back. "Oh wait, I didn't." I turned to go.

"Aren't you a fun little ray of sarcasm and bitchiness," he commented.

It was the second time in less than an hour that someone had called me a bitch. Coming from Maverick McKnight, it had been annoying. Coming from Torin Priest, it made me feel almost amused. My lips curled back and I continued for the library doors. "Is there a reason for you to be such an ass?" I called over my shoulder.

"Everyone has to excel at something, right?" he replied. I rolled my eyes as I shouldered my way out of the library and another one of those quiet laughs echoed at my back.

To keep from looking like I was two seconds from murdering the next person to talk to me, I took my time before heading to class. I walked the halls, pulling out my schedule and glancing over the room numbers listed. I found where each of my classes were located and memorized their locations before the first bell rang. Knowing where everything was made me feel more confident in my ability to navigate the whole concept of school. But as I showed up to my homeroom at the first bell, despite the fact that the class was barely even half full, a new feeling of anxiety crept into my chest.

St. Marion must not have gotten many new students because everywhere I went, it seemed as though people were staring. I adjusted my backpack on my shoulder and took a seat towards the back of the classroom, alongside the row of windows that overlooked the football field. Dropping my bag at my feet and kicking it beneath the desk, I folded my arms over my chest and turned my cheek, away from the lingering whispers hidden behind obvious hands. The early morning sun rose higher and higher into the sky, and I wished I could be done with school and get back to what I really needed to be focused on. Training and hunting.

Unfortunately, my desire to have the day end only made it drag by. By fourth period, nothing had really changed. People still stared. No one had talked to me. And almost everyone I passed on my way to lunch watched me with curious eyes. There were more whispers, and still, no one said a damn word to my face. It was beginning to grate on my nerves. So much so that I worried the first person that decided to be brave enough to talk to me was going to get a mouthful of my fist.

Though that didn't happen exactly the way I had expected, I didn't have to wait much longer for someone to approach.

I sat at an empty table with a tray of what the lunch lady had deemed pizza and fruit salad. It looked more like a triangle of cardboard with tomato sauce on it and a cup of peaches, but I doubted complaining would get me anything better. Though to be honest, for a private school, I was surprised. I took one bite of the almost pizza before giving up and pushing the tray away. No sooner had I done that and a shadow fell over me.

I looked up into crystal blue eyes, surrounded by dark smoky lashes set in a sharp angular face that was startling in its difference, though not unattractive. The girl cocked her hip against the table and stared down at me, pursing her lips as if she were trying to solve a rather difficult puzzle in her head. I blinked blandly back at her and waited. I had almost gotten to the count of thirty by the time she finally spoke.

"So, you're the charity case Maverick's family took in," she said. I tilted my head to the side and continued waiting. The girl flipped a lock of dirty blonde hair over one shoulder and folded her arms across her chest, pushing her breasts up until they strained against the top button of her low cut shirt. "Nothing to say?" she asked.

I shrugged. "You didn't ask a question," I pointed out.

Her lips turned down as if that hadn't been the

answer she expected. "Well, I just came to warn you," she huffed.

I licked my lips, reaching for my bag and slinging it over my shoulder as I slowly rose from my seat. "Oh? About what?" I asked. In my periphery, I could see that we had caught the majority of the cafeteria's attention. Including Maverick, himself, as he sat several tables away with what appeared to be a collection of bulky athletes. The football team, I presumed. I returned my attention to the girl before me.

"Not to expect special treatment or anything, of course," she said, casting me a smug look. "Trash like you is obviously low on the totem pole here. Haven't you noticed how you haven't made any friends yet? That no one has even bothered to talk to the new girl?"

I *had* noticed. But at the same time, I also didn't really give a shit. I shrugged again. "So? What's your point?"

The corners of her lips tightened. "Anytime we get someone new, they try to wheedle their way into the cliques and find their place in the school's hierarchy," she continued. "But that's different with you. You're not here because your parents moved into town and took a high-paying job. They're not doctors or lawyers or government officials. You're just a hanger-on, clutching at a family who's been going to this school for genera-tions. I wanted to make it clear that you shouldn't try anything. Trash like you has no place here. We don't care where you came from or why you're here. St. Marion is for people serious about their futures. And just looking at you,"—she paused to glance over me

—"it's a little obvious you don't have one. Not here, especially."

"Okay." I cracked my neck and stepped around her.

A gasp of outrage followed me. "That's all you have to say to me?" she snapped.

I stopped and looked back at her over my shoulder. "I don't want a clique, and I don't really care what you think of me," I replied. "In fact, this whole conversation has been a waste of my time. Feel free to say whatever you want if it makes you feel better. Bye."

I started forward only to slow and turn back as she began to laugh. With a weary sigh, I pivoted and stared at her with my hands on my hips. The girl giggled uncontrollably, one hand pressing against her stomach as if she could hardly contain herself. While the other hand wiped at the tears leaking from her eyes. I noted how not a single streak of black remained on her cheek.

It was obvious she had more to say and the entire room appeared to be centered on our exchange. Beyond her, though, something caught my attention—or rather, *someone*. Torin Priest stood with his back against the wall, other guys on either side of him, though none were as tall as he was. When he saw me looking, he smiled—his teeth white even in his pale face. My lips twisted as I jerked my gaze back to the bitch in front of me.

"—scared? I bet you think because you landed in the same house as Maverick McKnight, you're a princess in the making," she finished saying.

I shook my head. I had no clue what she'd started with, but I knew one thing for sure. There was no way a little girl like this could scare me. "Nope." I popped the end of the word with casual indifference. "I didn't know who Maverick was before I moved here and I didn't care and guess what, I still don't care."

"Oh really?" She smirked. "Pretty defensive for a girl who says she doesn't care."

I shrugged. "Not really, bobblehead bitches like you just annoy me."

She stopped laughing. "What the fuck is that supposed to mean?" Her growl reminded me of a chihuahua. I could suddenly picture her as one of those yippy little lap dogs. I fought against a grin as I pictured her shaking so bad she pissed herself.

"You know," I said, "bobbleheads are only good for one thing."

"Oh and what's that?" she said, clearly daring me to continue.

"Sucking dick," I deadpanned.

I could have heard a pin drop in the silence that followed.

"You're going to regret that," she grated out through clenched teeth.

"Hey," I said, backing up another step with my hands raised, "you were the one that came to me. I don't even know you."

"My name is Rachel Harris, you cunt, and I promise you're gonna wish you'd never come to St. Marion."

"I said I didn't know you," I sighed. "Not that I wanted to know you. I don't care what your name is, bobblehead, and I also don't care about your threats. You picked the fight, not me. I don't start fights, I just finish them."

With that, I pivoted once more and walked away, leaving the chick—Rachel—fuming as I strode right by Maverick's table and out the doors just as the bell rang to signal the end of lunch.

Today was turning out to be a great first day of public school.

EIGHT

BARBIE

"HOW WAS SCHOOL?" BETH ASKED AS WE SAT DOWN FOR dinner.

"Riveting," I replied dryly. Maverick shot me a look of disdain that I promptly ignored. Beth either didn't hear the sarcasm in my voice or she made the intelligent choice to ignore it because she nodded and dug into her pasta.

"When's your next game?" Jon asked, looking to Maverick.

"It's this Friday," he answered. "There's a party afterwards too, so I'll probably be out or stay at one of the guys.'"

Jon was a man of few words. He nodded and then followed Beth's example, shoveling a forkful of pasta into his mouth. I ate slowly, watching the three of them with a heart full of lead. I could picture Brandon in Maverick's spot. My mom in Beth's and my dad in Jon's. I felt like I'd somehow been cut from my old life and dropped into someone else's. Lucky Barbie.

I ate without really tasting anything. Jon was the first to finish and then Maverick. They both got up and returned their plates to the kitchen before heading off in their respective directions. Thankful to be alone with the woman I wanted to talk to, I set my fork down and turned in my seat.

I cleared my throat. "Um … so, Beth?"

"Yes?" She looked up from her plate and reached for a napkin to dab at the corner of her mouth where a drop of sauce had fallen.

"I was wondering if it'd be okay if I went out this Friday too," I said.

"Did you want to go to the party with Maverick?" she asked.

"Yeah," I lied, "but I probably won't be hanging out with him. I met some people in school today and I just thought…" I let the insinuation trail off. It wasn't a complete lie. I *had* met new people in school today.

"That's wonderful." She beamed at me. "I'm glad to hear you're settling in. Of course you can go. Oh, that reminds me—" Beth paused and set her utensils down, getting up from the table and disappearing into the living room before she came back carrying her purse. "I went and picked this up at the store today." She pulled out a cell phone complete with a pink and black case and set it down in front of me. "It's on our family plan so you have unlimited calls and text messages. Just be careful using the data, we don't usually run out, but between you and me," she looked over her shoulder as she lowered her voice, "I know I use a lot of it. I don't know if it's a girl thing or just me." She shrugged.

I looked down at the phone, shocked. My finger crept onto the table and brushed against the edge of it. "I've never had a cellphone before," I admitted.

Her eyes widened. "Delvina and Peter never…"

I shook my head. "No, they didn't see the point since we were homeschooled."

"Oh." Beth sucked in a breath and blew it out. "Well, this is just if you want it then," she said. "I think it'll be safer, though, for you to take it if you'll be going out. I've already programmed Maverick and Jon's numbers in there, as well as mine."

"Thanks, Beth." I meant it. I picked up the phone and turned it over in my grasp. "I appreciate it."

Another mega-watt Beth smile flashed my way. "It's nothing," she replied, returning her attention to the last of her food.

I bit the edge of my tongue. "There's something else I wanted to ask too." Chewing, Beth lifted her head once again. "I know you said you were thinking about getting me a car, but I don't really need one of my own. I was just wondering, however, if you wouldn't mind letting me borrow—"

"Oh, your car, yes!" Beth said. "I've already got one picked out. I had my assistant go and check it out today. I think she sent me pictures."

My mouth dropped as she grabbed her phone and began flicking through photos, turning it around to show me. I shook my head. "I don't want you to buy me any—"

"It should be here by next week, so you'll have to continue riding with Mav until then, but isn't it just darling?" She sighed as she looked at the photo she had pulled up. "It almost makes me want a little bug of my own. I was really hoping to get it in yellow—the sunshine color, you know? But all they had was a bubblegum pink and I didn't think you'd want to wait another two weeks for them to drive down a—"

She was talking a mile a minute, giddy excitement filling up her tone. This was too much. In less than a year I'd be out of her hair. I wouldn't be a concern anymore. Why was she going through so much trouble for someone she had just met days ago. "Beth," I said her name with more force than I intended, but it did what it needed to. She stopped talking and looked at me with a frown tugging her lips down.

"What's wrong?"

"You don't need to buy me a car," I said.

"It's no problem, really," she tried to assure me.

"You just met me," I replied. "I might legally be your goddaughter, but you haven't seen me in years. You're not adopting me. You don't have to go through all of this trouble. You don't have to do so much."

Beth's frown softened, and she reached towards me. I drew my hand back at the last second, turning my eyes down at the hurt look on her face. "Barbie, look at me," she said. I didn't want to. I didn't know what I would see in her expression. "Barbie." She said my name in a harder tone, one that brooked no argument. I sighed and angled my head back around. "Yes, it's true," she confessed. "I haven't seen you since you were a baby. I hadn't spoken to your parents in well over a decade. Closer to fifteen years, I think. To be honest,

77

I'm not just doing this for you. I'm doing it for them too."

My head jerked back. "What do you mean?"

"Some people grow apart when they move and don't see each other anymore. But that wasn't the case with Delvina and I. We were best friends all throughout college and when she moved away and went on to get her Master's and Doctorate, we still kept in contact. Even when she spent a year in Italy, we were closer oceans apart than I was with the girls I saw at work every day," Beth said. "She was in my wedding. She congratulated me when Maverick was born, just as I did for Brandon and then you. I thought we would have one of those friendships that lasted until we were old and gray. Hell," she laughed good-naturedly, "at one point, we contemplated setting you up with Mav so that we could bring our families even closer together."

I grimaced. *Fat chance that would've happened*, I thought. My fingers tightened on the phone as something occurred to me. I looked up at Beth with a frown on my lips. "If you were so close," I said, "what happened to cause you to stop talking?"

Beth grimaced, but she didn't shy away from the uncomfortable question. In fact, she appeared as though she'd expected the question and with a resigned sigh, she answered. "Well, first I suppose you have to understand that Vina was really close with her parents. They had no other children, so they doted on her. When they died, things started to change. She was wrecked—it was to be expected—but there was more. Vina became withdrawn. We had a horrible row," Beth admitted. "I was hurt that she was ignoring me so willfully. It was months later, and she still didn't seem okay. She seemed more obsessed than ever with something, but she wouldn't tell me what. I felt like it had something to do with her parents' deaths, but—"

"How did they die?" I asked. My free hand latched onto the edge of the table and I found myself leaning forward, listening intently. This was far more information than my parents had ever deemed to give me or Brandon. They had never told us how they knew of the existence of vampires.

"That's just the thing," Beth replied, "I don't know. She never did say."

I bit my lip. I was almost sure that whatever had happened to my mom's parents—my grandparents—had been the very thing that had driven my parents to find out about vampires. Perhaps, my grandparents had been killed by vampires. Considering how greatly my parents seemed to hate them and how harshly they had trained Brandon and me, it wasn't unlikely.

"But I digress, Barbie." Beth reached out and took my hands in hers, causing me to drop my new phone back next to my nearly empty plate and release the ledge of the table. "I should have tried harder to understand where your mother was coming from. She was my best friend and I allowed her to pull away out of grief. Even though I'm sure she and Peter likely meant to change their will and entrust your care to someone closer to them before they passed, I like to think that fate has brought us together." Beth spoke with such sincerity that it made me uncomfortable. Her eyes beseeched me with willful hope and I had a hard time looking at them. "For me, you're my second chance to make things up to her. I really want you to think of this home as your own. Jon and I haven't adopted you yet, but that's not because we don't want to. The choice has to be yours. If you want to stay after you're eighteen, we'd love to have you."

In the glaringly loud silence that followed, I was left, for the first time in a long time, utterly speechless. Thankfully, Beth recognized that tidbit, and with a kind, gentle smile she released me. "Of course, that's for the future. For now, why don't you go upstairs and get ready for bed? I hope you have another wonderful day at school tomorrow. I look forward to hearing all about your new friends."

My lips pinched tight to ward off an oncoming grimace as I nodded my acquiescence and stood from the table, grabbing my phone and plate and hurrying to the kitchen. The reminder of just how *well* my new school life was going was unwelcome, to say the least. It did, however, serve as a hint of what I should prepare for.

Even so, Beth's story about the death of my grandparents followed me into my bedroom and later into my dreams as, once again, I was dropped into a nightmare surrounded by nameless, faceless vampires and this time, I was not watching my parents and brother die, but a wrinkled and gray-haired couple that I supposed was an imitation of the grandparents I had never met.

I hated watching people die. Even in my dreams.

NINE

TORIN

"How many of your friends did you invite to our little soiree this weekend?" I scowled at the question a split second before the speaker's arms slithered over my shoulders. The scent of rust tickled my nose. I flung the book I'd been reading onto the coffee table and stood up, effectively removing Eloise's grip from me.

"Why do I smell fresh blood on you?" I snapped, rounding on her.

Big blue eyes blinked up at me. "Probably because I just came back from having dinner."

"You know the rules about feeding in town. If you—"

"If I what?" she interrupted. "Killed someone? Please, darling, I've been a good girl lately."

"Drinking from the vein is not being a 'good girl,'" I quoted. "I still have another year to finish. For fuck's sake, can't you keep your fangs in your mouth?"

"Why would I do that?" she replied with a smirk, slinking over the top of the couch and landing in a stretched out position before me. "I haven't killed anyone or taken any unwilling donors. I should be rewarded." Her claw like grip found the edge of my shirt and tugged sharply. I slapped a hand out against the back of the couch to keep from falling on top of her. Eloise's pink tongue peeked out.

"If you don't keep your fangs to yourself, I'm sure Arrius will have something to say about it," I growled, jerking away from her grip.

The tinkling sound of her laughter grated in my ears.

"El, why are you torturing my brother?"

I lifted my eyes as Katalin descended the staircase and strode across the tiled floor until her booted feet met the edge of the couch. Eloise grinned up at her. "Katalin, dear!" She popped up into a sitting position. "You're home."

"I am. What are you doing here?"

"She was asking about the party this weekend," I answered for her, slanting a look Katalin's way.

"What about it?" Katalin arched a brow, but not at her friend. No, she leveled that knowing look right at me.

I folded my arms across my chest. "You tell me, Katalin. Why are we having a party? What's changed?"

"Are you still upset about that boy?" Eloise groaned even as her eyes rolled into the back of her head. "You seriously have to get over it. Besides, it's not like you don't still see him at that little school you go to." Eloise folded her fingers together and stretched her long slender arms up before she dropped them and rose from the settee. "But I suppose I could be convinced to see the appeal. I bet he tastes delicious."

I scowled. "Regardless, he hates my guts," I reminded her. "Therefore, he won't be coming back."

She hummed low in her throat. "He might for the party."

When neither Katalin nor I said anything more, Eloise shrugged and turned, drifting from the room and leaving my sister and me alone. After a beat, Katalin spoke. "I didn't request this party," she said quietly.

I cut a glance her way out of the corner of my eyes. "Then who did?"

"Who do you think?" she countered.

"If you didn't want the party, then *he* did." I hissed in outrage. "Why?" I demanded. "He's not even here."

She shrugged as if it didn't matter to her. It probably didn't. "How am I supposed to know?" she replied, taking a seat where Eloise had vacated. Honeyed tresses sifted over her shoulders as she arched her back and settled in comfortably. For a moment, I was arrested. Not because of her, but because her hair reminded me of another blonde. One with much lighter hair—so light it appeared to have been bleached by the sun.

Thirst wrapped bloody fists around my neck and squeezed as I imagined a completely different neck under my hands. Suckling at my sister's vein would do very little for me, but the new girl that had arrived this week … my whole body tightened in unnecessary anticipation. I swallowed against my fangs as they prodded at my gums. I was not an animal. I did not cave to the desires of my vampire side. No matter how much it desired Barbie Steele's blood.

Clearing my suddenly parched throat, I distracted myself by focusing on my sister. "Why do you allow her here?"

Katalin closed her eyes and rested her head against the couch cushions. "Eloise is one of Arrius' most trusted advisors—"

"You and I both know she's not an advisor," I interrupted.

Katalin's eyes open once more. "Regardless," she said, "that's her title and she's here under his orders. You'll just have to deal with her. She's not as bad as his other girls."

I scowled. "She's a leech."

White teeth flashed as Katalin's full lips parted. "Aren't we all, darling?"

True as it was, I wasn't like them. I was apart. Separate. While their hearts had long ago shriveled up and died as they were frozen in time at the age each of them were turned, I grew. I aged.

She flicked a hand my way. "Why don't you go grab me a drink, I could use one right about now."

The front door opened before I could reply, and one of Eloise's favorite children sailed inside with arms full of shopping bags. "I'm back," Delia said in a bored tone, flinging the bags at the bottom of the couch and striding forward. I grimaced, stiffening, as she hugged her arms around me. The cloying scent of her perfume burned my nostrils. How she could bear the overly floral smell with her own senses was a mystery to me. I carefully extracted myself from her octopus-like hold.

"Wonderful, perhaps you can keep my sister company," I said. "Or better yet, get her a drink."

In response, Katalin chuckled.

Delia, however, acted as though she hadn't heard. She advanced on me, fingers curling into the fabric of my shirt. As I backed up, she pressed herself against my chest, her breasts plumped up and rubbing with intent. She practically purred as she flicked a lock of dark hair over her shoulder and puckered her full lips at me. "I'd much rather keep you company, Torin," she rasped. "What do you say we go upstairs and have a nice…" She slid one hand down my abdomen. "Long…" When she reached the edge of my jeans, I snatched her hand and squeezed until I was sure—had she been human—she would have felt the fracturing of her bones. "Rest?"

"No offense," I said blandly, "but getting into bed with you would be like sleeping with a snake."

I was sure to any average man, she would have been irresistible, but to me, she was nothing more than yet another viper, slithering her way into the bed of anyone who had power. I knew for a fact that she, like Eloise, had slept with my father and that alone would have warned me away. The only women my father slept with were as cold and dead inside as they were on the outside. And both Delia and Eloise had been dead for many centuries.

Delia laughed and tugged her hand away from my grip. "Even snakes need mates," she said flippantly, gliding to the couch and reclining next to Katalin who lifted her brows at me. "I'm sure your father will choose someone for you soon enough. You really should have fun while you still can."

I scowled. "It doesn't matter who he chooses," I snapped, "I'm not some pet to be ordered about or a pawn to be paired off and sacrificed."

Delia laughed as though my words were the most amusing joke she'd heard in years. "You're so adorable," she chuckled. "But so naive. Everyone in Arrius' world is a pawn. Everyone is expendable."

I looked to Katalin, but she avoided my gaze as she too, responded. "Just make sure that you have enough people for the party to be a success," was all she said. "Father has invited a few friends."

My frown deepened. I didn't like that. Any friend of Arrius Priest was bound to be as soulless as he was. And if Barbie came … my fangs practically throbbed. The thought of her in a roomful of hungry vampires sent spikes of volcanic anger and fear through me. The thought of her alone in a room with me, however … I sucked in a breath and shoved away the image that formed in my mind—all that blonde hair, that pale skin under me.

As if she could sense my internal battle of wills, Katalin scoffed in amusement. "Careful there, brother darling," she said with mock concern. "If you don't take care of that thirst of yours, you're bound to take it out on one of your classmates this weekend."

"You'd like that, wouldn't you?" I growled as I headed for the kitchen.

"I never said anything of the kind," Katalin called after me.

"I might," Delia piped up. "I'm feeling rather parched. I do hope you invited some of those football players. Athletes always have such a thick taste." She clapped her hands together. "Oh, I have an idea. Let's make a game of it. Whoever tastes the best will be shared between the three of us. Katalin, what do you say? You, me, and El?"

I stopped at the doorway and looked back over my shoulder. "If you kill any of my classmates, how the fuck am I supposed to graduate?" I growled. "Even if *he* did order the party, keep your fangs to yourself or I'll remove them for you."

Delia's laughter echoed up the walls as I turned and left the room. It was difficult to intimidate a vampire as old as either of them, no matter that I was completely serious. They had seen much in their long lives—far more than I. But Katalin was right about one thing.

I went to the kitchen, spying the refrigerator as soon as I entered and made a beeline for it. Snatching a bag of A positive from the top shelf, I finally let my fangs descend and as they did, I plunged them into the top of the plastic. As my fangs worked, and my thirst dissipated. No matter that I tried to deny the truth, human food simply wasn't enough to sustain me.

TEN

BARBIE

THURSDAY. THAT'S HOW LONG IT TOOK FOR SOMEONE TO work up the nerve to talk to me, and it wasn't who I thought it would be.

"Hi, I'm Olivia."

Amidst all of the available seats still left open in study hall, a flash of curly red hair sank into the seat next to mine and looked at me with expectant bright blue eyes. I turned to the side, half expecting someone else to be there. When there wasn't, I finally resigned myself to the realization that the introduction was, in fact, meant for me.

"Not. Interested." *There. Straight to the point,* I thought.

Giggling, the girl pulled out a textbook and flipped it open before promptly pivoting her entire body away from it and towards me. "I know no one else has talked to you yet. I couldn't help myself anymore. We haven't gotten a new student in ages, and to be honest, you're the first person aside from maybe the guys on the football team or Torin Priest to ever talk back to Rachel, and Jesus, girl, the things I've heard—"

"Don't care," I interrupted, sighing as I focused back on the calculus equation I had been working on prior to her entrance.

"Well, that's obvious," she replied. "You don't seem to be even a little bit uncomfortable. I don't know how you do it. The students here aren't exactly subtle." *Why was she still talking? Had I not been clear in my physical 'go away' and 'do not disturb' signals or was she just stupid?* "Rich kids," she confessed. "They just don't care if anyone hears them; if Mommy and Daddy can get them out of any trouble they get into, be it a libel or slander lawsuit—"

"And let me guess, you're not one of them?" I gave up on the equation.

"Oh no, I am," she admitted without a shred of guilt. "I'm a born and bred heiress." Flicking her hair back, she gestured to the diamond choker on her neck. "Both sides of the family."

"Then why, pray tell, are you talking to me?" I asked.

"Boredom?"

Behind my sealed lips, I shoved my tongue over my teeth and sucked in hard. "Lovely," I finally said. "At least you're honest."

"And so are you." She beamed. "But besides that, do you want to know why no one else has talked to you yet?"

"Not particularly," I said, "but you're going to tell me anyway, aren't you?"

She nodded vigorously, sending the cascade of her cherry locks over one shoulder. "It's not because Rachel has deemed you undesirable. She can't really give that edict. Drives her insane, but it's true. Everyone here is rich, so that kinda evens the playing field. Though, she'd like to believe she's her own little Regina George—movie deal included."

Mrs. Echolls, the teacher in charge of supervising study hall, paused between our desks. "Miss Jones, can you tell me why your textbook is out, but no work is being done?"

I was almost thankful for the teacher, but instead of sinking down and turning back to her textbook, Olivia waved her fingers dismissively. "Because it's all done," she answered.

Mrs. Echolls' lips turned down, making the wrinkles lining the corners of her lips deepen into grooves. "Well, see that you don't make Miss…" I could tell when the teacher swung towards me, pausing as her lips parted midsentence, that she had no clue who I was.

I sighed. "Barbie," I offered blandly. "Barbie Steele."

"Right." She cleared her throat, looking back to Olivia over the rims of her glasses. "See that you don't interrupt Miss Steele's study time. You're not the only one in here, Miss Jones."

"No worries, Mrs. E." Olivia grinned. "I'm helping her out." Mrs. Echolls hummed doubtfully as she strode off. I went back to calculus.

Not even a minute went by before she started again. "So anyway…"—I slapped my pencil against my desk. If there was a devil, Redheaded McChatterbox was certainly a punishment from his domain. "People aren't talking to you, but it's not because they're scared of Rachel. Half of the guys on the football team already think you're hot. Standing up to her definitely gained you some cool points. I heard Calvin Wallace—"

"Is there a point to this, or are you just going to keep talking until someone shuts you up?" I asked. "Because if you're looking for someone to stop you, say the word. I know how to knock a bitch out in less than three seconds and I'm cheaper than duct tape or sleeping pills. In fact, I'll do it for free."

"You're unapproachable," she said, not seeming the least bit put off by my threat. "That's why people aren't willing to talk to you."

"Well, I'm obviously not unapproachable enough," I pointed out. "Since here you sit. What do you really want, Lindsey Lohan?"

"I feel like I'm more of a Lucille Ball," she countered. "The classic kind of pretty rather than the strung out on drugs kind." I placed my hand on the desk and slowly but deliberately tapped my fingers, letting them click against the faux wood of the desktop one at a time —waiting. "Okay fine, I want gossip," she said. "You're living with Maverick McKnight. You've got access to the King and I want in."

My fingers stopped. That caught my attention. "King?" I repeated. "I thought Torin Priest was the 'King' of St. Marion?" I rolled my eyes even as I air quoted the title the girl who'd been my tour guide had given him.

Olivia's lips curved into a slow, seductive smile. She

looked like a cat ready to eat the cream. "So, you have been paying attention to the school's hierarchy," she said knowingly.

"No, I haven't," I snapped. "Some girl just told me—"

"Don't worry about it." That damned grin of hers was still there and it was starting to piss me off. "But to answer your question, Torin is … was … well, it's actually complicated. They used to be the Kings of St. Marion, like co-ruling monarchs or whatever." She waved her hand nonchalantly, as if she hadn't just proclaimed two teenage boys royalty. Was this what public school was like?

I told myself to just let it go, to leave it at that. Torin Priest was none of my business. He was just another guy like any other. And Maverick McKnight was just an unfortunate jackass I had to spend the next year or so living in the room across from his. I had more important things to do—namely more important things to *stake*.

"Torin and Maverick used to be best friends," she admitted.

I frowned, trying to picture a scowling Maverick in all his football finery being best friends with pretty boy Torin Priest in his boots and t-shirts. One made me want to shove a baseball bat down his throat and the other … unsettled me.

"Why used to be?" I found myself asking.

As if sensing someone willing to listen to her gossip, Olivia crossed one leg over the other and leaned forward. "Torin and Maverick were friends back in pre-school and up until two years ago, they were as close as two guys who aren't boning could get. And if the rumor mill on their sex lives is anything to go by, those guys are anything but gay. Besides, Maverick had a girlfriend up until about two years ago."

I bit my lip. *Don't ask, Barbie. It's not important,* I said to myself. *Learning about Torin or Maverick won't help you find vampires or kill them.*

While my brain definitely got the memo, my mouth did not. "What happened?" I asked.

Olivia smiled, showcasing two rows of teeth that had been perfectly bleached of any stains. *Did the girl even eat or drink anything?* "Well, no one actually knows for sure," she started. "But one day they both came to school and Maverick kept trying to talk to Torin and Torin cut him off completely. He changed out of all the classes he shared with Maverick and quit the football team."

"Torin was on the football team?" Huh. For some reason, I couldn't picture it. To be honest, if I hadn't seen how well Maverick filled out a uniform, I wouldn't have believed he was a football player either. I always pictured football players as these huge, hulking guys with thick necks and shoulders so wide they had to shimmy sideways into doorways. And while both Maverick and Torin were large guys, they were also fairly normal. You know, if you ignored the penetrating intensity from both, the asshole behavior of one, and the searing sarcasm from the other. Totally normal. Maybe. Ish.

In response to my question, Olivia jerked her head up and down in a quick nod. "Oh yeah. They were, like, the best players. Torin was the quarterback before he quit. He didn't even give a reason. It was so weird. But then there was the whole thing with Maryanne, and after that, I knew their friendship was well and truly over. I mean, some people can survive that but it's pretty rare."

I pressed my lips together and when she didn't elaborate, choosing to drone on about friendships and the loss of theirs, I stopped her. "Who is Maryanne?"

"Oh, right!" Olivia shook her head. "I forgot you didn't know about her. Maryanne was Maverick's girlfriend."

"Was?" I clarified.

"Yeah." Olivia's eyes brightened. "They'd been together since freshman year. She was on the cheer squad. Maryanne had it all, girl. You have no idea. But not long after Torin and Maverick stopped being friends—Maryanne was trying to get them to talk it out —Torin came to school on this black—get this— motorcycle!" I failed to see the importance of the motorcycle, but I nodded so that she would continue. "It was so hot. And guess who was on the back of it with him?"

"I await with bated breath," I said dryly.

"Maryanne!" she exclaimed, earning a hissed shush from Mrs. Echolls from the front of the room. "Oops." Olivia grimaced and then shrugged, going right back to her story, though she lowered her voice as she did. "Anyway, apparently, he gave her a ride to school or so she said. But I talked to Stella Grant, and she said that Rex Dorphin's mom saw them—"

"The human body has something like seven trillion nerves," I said through gritted teeth, "and somehow, you're managing to get on every single one of mine. Get to the point, Red."

"Right, well, suffice it to say that there were some pretty nasty rumors about Maryanne jumping from Maverick to Torin. Personally, I think that was just the thing to seal the deal between them. If Maryanne did sleep with Torin, I don't think Torin cared about her. She ended up moving not long afterwards. That wasn't the start of the end for them." She bit her lip and leaned forward a bit more conspiratorial. "Apparently, in all their years of friendship, Maverick never met Torin's dad and I heard that the senior Priest was in town the weekend before Torin quit football and cut Maverick off. Maryanne wasn't the beginning, she was the end."

My lips parted as I narrowed my eyes on her. "What does Torin's father have to do with anything?"

Olivia blinked at me. "Isn't it obvious?" she asked. "Maverick and Torin knew each other for years and Maverick never met his dad. *Years*, girl. Yeah, Mr. Priest apparently travels a lot, but from what I hear, Torin's real guardian is his sister." She paused, tightening her fingers into a fist over her jean clad thigh. "But it's Katalin's friends that are the chicks you don't want to piss off—I've only seen them at the parties Torin used to throw, but I wouldn't want to be alone in a room with them if you know what I mean. Eloise just seems so ethereal, you know? Like nothing can touch her. Delia, though, she's the one to watch out for. At one of the last Priest parties, I saw her toss this guy into their pool."

"Okay?" I squinted, not understanding.

"He hit his head," Olivia confessed, biting down on

her lower lip. "There was a lot of blood, and he had to get stitches. She just laughed."

I hummed. "That is crazy." It was downright incriminating.

"She's just got this look in her eyes. You know—like crazy eyes." Olivia paused with a shudder. "But don't worry, you don't have to worry about seeing any of them out and about, though. I've heard they've all got this allergy to the sun or whatever. No one ever sees them out before dark and whenever there's a parent teacher conference or something, his sister has to schedule it after the sun goes down. To my knowledge, they don't work—just sponge off Mr. Priest, not like he can't afford it, but anyway—Maverick and Torin." She shifted her legs again, switching which one was on top and scooted to the edge of her seat. "So anyway, like I said, around the time Maverick and Torin stopped talking to one another, Mr. Priest was in town. Candace Roloson saw a limo at their mansion and there was a whole bunch of security. You know, guys in suits and leather, sunglasses. The whole shebang. Next thing you know, Torin and Maverick are on the outs. Major weird."

"That is weird," I admitted. My mind was churning. Maybe learning about Torin Priest was going to help me find vampires. *A sister and friends with an allergy to the sun? Was that even a real thing?*

"Yeah, totes weird. I think it's Mr. Priest. He didn't want them hanging out or Maverick said something to piss him off—"

"He does seem to be able to rub someone the wrong way," I remarked.

"Yeah, well after Maverick and Torin had their split or whatever, Torin stopped throwing those parties too. Which was a major bummer. They were *killer* ragers. Mr. Priest is never around and Katalin didn't care if there was underage drinking or anything. The cops never got called. Even if parents found out about them, they didn't dare try to come after the Priests. No one would."

"Because they're rich?" I clarified.

"Well, yeah, that and they're totally scary. My bet is that Torin is actually the heir to some overseas mafia or something." She laughed as if the idea was ludicrous. "But Torin's finally come out of his shell again. Apparently, there's going to be another party tomorrow night after the football game. First one in two years," she said. "Everyone's going to be there. People are starved for a Priest party."

A part of me actually kind of hoped she was right in guessing that Torin Priest was the son of some mysterious foreign mafia. Because if what I was thinking was true, then what was a human doing living with a vampire? Whatever the case. I had to find out.

"So," I finally said, "are you going to this Priest Party?"

Olivia lowered her lashes and looked up at me through the thin veil of spiderweb thin curled black lines. "Maybe."

And there it was. The kicker. Sticking the tip of my tongue between my teeth, I couldn't help but laugh. She'd done it. Drawn me in and hooked me like a damn fish. I leaned back and flicked my Calculus book closed.

"Alright, out with it," I said. "What's it going to take to find out where this party is?"

"I want you to invite me over to your house," she said.

"Why is that?"

"Because, like I said, you live with Maverick McKnight. *The* Maverick McKnight."

More like *the* pain in my ass. "Fine," I said. "When?"

"You invite me over today,"—my right eyeball twitched—"and not only will I tell you where the Priest Party is being held, I'll drive you there myself," she offered.

What else could I do? I needed to get to that party. I needed to find out if Katalin Priest was just an unusual human living like a vampire or an even more unusual vampire who needed to get herself staked and baked by none other than little ol' me.

"I think you've got yourself a deal, Merida."

She flicked another strand of hair off her shoulder and grinned. "I always knew people thought I was a princess."

ELEVEN

BARBIE

Olivia, as it turned out, was true to her word. Despite her request, I didn't let her come over the same day. We exchanged numbers and she met me after school in the stands of St. Marion's football stadium the following day. The school's football field was college level professional. It was mowed to perfection with bleachers cleaner than I'd ever seen on TV. A dozen or so players ran the length of the immaculate football field in their gear, and even though the day had a breezy chill to it, I could imagine that they must have already been sweating up a storm.

"Look, there's Maverick," Olivia said, pointing across the field.

I followed Olivia's finger and grimaced when I saw that Maverick had already been made aware of my arrival. Unlike the others, Maverick stood on the sidelines, his hair drenched in what I could only assume was sweat. It looked like I'd missed his round of practice. Maverick's scowl deepened when our gazes locked.

Unfortunately for him, I didn't scare so easily. Lifting my fingers, I wiggled them at him with a smug grin. His upper lip curled back and he whirled around and stomped away.

"Awww, trouble in paradise?" Olivia grinned, unperturbed by Maverick's hasty retreat.

"If this is what you think paradise is," I replied, "I'd hate to see your idea of Hell."

Together, we headed off the bleachers as the coach called in his remaining players. My guess, they'd be allowed to chill before the big game that night. Personally, I didn't care about the game. My entire focus was on the party that would follow and what information I could glean from it. There was just something about Torin Priest that rubbed me the wrong way.

I said nothing as Olivia took me to her white Porsche. She hadn't been kidding when she said she was an heiress. If she wasn't, then I had good reason to believe that my new friend was into some pretty illegal shit—shit that could afford her the nicest of everything, including cars and the diamond encrusted Rolex that hung from her rearview mirror.

We drove to the McKnight house in relative peace. I considered it relative because as I sat back and listened to her drone on about the school and what so-and-so said to who, I somehow managed to block most of it out. The more she talked, the less I heard. She was skilled at managing to hold an entire one-sided conversation by herself without much more than a few grunts of acknowledgment from me. When we pulled up to the house, I nearly tripped getting out of the damn car just to get away from her incessant chatter.

Olivia's slow whistle drew my eyes. "What?" I asked as I led her up the staircase. We bypassed the hallway and headed straight for my bedroom.

"This place is adorable." She whirled around as I stopped at my door and pushed it open. Olivia twisted right by me and turned, landing on her back in the center of my mattress. "I bet you never lived in anything so cute," she gushed. "You're living the high life now, girl, and you don't even know it!"

"Oh, believe me," I replied. "I know exactly what kind of life I'm living." I dropped my backpack by the desk and kicked it out of sight. Hopefully, the age old saying of out of sight and out of mind was true for this girl because she seemed like the snooping type and I really didn't need a wannabe gossip going through my shit.

Why had I allowed her to come over again? I asked myself. In the next minute, I answered my silent question. Because a) she was my key to getting to the Priest party and b) having someone who knew all of the latest gossip on the Priest family was probably going to come in handy—especially if it turned out that one or more of them were vampires. I had no clue what vampires would have to do with a human guy like Torin—because there was no way he could be a vampire. He had walked through sunlight and eaten real food. I would just have to suffer through Olivia's attempt at a makeover.

"Okay, Cinderella," Olivia said, sitting up as she clapped her hands. "Hair." She looked me up and down. "I'm thinking side-braid, a fishtail. Then makeup. Do you have any?"

I gave her an unimpressed look. "What do you think?"

She shrugged. "Can't judge a book by its cover," she countered. "Now, do you want to go to the party or not?"

Touché.

"I've got a few things in my desk," I said, spinning the chair and opening drawers. "But don't hold out hope for the good stuff." I pulled out an old dollar store pallet along with a singular brush, a tube of chapstick, and an eyeliner pencil. The sound of shifting sheets behind me caused me to look back. Olivia left the bed and moved closer, peeking over my shoulder.

"*Yeahhhh.*" She drew out the word, starting high pitched and ending on a pathetic note that said more than the actual word itself. "I think we'll make do with what I brought with me."

I sighed and shoved the makeup back into the desk drawers as Olivia snatched her purse up from where she had dropped it by the bed. Popping it open, she upended the contents across my mattress, spilling tubes of lipstick and gloss, sticky notes, and mints across the coverlet. Olivia hummed as she perused the supplies she'd revealed before she selected what she thought she'd need and turned back to me. And with an evil grin, the woman before me brandished a tube of dark purple lipstick and an inked eyeliner pen at me right before she spoke.

"Alright," she said, "time to get to work."

Olivia went through the new clothes Beth had bought me, pulled out new underwear and enough outfits to cover the mattress. Then, she set to what she considered work and I considered three hours of torture. My lips were painted purple. My eyes lined in kohl. My face smoothed of any imperfections.

"Does it come naturally to you?" I asked after she had plucked and tweezed my eyebrows into twin slender lines. "Or did you graduate from Dante's Infernal School of Torment? Let me guess, top of your class?"

Olivia giggled and pronounced me done. "That's it," she said. "All that's left is to get to the game and the party." She pulled out a small bottle of vodka. "Want to pregame a little with me?" she asked.

I shook my head. "No, but maybe you should let me drive if you're going to do that."

She shrugged and nudged the keys on the bed my way before she upended the bottle and swallowed, her eyes pinched shut against the burn.

"Alright," she said, popping off the bottle with a sigh and a hiccup. "Time to go meet the girls at the game."

With a grimace, I gestured for her to precede me. "Lead the way."

I READ AN ARTICLE ONCE ABOUT THE EFFECTS OF HAVING money on IQ levels. Researchers found that the more money someone had, the higher their IQ was. Something about being able to see the bigger picture and not having to worry about survival, allowing the people they based their study on to think more critically than those who had less money.

I don't know about the researchers, but I was pretty sure they didn't take into consideration the children of wealthy people. Because as I stood in the stands of St. Marion's stadium and watched the students of St. Marion, I was hard pressed to find anyone with an IQ in the double digits.

Booze flowed freely. The teachers attending were either being bought off or weren't paid well enough to care because even when a freshman nearly fell over one of the railings, nothing was said or done. And parents? I might have seen Jon and Beth somewhere when the game had first started, but Olivia had dragged me away and now they were lost in the crowd.

"So, are we winning?" I asked.

"I don't know," Olivia replied lifting a cup she'd purchased from the concession stand, now filled halfway —a mixture of Dr. Pepper and the Fireball one of her friends had smuggled in. She took a long drink and hiccupped.

Wonderful, I thought. The one girl that was willing to talk to me was already well on her way to being drunk.

"Hey, you're that new girl, right?" I turned and looked up as a tall, lanky guy in a yellow polo sidled up to my side.

"What gave me away?" I replied.

The guy grinned, flashing a somewhat crooked smile. "Never seen you here before; you going to the party afterwards?"

I glanced back as one of Olivia's friends began to

pour more Fireball into their drinks and considered the possibility that I'd be dropping my new friend off long before the Priest party actually started. My dad always said plan B's were a necessary part of life. I turned back to the yellow polo guy. "I sure am," I said brightly. "And I'm super pumped about it. Are you going too?"

He laughed, turning his head as he shrugged. "Yeah, I thought I'd go, see if there was anyone worth talking to there." He looked back at me and I waited a beat as his gaze slid down, slowly crawling up the skin tight jeans and low cut t-shirt I was wearing. "I might see you there."

I bit my lip and batted my eyelashes. "I forget, where is it again? My friend's supposed to take me,"—I paused, looking back to Olivia meaningfully—"but I'll probably have to go alone now. If you're gonna be there, I don't wanna get lost."

"You got a cell?" he asked.

I pulled it out and handed it over. "It's new," I confessed as I punched in the code. "Still getting used to it."

"Here." He handed the phone back—with a new name and phone number that I knew I'd delete before I left the stands—but more importantly, with a new address in the GPS map coordinates. "Come find me when you get there," he said. "I'll ask you to dance or something."

"Ohmygod," I gushed. "Totally. Thanks!"

Almost as soon as he had wandered off back to his friends, who all hooted and clapped him on the back, Olivia stumbled into my back and nearly made me drop the phone. "OhmyyyyyGaaaawwwwwwwddddddddd," she slurred. "Do you know who thash was?"

I grimaced as the smell of burning cinnamon lit fire to my nose. "Don't know, don't care," I said as she slung an arm around my waist.

Cheers rose up from the stands as people all around us screamed at something on the field. Over the sea of different colored heads, I watched as Maverick was rushed by his teammates. "Well," I said, "it looks like we won."

"Barbie?" I stiffened when Olivia's hand slapped over her mouth. "I don't feel so good."

I had a split second to either dive out of the way or let my new friend vomit all over my shirt, and in that split second, I chose option number three—turn her back towards the friends that had been encouraging her to drink more and let them take the brunt of her sickness.

Outraged screams ensued, male groans echoed in my ears, and the sounds of Olivia vomiting up the fifth of Fireball and twenty-four pack of light beer she and her pals had downed in the thirty minutes before the game had started.

Beer before liquor, never been sicker and all that.

Once she was done puking her guts up, I hauled Olivia off the bleachers and back to her Porsche. "Great friends," I commented sarcastically. Not a single one of them had asked if she was okay. Instead, every single one of them had cried over their ruined clothes, and those who had managed to escape had quickly booked it.

"Nooooooo," Olivia mumbled, stumbling along, clutching my arm. "I was supposed to see Mav'rick tonight."

"Yeah, well, maybe next time don't get drunk before the game is even over." I snatched her keys from her purse and hit the unlock button; her headlights flashed.

"I'm shorry," she sniffled. "I jush, I dunno…" I propped her against the side of her car and opened the passenger side door. "I was nervous."

When she didn't move from the place I put her, I hefted her against my side once more and shoved her into the car, ducking inside long enough to clip her seat-belt for her and listen to a few more seconds of her grousing.

"You're going home," I said as I closed the driver's side door behind me and started up the car. The Porsche revved to life, giving me pause. Silent and deadly. I smoothed my hands over the leather steering wheel. Damn. Maybe I was in the wrong business.

"Noooooooo." Olivia's cry sucked the smile right off my face.

"Yes," I said, putting the car in reverse. "And"—I whipped the wheel as I sped out of the student parking lot—"you're going to let me borrow your car."

TWELVE

MAVERICK

Sweat dripped down into my eyes as I stared straight ahead and made my way off the field. My fucking bones ached. Tonight had been a goddamn good game, but it'd been a battle. The other team had been just as good and their defenders—those mother-fuckers had definitely tried to wipe us out.

As soon as I hit the locker room, I went straight for my locker, stripping out of my jersey as I went. Coach followed the lot of us into the room. The team spread out. Milner and Rosso popping a squat right in front of my goddamn locker. I scowled down at the pathetic excuse for a defensive lineman. It was a fucking wonder he'd blocked anyone tonight with his head so far up his ass.

Milner leaned back, his fingers curling around the edge of the bench as he looked at me and smirked. I slammed my locker closed and turned, crossing my arms over my chest and ignoring the little shit's presence as best I could as Coach started his post-game wrap up speech. When we lost, these little speeches were long and grueling. He would point out every goddamn mistake we'd made on the field. But since we'd won, he was finished within a few minutes—telling each and every one of us to take a day to relax. Had we lost— he'd have ordered us back on the same field we got our asses kicked on at dawn the next day.

I was damn glad we'd managed to pull through tonight because if there was one thing I didn't need, it was the concern of making practice in the morning.

I headed for the showers and washed the sweat from my skin. Some of the guys hit their own shower stalls. Some packed up their shit and left—heading home to shower there and probably get some well deserved rest. And some—unfortunately for me—stayed behind to shoot the shit. I waited a good twenty minutes, ten minutes longer than it usually took for me to finish showering in the hopes that Milner and Rosso would leave, but no such luck.

Finally, I shut off the shower, grabbed a towel and went back to my locker. They sat in the same fucking place they'd been when the coach had finished up. I reached into my duffle bag and grabbed the set of clothes I'd placed in there earlier that didn't reek of wet grass, dirt, and sweat. Quickly changing, I stuffed my dirty uniform into the bottom of my bag.

"Did you catch that new chick? She was smoking hot."

I stiffened at Milner's comment. There was only one new chick. Barbie.

"Smoking?" Russo replied. "That girl's on fire. With

an ass like that and those tits—she can't be a fucking virgin."

I grabbed my bag and slung it over my shoulder.

"Who gives a shit if she's a virgin," Milner chuckled. "Virgins can fuck as well as experienced women."

Russo groaned in dismay. "Nah, man. Virgins are all shy and shit. I don't want a girl who doesn't know what she's doing."

My knuckles went white against the strap of my duffle.

"Virgins can be taught," Milner said nonchalantly. "Besides, it doesn't matter if she's a virgin or not. After I'm done with her, she definitely won't be. Do you think she'll be at the Priest party tonight?"

"Saw her with Olivia, she'll definitely be there," Russo replied. The tension in my body coiled tighter and tighter.

"Then maybe I'll see if I can't find out just how innocent the new girl is," Milner paused, a cocky grin lifting the corner of his mouth, "tonight," he finished.

Slamming the door to my locker shut, I turned slowly. Russo glanced back and had the decency to appear somewhat apprehensive. Milner, however, merely tipped his head back and looked at me.

"Oh sorry, man, she's like your new sister, right? Hope you're not offended or anything. It's a compliment, really. Your new sis is hot as hell."

"She's not my sister," I said, "but I'd stay far away from her if I were you."

"Oh?" He lifted a brow, his lips quirking with barely

restrained amusement. "Why is that? Is she off limits? Did you already call dibs? Gonna get a little action close to home?"

Russo—despite his apprehensiveness—released a weak chuckle. The sound was quickly cut off when I shot him a look that promised retribution if he kept that shit up.

Hitching my duffle up further on my shoulder, I rounded the bench before Milner. "You put your hands on Barbie Steele," I said, keeping my tone low and even, "and you and I will have a problem. We clear?"

Milner's eyes sharpened and he gritted his teeth. Milner was still a new player on the team. I, on the other hand, had been defensive captain for at least two years. It was rare that I ever used my authority against anyone, but I wouldn't back down when it came to something as important as this. Barbie Steele was trouble with a capital fucking T. I felt that in my gut.

Yeah, maybe I found her sharp crystal blue eyes striking. And yeah, she had a body that could turn a fucking monk to rock in his pants. But there was no way in hell I was going there. And neither would Jeremy fucking Milner.

After another moment of tense silence, Milner held his hands up in defeat. "Yeah, man, we're clear." He pushed himself up from the bench and came toe to toe with me. I didn't let an inch of the irritation I felt show on my face, but instead, remained as placid as fucking possible. This little dickweed wasn't going to push me.

"Stay away from her," I said, "or else."

With that, I turned and strode towards the double doors leading out of the locker room. I punched through and headed for the parking lot. Would she be at the Priest party? Milner had asked. I'd heard about the after party of course, but I'd never considered that Barbie might go. My plan had been to go, see some of the guys, show my face, and leave.

Torin hadn't thrown a Priest party in two years. Not since everything had fallen apart. Not since … Maryanne. All I wanted to do was show him that I didn't care. I could treat him just like he treated me. I could be apathetic. I could act as though we didn't know each other, as if we hadn't been as close as brothers once. Though that's all it would be—an act.

I clenched my fist and headed for my truck. My phone buzzed in my pocket. I pulled it out as I tossed my duffle into the backseat and got into the front.

Mom: GREAT GAME HONEY! YOUR FATHER AND I ARE SO proud of you. We're gonna head into the city for the weekend. Text us if you need anything. Love you.

I TOSSED MY PHONE INTO THE CUPHOLDER AND CRANKED the engine. My parents were good, well-meaning people. They were smart. So, why the hell had they let someone like Barbie Steele into our lives?

I could tell as soon as I saw her—all pale skin, blonde hair, sharp tongue—she was going to be bad news. Bad news with a side of bitchiness and a whole lot of lip. As searing as her sarcasm was though, it only made me want to shove her against a wall and devour the place from which all her smartass comments came. Barbie was a temptation I didn't want or need.

THIRTEEN

BARBIE

Irritation continued to eat at my insides as the back tires of Olivia's Porsche spun and spit out gravel from the small road leading towards the Priest estate. She was a sweet enough girl—willing to talk to me despite the bullshit of Rachel fucking Harris—but she was also a hot mess. Hot messes could get me killed. It was actually probably a good thing she hadn't been able to attend the post-game after party.

As I swerved into the opening of the estate's driveway following the GPS directions, my mouth dropped. All Olivia's talk of possible mafia connections suddenly made sense. A tall, stone building came into view—with no less than three balconies across the front upper floors. At minimum, there were three stories, but as I rounded the side of the mansion, I spotted a cluster of smaller buildings several yards beyond the main building.

I released a slow whistle as I followed the line of cars

pulling up to the valet at the front door. Lights. Cameras. A fountain five tiers high with a spring of water raining down in the middle of a lawn that could grace the covers of any garden and home magazine. I was starting to think a t-shirt and jeans would be severely underdressed when I noticed the people getting out of the other cars.

I recognized the two girls that exited the car in front of me, tossing their keys to a lanky young man who promptly got in and drove their car away as they teetered in high heels and short skirts towards the front door of the mansion. *It wasn't that I would be underdressed*, I thought, *more like ... overdressed.*

"Here you are, Ms. Steele." Another valet handed me a small slip of paper as I got out of the running car. "The number to your Porsche. We'll have someone grab it for you when you're ready to leave."

"Thanks," I said without bothering to correct him.

I headed for the double front doors. Golden light spilled out as they were opened by two ushers and pounding pop-rock music drifted out.

My eyebrows shot up as I came to a screeching halt just twenty feet inside the doorway. There, in the main hub of the mansion, was a nearly floor to ceiling painting. Torin, and what I guessed were his infamous sister and father, in 19th century Victorian regalia. While my eyes were automatically drawn to the one person in the painting I had met, I yanked my gaze away from Torin and scanned the images of his sister and father.

While Torin's sister was a beauty—thick caramel

hair that was tied back into a careful chignon—it was the image of the older man in the picture that gave me chills. Even from a painting, I had never seen eyes so devoid of emotion. He stood like a regal monarch of old, but there was no pride in his stance. There was no pride for a man who truly believed all he wanted was at his fingertips, and that was what he looked like—more God than man. And if he was truly a vampire, I had no doubt in my mind that he was beyond dangerous.

Which begged the question: *Who was Torin Priest?*

Was he the son of a business magnate? Or a vampire progeny not yet turned? Why would vamps want a human child?

"Hey, you're Liv's new friend, aren't you?" One of the girls I'd seen just outside getting out of a bright red Maserati interrupted my thoughts when she stopped next to me at the top of the small staircase leading into the main part of the mansion. "Is she here with you?"

"I took her home," I said. "She got sick."

"Awww, bummer. She's missing the greatest Priest party yet."

"Hey." I grabbed the girl's arm before she could walk off. "Where's Torin?" I needed to know where he was so I could make sure he wouldn't catch me when I went snooping.

The girl lifted one perfectly sculpted blonde brow, just slightly darker than my own. "Why do you want to know?"

I sighed and gripped her arm harder. "Because I do," I said.

"If you're planning on seducing Torin Priest, you've

got a lot to learn, *new girl*," she spat at me, all venom and unnecessary jealousy.

I blinked slowly. "Location?" I prompted when she said nothing more.

"I'm not going to tell you," she growled as she tugged on her arm. I clamped down harder, digging my nails into her skin with an annoyed sigh. "Ouch! Let go of me!"

"Just tell me where he'd be," I said.

"You wouldn't—ow! ow! Oh my God. Carrie, get this bitch off of me!" I frowned. What a drama queen. I twisted the girl's arm behind her back and used my hold to march her out of the way of incoming traffic. It was just pressure. It's not like it actually hurt the girl. "He's probably out by the pool," she shrieked, eyes widening in panic. "He and his friends always sit out there until people stop showing up."

I released her immediately and stepped back. "Thanks."

"Crazy bitch," she sneered, storming back towards her friend, Carrie—the same one who apparently hadn't heard her cries for help, too busy flirting with one of the guys by the fireplace.

I headed for the backdoor, dodging sleazy jocks bumping chests and girls in skimpy clothing, stumbling along while sloshing their drinks over the rims of their cups. Multicolored lights lit up the pool, throwing shadows of all the people across the tiles surrounding it as they danced to the DJ's music thumping through unseen speakers. Girls in bikinis danced together on a makeshift dance floor while more played in the pool. I bypassed them all, scanning the crowd. Searching for a hint, a sign of Torin or his mysterious sister.

A firm hand gripped my elbow and jerked me around. My shoulders tensed, my fist clenched. As soon as I made the full turn, I popped the man latched onto my arm in the face and stood back when he stumbled, barely hanging onto me as his free hand cupped his now bleeding nose.

"What the fuck?" Maverick's sharp inhalation was muffled as he glared at me.

"Maybe you should learn to ask permission before you touch a girl," I said with a scowl as I quickly extracted my arm from his grip. "What do you want?"

"What the hell are you doing here?" he asked instead, steering me with the sheer size of his body towards a more sequestered alcove between two potted palms. A woman's high-pitched scream assaulted my ears and seconds later, one of the football team guys ran by with a dark haired brunette thrown over his shoulder as he leapt with her into the pool.

I ignored them in lieu of staring up into Maverick's honey brown gaze. "It's a party," I said. "I'm allowed to be here."

Maverick pulled his hand away and I was satisfied to see that though his nose wasn't broken, blood still seeped from each nostril. He scoffed and reached down, lifting the hem of his dark t-shirt to his upper lip, wiping away the red there. My breath caught. Holy shit.

Saliva saturated my mouth as I could do nothing more than stare, open-mouthed, at the fucking rock hard lines of his abdomen. It wasn't fucking fair. Maverick was an asshole. A hot one. Built like he was smuggling paint rollers under his fucking skin. I could feel the heat under my skin rising as I forced my eyes to avert.

"Fuck!" he hissed.

I sighed. "Tilt your head down," I said, turning back to him. He, thankfully, dropped the hem of his shirt and did as I commanded. "Do you taste blood in your mouth?" I asked, recalling all of the times I'd done this same thing to Brandon in training.

"No," he said, keeping his head bent.

"That's good," I said. "Means it's not going to your stomach. Just wait like that until you stop bleeding and then you can ask your damn questions."

"I wouldn't have to if you hadn't punched me. What the hell was that for?"

I shrugged, realizing a bit belatedly that he couldn't see it with the way his head was canted forward. "You grabbed me," I answered aloud.

"And that gave you a reason to punch me?"

"You're an asshole." When he didn't respond, I assumed he wouldn't deny it and that was reason enough.

After another minute or so, he slowly lifted his head and looked down at me. "What are you doing here?" he repeated.

I rolled my eyes. "I already told you."

Above his reddened nose—which would likely bruise later—he narrowed his eyes. "What are you up to, Barbie?"

"Your trust in me is inspiring," I deadpanned. "What makes you think I'm up to anything?"

"You're new. You don't have any friends. What could you possibly be doing here other than scheming?" he replied.

"Maybe I'm trying to make friends," I argued.

"Yeah, you're real friendly," he said, gesturing to his nose.

Before I could respond, a tall, voluptuous woman appeared at our sides, peeking through the leaves into our hideaway. "Maverick? Is that you?" She reached inside, latching onto his arm and pulling him out. "What are you doing hiding over here?" she asked playfully as she lifted an elegant hand and draped herself over his chest. "I haven't seen you in so long. You never come over anymore." Full pink lips pouted up at him.

"El," Maverick was stiff as he greeted her, "you haven't changed at all."

The woman—El—sniffed delicately and perhaps it was my focused attention, but she appeared to pause for a moment, her eyes darting to the hem of his shirt before lifting to his lips. I squinted at her. Though her eyes didn't flash red, her mouth opened and her tongue darted out to lick over her lips before she moved in closer. "I know you and Torin don't talk much anymore, but you really should visit. If not for him"—She paused, stroking a lone finger down the center of his chest between his pecs. For some reason, that made something inside me tighten in revolt.—"then for me."

"Maverick," I barked before I could stop myself.

Maverick's head turned my way, one dark brow

lifting slightly. El, however, fixed her gaze on Maverick for a moment more, looking specifically at his throat before she, too, slowly tilted her head my way.

"Who's this, Mav?" she inquired lightly. "She can't be your girlfriend. Have you moved on from Maryanne? So soon?"

Maverick jolted as though he'd been electrocuted, his arms coming up and pushing El away. "Maryanne's gone."

"Is she?" El's lips curled, but there was no surprise on her face. She'd already known that.

"Maverick."

"Fucking bloodhounds," I muttered as Torin strode up between the three of us. Everyone was just popping up tonight. Torin's expression was thunderous as he moved between Maverick and El, cutting an arm between them and pressing the other woman back. El's gaze snapped to me at my comment, and her eyes dilated briefly before she turned back to Torin.

"Torin, darling—"

"Not now, El," Torin said, cutting her off. "Why don't you go find a boy toy to play with?" Though phrased as one, it wasn't a suggestion.

El's lips curled upward once more as she fixated on Maverick. "I already have."

A deep rumble of irritation erupted from Torin's chest. "Go," he ordered.

Maverick glanced at me. "You should go as well," he said.

I shrugged and stepped away. That was fine by me.

With Torin distracted by Maverick, I knew I'd have time to search the house on my own without worry.

Keeping my gaze fixed on them, I melted back into the crowd and retraced my steps until the cool wash of air conditioning filtered over my skin, leaving a trail of goosebumps rising along my bare arms. Time to get to work.

FOURTEEN

BARBIE

IF WEALTH AND OPULENT WASTE HAD A STENCH, IT WAS the combination of alcohol and expensive perfume. I passed by the third crystal chandelier dangling from the arched ceilings of the second floor and made my way to the end of the hallway through the sparse crowd that had been allowed up here. The farther up I went, the less people there were. As I went, I examined my surroundings.

The house itself was a lot older than I had originally thought, the internal structure unusual and somewhat confusing. I could see areas where the old pieces of the house met the new. The floorplan I expected didn't match what I found. Some rooms were far smaller than any architect would normally create, more the size of closets than actual rooms. When I peeked in a few of the bathrooms, I noticed that some of those, too, were awkward looking. *A clawfoot tub ... who even had those anymore?*

I took out my phone and snapped a few photos of

the rooms. A backup plan was always smart. It would be best to get familiar with the layout of the place, nonetheless, and photos would help me plan if I needed to return to finish the job. Regardless of who these people were, or where they came from, if they *were* vampires then they might know why my family had to die. There was no doubt in my mind we were targeted. The entire night ran through my head on repeat whenever I thought about it. Travis had known who I was when he had first met me. He'd known who my parents were. He'd come there to torture and kill us all.

Unfortunately for him, he failed—with the killing me part. But at least he solidified what my parents had tried and failed to teach me. Vampires couldn't be trusted and it wouldn't do to leave any of them alive.

I hit the third floor and froze at the top of the stairs when voices drifted out of one of the open doorways farther down the hallway. The sound of footsteps drew nearer, causing a small amount of panic to rise within me. I knew I couldn't make it back down the stairwell and out of sight before whoever it was entered the hallway. So, instead, I darted into the nearest bedroom and scrambled across the carpet as the voices behind me—female, I recognized a split second later—grew closer. I ducked behind the blackout curtains and cupped a hand over my mouth to keep the sound of my breathing muffled. Even behind the thick fabric of the curtains, it felt like I was practically screaming rather than quietly drawing sparse breaths in and out.

"It's beautiful," a woman said. My brows lowered as

I tried to decipher where I'd heard that high-pitched feminine voice before. "It's just gorgeous, really."

"You like it?"

I pressed my lips together and tried to breathe through my nose. I didn't recognize the second voice.

"Oh yes, it's the prettiest necklace I've ever seen. I'll have to ask my father to get me one just like it."

"Would you like to keep it?" the second woman asked.

"W-what? Oh my gosh, I c-couldn't possibly—"

"Here," the second woman interrupted. There was the sound of an audible gasp.

"It's so heavy," the first said in wonder.

Sidling to the side, I peeked between the curtains and nearly cursed my horrible luck. The two women stopped just outside the room. The light from the hallway spilling into the opened doorway of my hide-away room. I had been right. I did recognize the first voice. Rachel. I scowled into my palm before my brain caught up with my feelings.

What the hell is she doing on the third floor? It was practically deserted, while the first two floors and the grounds of the estate were crowded with people. What reason could she have for being up here? And who was the second woman?

I craned my neck, trying to see further without alerting them to my presence. The second woman was taller than Rachel, her hair dark and curled on the ends. Her face was turned half away, so I could only catch a glimpse of her profile, but from what I saw she was a beautiful woman. A sharp looking nose, petite chin, and slender neck. It was clear, though, that she was several years older than Rachel. In her twenties, at least.

The woman's hands lifted to the jeweled necklace dangling in Rachel's grip as the younger girl stared in awe at the glittering emerald. On anyone else, the small curve of the unknown woman's lips might have looked innocent, but to me—for some reason—it felt … wrong.

"I can't keep this," Rachel was saying, though her words held no heat. It was clear she wanted the necklace. She couldn't tear her gaze away from it. It was as if she were entranced.

I rolled my eyes. It was just damn jewelry.

"Please, I insist," the woman said. "Think of it as a gift from me."

"Oh Delia, thank you!" Rachel finally gave in, quickly clasping the necklace to her chest before she yanked it up and undid the clasp as she fastened it around her own throat. "I'll wear it always."

Delia. Where had I heard that name before? I searched my memory. It was in there somewhere. Delia. Delia. Del—I dropped my hand away from my mouth as realization struck. This was one of the women Olivia had talked about. I narrowed my eyes and leaned further to the side so that I could see more. What was she doing giving jewelry to Rachel Harris?

"You should totally wear it always," Delia agreed. Her hand came up to Rachel's shoulder, her nails stroking the silky fabric of Rachel's loose fitted top. "In fact, you should never take it off."

My breath caught in my chest as Rachel's whole body grew lax and she bobbed her head up and down.

"Never take it off," she repeated, the syllables slurring slightly.

Anxiety settled in my gut. I reached back, my hand sliding beneath my t-shirt to the dagger anchored at my back. I'd doused it in holy water before I'd left and I had never felt so relieved to be prepared in my life. I knew what Delia was doing. It was the same trick Travis and Kent had used on me and Brandon to get us to invite them into our home. Mind control.

I slid the dagger out from beneath my t-shirt and held it at my side.

"Now, why don't you go downstairs and join your friends?"

Rachel bobbed her head once more, turned on her heel, and left—disappearing from my view as I assumed she headed for the stairs. In a few short minutes, Delia's mind control would fade, but by then she'd be swept away by the party. It was hard to realize you were being controlled, even harder when you didn't even know such a thing was possible. My fingers tightened around the hilt of my blade.

"Something smells delicious." I stiffened as Delia turned towards the room I was in and strode through the doorway. She touched the light switch, letting the room glow to life as she moved silently across the floor.

I should've known better, I realized. To think that she couldn't smell me.

FIFTEEN

BARBIE

My heartbeat pounded in my ears. I was trapped, unable to move or escape. Not that I would have. A vampire was before me, and it was my sworn duty to kill it. Preferably before *it* killed *me*.

I stepped out from behind the curtains and the creature—Delia—halted at the center of the room, just beneath the light. It illuminated her pale cheeks, her glowing blood-red eyes, and the wicked smile she sported. Two dainty looking fangs peeked out over her lower lip.

"What happened, pet?" she asked. "Did you wander away from the party?"

I clenched my teeth as I held the dagger against my back with one hand, out of sight. For now. "I'm sorry," I started, feigning an awkward giggle. "I heard voices and I just … panicked. I didn't mean to eavesdrop, really!"

Delia's head tilted, her jaw angling to the side as a thick hunk of her dark brunette hair slid over her bare shoulder. "You smell like blood," she said, inhaling deeply.

I looked, automatically, down to the remaining hand that still rested at my side. Wrong move. In the next instant, Delia had crossed the remainder of the space between us and reached out, her hand locking around my throat. Without thinking, I swung my blade out and sliced across her chest. The edge of my dagger cut through the front fabric of her dress easily enough and a thin line of blood rose from her bared flesh. She cried out and released me just as quickly as the edges of her wound festered and blackened.

"What the fuck!" she shrieked. "It's not healing. Why isn't it healing?" Red eyes flashed at me as she lunged. "You little bitch!"

I dodged, swinging around as she ripped through the drapes, yanking them from her nails with such strength that the bolts holding up the rungs were jerked from the wall and the whole thing came down at her back. Moon-light streamed into the darkened room, washing her back in a low blue hue.

I didn't wait for her to move again. I struck—my arm swinging out once more. I ducked and rolled when she easily evaded my attack. Her upper lip curled back into a snarl. "Hunter." She spat the term as though it were a curse and I was sure, to her, it probably was. "I wonder, who let you in?"

I went down on one knee, reaching beneath my pants leg and withdrawing my second dagger. Having two in hand made me feel far more prepared. I didn't answer her question. I threw my first dagger and when her arm arched out—slapping the thing away as though it were a pesky bug buzzing about her head—I rushed her, dagger up and at the ready.

The tip slid easily between her ribs. The sound of her surprised gasp drew a smile to my lips. They were always shocked when a mere human caught them off guard. Vampires had a nasty habit of underestimating people they considered livestock. I gritted my teeth and shoved the blade in harder until I hit something and blood gushed over my palms. But it was too low, I hadn't hit the heart.

I cursed and jerked back, withdrawing the blade, but not quick enough, it seemed. Once again, a cold hand closed over my throat and squeezed. Another hand wrapped around the wrist of the hand that held my remaining dagger and squeezed. I could feel my bones on the verge of cracking. The second I released the dagger, Delia's grip stopped contracting. She turned abruptly and slammed my spine into the tall windows that stretched halfway up the wall so hard that it gave an explosive cracking sound as fissures raced up along either side of me.

"Oh shit!" I gasped as the glass fractured. Large shards fell outward, but several smaller pieces rained down over my shoulders. They stuck in my hair and fell into the low cut neckline of my shirt. I winced when I felt one of the falling shards cut me, warm blood soaking the inside of my t-shirt.

My eyes widened when I realized that Delia didn't seem to care about my blood. Instead, she kept going, pushing my upper body out of the window until I was half bent backwards, hanging suspended above the open air. Glancing back, I saw that one of the balconies from the second floor was directly beneath me, but it was still at least a ten foot drop.

I kicked out, struggling to maintain some semblance of control and balance as I shoved my lower back against the windowsill. I clenched my teeth when I felt another shard of glass cut me—this time slicing right through the fabric and into my skin.

"What the hell did you cut me with?" she demanded.

Gasping, panic clawed at my throat. Black and white dots danced before my eyes. I couldn't breathe let alone answer her. She shook me, nonetheless. "Answer me!" she screamed. "Why isn't it healing!"

Fuck. This. Bitch, I thought. Though it hurt against her powerful grip, I jerked my chin down, loosening her hold, and reached up to clasp my fingers around her wrist with one hand as I dove into my pocket with my other. I uncapped the bottle I'd stowed there—my last fucking bottle of holy water—and splashed it right in her face.

Delia dropped me so quickly, I nearly careened out of the window. My fingers released the bottle and latched onto the windowsill just before I fell completely through as Delia shrieked—her hands covering her face as she screamed and her skin sizzled. Her blackened flesh was caved in against one cheekbone, pain echoing across her features as she cupped her fingers over decaying skin.

I leveraged myself up and scrambled across the floor

for my daggers. Just as my hand closed around one, I heard the sound of voices coming up the stairs. I glanced at Delia and paused. I could choose to stay and kill her and risk having to explain not only *why* I stabbed her but having to explain why she turned to ash when I did—assuming, of course, that whoever was coming was human—or I could get the hell out of Dodge.

I chose to get the hell out of Dodge.

With a curse, I snatched up the curtain rod, ripped the drapes free and threw them over the shattered glass in the window. Placing my hands over the fabric, I lifted one foot over the sill as the voices reached the third floor. *It would really suck if I broke something*, I thought as I swung my other leg over and with my fingers clutched in the fabric of the curtains, I leapt down to the balcony below. I tucked my arms and legs in as I landed, rolling to a stop when my side slammed into the balcony railing. The curtains fluttered down over my head.

I yanked the heavy fabric off and dove for the doors leading inside, slamming into an occupied bedroom. The couple writhing on the bed stopped, the man cursing and the girl squealing in surprise, but I didn't stop. I dashed across the room and into the hallway, turning and barreling through the crowd drinking and laughing and chatting. The music was loud, even up here, which told me that the people who had heard Delia's screams were vampires as well. What had I fallen into? How many were there?

One, I could take. Two, maybe. But more than that?

I was forced to slow down to stay as inconspicuous as possible, but I definitely stuck out like a sore thumb. My hair was matted to the side of my face. Sweat coated my skin. I was lucky I had opted to wear darker colors. Had I chosen the baby blue tank top Olivia had tried to shove me into, I would have bled right through it.

As it was, I could feel blood leaking from my wounds, making the inside of my shirt stick to my cuts. My body ached. My throat in particular, but I dared not stop. I hit the bottom floor and turned for the front door when my mind caught up with me.

Maverick.

Shit.

I couldn't leave him.

Cursing, I whirled away from my escape and headed out the back. My head was pounding by the time I reached the pool, my heart hammering in my chest. The noise escalated when someone turned up the volume on the speakers as they blasted a dance song. I scanned the nearby area looking for the top of Maverick's dark head.

People crowded around the pool, bumping and grinding against each other, making my task all the more difficult. Across the yard, I saw Rachel and then … Maverick. She stroked her fingers down his chest as another guy talked to him. From where I could see, it was as though he didn't care about her presence, but neither did he stop her from touching him. Torin was nowhere in sight. Good.

I shoved my way through the dancing crowd and when a girl whirled on me with a scowl, I shoved her— glittering dress and drink in hand—into the pool and kept going, making my way to where Mav stood.

"Maverick," I barked his name as my sneakered feet hit the grass, "we gotta go."

He turned and frowned. "Where——"

I didn't let him finish, instead choosing to grab Rachel by her wrist and pry her off. "Sorry," I sneered. "If Mav gets desperate for attention, he'll give you a call later."

Her eyes lit with indignation, but before she could slap me or say something equally scathing, Mav stepped in front of her. "Barbie."

I shook my head and reached for his arm. "No time," I said. "Gotta go. Now."

He must have been surprised by my willingness to touch him or perhaps it was the strength with which I dragged him along behind me, but he didn't argue. I darted a glance over my shoulder. Rachel's gaze was fixed on me—no, not on me—on Maverick. I frowned at that but continued forward. Whatever teenage lust hormones were floating through her system could be taken care of with someone else—preferably, someone I didn't feel responsible for.

"What are you doing?" Maverick finally asked, his tone low and warning.

I stopped in front of the valet, handed over my ticket and spun towards Mav. I held out my hand and his dark eyes narrowed, but thankfully he pulled his out and gave it to another valet. I regretted letting someone else park the car for me, now. "What's this about?" Mav demanded.

"I——" My eyes shot up to the front of the mansion, skimming the windows. The curtains had been retrieved and put back up, but a gentle breeze fluttered through the window three stories up. "I can't say right now." It wasn't safe and really, I needed time to come up with a plausible lie.

A bolt of unease whipped through me. When the valets returned, I looked up at Maverick. "Follow me to Olivia's," I said. "Stay close."

"What—"

I didn't stay to answer anything else, but instead hopped into the Porsche and buckled in. Maverick's growl of frustration reached me moments before I pressed on the gas and headed for the end of the driveway. In the rearview mirror, I watched as his truck was brought to him. Casting a glance my way, he got in and followed. I was more than a little surprised by the lack of fight from him, but I wasn't in any way under the illusion that he trusted me. No. Maverick McKnight would want answers and soon.

Those answers though—the truth, anyway—would get him killed. I was almost positive. Despite my concern for him, the farther we got from the party, the more my mind turned to Torin. He had walked in the sunlight. He had eaten food. He was in high school for fuck's sake.

So then, what the hell was he doing living in a house full of vampires?

SIXTEEN

BARBIE

THE CUTS BENEATH MY CLOTHES HAD BEGUN TO BURN. The bleeding had slowed, but the fabric of my shirt was now stuck to my wounds—pulling them open each time I tried to shift it away until finally I just gave up and left it alone. I parked Olivia's Porsche in her driveway and left her keys on the driver's seat after checking to make sure I hadn't bled all over the fine German car as Maverick's truck pulled up alongside the curb.

"Want to tell me what that was about?" he asked as I hopped in the cab.

I left my seatbelt off and sank into the seat. "Not particularly," I answered.

"I'm sorry, let me rephrase," he replied. "Tell me what the fuck that was about or else."

"Ohhh, so badass." I groaned and slapped a hand onto the dash to keep myself from careening forward as he braked hard and snapped his head to the side to glare at me. "Okay, I thought I could trust your driving abilities," I said, reaching for the seatbelt, "but not if you're going to slam on your brakes for no damn reason."

"You just dragged me out of a party without warning and without explanation, Barbie. What the hell is going on?"

I clipped the belt in place and leaned back once more. "Can we please get back to the house first?" I asked. "I'm tired and I'd really like a bath."

"If—and I mean the if part, Barbie—I take you back to the house without argument, will you tell me what the hell that was all about?"

I waved my hand at him. "Yeah, yeah, sure," I lied.

He stared at me for a moment as if trying to assess my honesty. Either my poker face was damn good or he was awful at judging people because, with a heaved sigh, he lifted his foot off the brake and faced the windshield.

Great, I thought. I'd managed to buy myself about twenty minutes to come up with a plausible story. Forty, if he let me take a shower and get changed first. The vision of mansions and trees outside the car blurred past as he drove in silence back to the house.

When we pulled into the driveway, Maverick slammed out of the truck as if it were on fire while I, on the other hand, moved slower in deference to my wounds. Maverick was already on the porch, keys in the lock, and front door hanging partially open as he waited for me to catch up.

"Awww," I said with a grin as I ambled up. "Maybe there is a gentleman under all that asshole veneer."

"Not on your life," he snapped. "Get inside."

"Can I take a shower first?" I asked, subduing my panic. "Before you start in on the Spanish Inquisition, that is." I still had yet to come up with a story.

He glared at me and gestured for me to go up the stairs before him. "Shower now or shower later, you're still not getting out of telling me what I want to know," he said.

I swallowed around a thick throat. "I know."

Considering how close Maverick was sticking to me, I was slightly surprised that as I entered the bathroom he told me he'd be downstairs when I was done. I almost thought he'd been prepared to wait outside the bathroom until I finished. Grateful for the distance, I closed the bathroom door and began to lift my shirt away from my skin.

I bit my lip hard as I slowly pried the fabric from my wounds and tugged it the rest of the way over my head. Most of the cuts were small, but there were at least two that had gone a bit deeper. I pressed my fingers against the outer edges of the one on my abdomen and winced. No wonder they were still burning, there was still fucking glass embedded in me.

With a sigh, I got down on my knees and went digging under the cabinet for tweezers. I found a pair still in the package, and after tearing it open, I used them to pick the shards out of my cuts. Red flowed against the white plastic bag lining the bathroom trash can as I plopped each piece of glass right from my skin into its contents.

When the burn subsided, I assumed I'd gotten it all out and divested myself of the rest of my clothes, leaning into the shower and cranking the water on full blast. As soon as I stepped inside and the water hit my cuts and bruises, I hissed out a pained breath.

Punching the tile, I inhaled sharply and cursed. *Fuck! It hurt.* As the initial discomfort faded, I slowly released the breath I'd been unintentionally holding and set to work on soaping up. I scrubbed over the cuts, trying to get them as clean as possible and even bent over and shoved my scalp under the showerhead so I could make sure to get any and all remaining glass fragments out of my hair.

As the water began to grow cold, I flipped around and leaned against the shower wall and finally let myself consider a story. What was I going to tell Maverick? What *could* I tell Maverick?

Hey, sorry for pulling you away from your ex-bestfriend's party, but I'm pretty sure he's shacking up with a bunch of vampires and one of them just tried to kill me. It's not a big deal, but maybe you should start carrying around a cross and some holy water. You know, just in case.

Yeah, that was sure to go over splendidly. Probably about as well as him calling his parents and having me shipped off to a white padded room with comfy strait-jackets and a routine schedule of pills meant to keep me calm and happy. Not only would he not believe me, but he would think I was crazy.

I shut off the shower and got out, wrapping myself in a towel before padding out into the hall and towards my bedroom. I froze just inside the door at the figure reclining on my bed.

"I thought you said you were going downstairs," I said.

Maverick shrugged, unashamed, as he laced his fingers together behind his neck and leaned against the headboard. "I thought better of it," he replied. "I wouldn't put it past you to climb out the window to get away from answering a few simple questions."

There was nothing simple about this coming conversation. "I'm not really in the climbing mood right now." I cut across the room, reaching for the top drawer of my dresser as I began to pull out clothes. "Are you going to stay and watch the show or can I have a little privacy to change at least?"

He lifted a single brow. "You don't have anything I haven't seen before," he said. "I'm not leaving until I get some answers."

The sheer fucking audacity of this asshole. He thought I'd run. I could see the challenge in his eyes. Turning away from him, I let the towel fall to the floor and then bent over to slide my underwear up my legs. The intake of his breath brought a grin to my lips. *Oh, how easily men fell,* I thought with a roll of my eyes.

"Barbie." I finished putting my panties on and then reached for a bra, snapping the front clasp as I ignored him. "Barbie," he repeated my name harder this time. I yanked the soft stretchy workout shorts on and turned to face him, pausing at the look on his face. Maverick's brows were drawn down low over his light brown eyes, his lips thinned into a straight, pinched line. I blinked at the ferocity of his gaze, fixated now on my chest. I looked down reflexively and cursed my stupidity as I reached behind me for my tank top and pressed it to my front.

Maverick swung his legs over the side of the bed and stood up. I didn't move a single muscle as he approached, not even to slide the shirt over my head. "Maverick?" My voice was hoarse as he stood over me. I tipped my head back so I could keep my gaze on his face as I tried to determine what he would do or say next.

He reached up and tugged the tank top in my fists down, his eyes sliding over the cuts and bruises. One thumb graced the edge of one of the cuts on my chest. "Your back..." he said, swallowing around a thick throat. "Why is it covered in bruises? Why are you all cut up?"

I sucked in a breath. I hadn't even thought about that. It must have happened when I went through the window. My lips parted, but no words escaped. What could I say? I put my hand on his chest and pushed him back a step. Though I didn't press hard, he went willingly, keeping his eyes on me the entire time as I lifted my tank top and slid it over my head, tugging it down to cover the rest of my front.

"It's a complicated story," I said.

"I think we have time." He gestured around. "Maybe it's escaped your notice, but my parents aren't here. They went into the city for the rest of the weekend. It's just you and me, Barbie." Maverick lifted one arm over my shoulder and braced it against the dresser at my back. He leaned close, his breath washing over my face, smelling of something citrusy.

I grimaced. As much as I hated to admit it, it was

probably a good thing Beth and Jon were out of town. Soon enough, Delia would want her vengeance, and unless Torin was an idiot—which I highly doubted—then he'd know exactly who had attacked his vampire friend based on her description of me. But if Maverick was going to stay safe, he needed a goddamn good reason to listen to me.

I girded myself as I stared into his expectant gaze. "I think you're going to want to sit down for this one," I said. When he still didn't move, I closed my eyes and took a breath, pushing out the next word on my tongue through clenched teeth. "Please?"

I opened my eyes as Maverick's hand fell away from the dresser. He took one step back and then another and another, until he was at the end of my bed. Folding his arms across his chest, I gathered that was the best I was going to get from him and I started talking.

"The night my parents and brother died," I started, "I was there."

He blinked. "I thought—"

"I lied to the cops," I said. "I didn't get into a fight with my brother and spend the night at my neighbor's house. The house didn't burn down on its own, and I … I saw how they died."

Maverick unfolded his arms, but he didn't seem to know what else to do with them. His muscles tensed. His fists opened and closed at his sides. "Why the fuck didn't you tell the cops then?" he asked.

"Because I couldn't prove it and the men who killed my family were already gone." I left out the fact that they weren't men at all, but vampires, and that they were dead and I had been the one to kill them.

"What does this have to do with tonight?" he demanded.

"The men who attacked my family said that there was someone else in charge. They insinuated that it had been preplanned. Tonight, I—there was someone at the party that…" I trailed off with a wince. I didn't know how to keep going without giving away too much.

"If you saw someone you recognized or someone you think might be involved in your family's deaths, you need to call the police." Maverick was already taking out his cell phone and punching in numbers when I slapped his phone out of his hand.

"No!" I grabbed his wrist. "No, we can't do that."

"Why not?" Maverick growled. He broke my hold on his hand and reached up, his fingers closing over the sides of my arms as he shook me. "I may not fucking like you, Barbie, but that doesn't mean I'm going to let your family's murderers get away."

I shook my head. "It's more complicated than that," I insisted. "There's no evidence and despite what crime television would have you believe the police aren't going to want to open up a case they already closed six months ago."

"So, you're just going to leave it at that then?" He stared down at me, his mouth gaping open as he shook his head in disbelief. "Why?"

"Please," I said. "Just leave it alone for now. Stay in the house this weekend. Don't go anywhere and don't let anyone know about this."

He tilted his head, slightly shaking it from side to side. "What would that do?"

"Just…" I reached up and latched onto the front of his shirt even as he squeezed my arms. "Trust me," I said. "Don't leave. Don't tell anyone. And most importantly, don't invite anyone into the house."

"Wha—"

I yanked on the fabric of his shirt until he had to bend slightly or risk me tearing it. "Don't invite anyone into the house," I repeated. "Promise me that."

Our gazes locked and held for several moments—it felt like eons but was likely only a few seconds—before finally, he nodded. "Okay, fine," he conceded.

Relief echoed through me and I sagged against him. The soreness and aches in my muscles came screaming back as I pressed my forehead against his chest. "Thank you," I whispered.

Maverick's fingers loosened their hold and he slipped them around my back until they were pressed to my spine. "Don't thank me just yet," he replied. "I know there's more to this story than you're letting on." My body clenched, but he soothed his fingers up and down my back gently. "I'll let it go for now," he said. "But you'll have to tell me everything at some point. You'll have to tell someone."

Maybe he was right, I thought. *But…* "Who said anything about that someone being you?"

"Do you see anyone else here?" he asked.

I didn't. I didn't have anyone else, but I knew—no matter how good it felt being in Maverick's arms, to tell him about my family, even just a little bit—I shouldn't allow myself to. I needed to protect him and his family. At least as long as I was living under their roof, but as soon as my eighteenth birthday hit, I knew I'd be gone.

It'd be safer for everyone that way.

SEVENTEEN

TORIN

GLASS SHATTERED AGAINST THE WALL AND A SMALL BODY slammed into me, shoving me into the door frame at my back.

"Who is she?" Delia spat, her form vibrating with barely suppressed rage.

"Who is who?" I asked keeping my tone even and my face passive. It only served to piss her off even more.

"Do not fuck with me, Torin." Delia slammed a fist through the drywall next to my head. For a creature so tiny, her vampire was a bloodthirsty little beast and all of that otherworldliness that she now had in place of her humanity was bordering on out of control. "I want the name of that little bitch. The one who did *this* to me!" She turned her cheek so that I could plainly see where something—it looked as though it were some kind of acid—had melted through half of her face.

Whatever it was, it was obviously disrupting her vampire healing capabilities because the wound had yet to heal; the right side of her cheek was sunken in and blacked at the edges where pieces of her flesh were missing, revealing the top and bottom row of her teeth all the way back to her molars.

My lips twitched in amusement. She must have been in considerable pain. A small feminine hand wrapped around my throat and used its hold to yank me forward and slam me back even harder against the frame of the door until the wood cracked.

"Releasing your anger on me won't get you the name you want any sooner," I said.

"It makes me feel better," she growled. "Name. Now."

"How am I supposed to know?" I asked with a shrug. "I wasn't there when you were attacked."

"Blonde. Short. A bitch. Anyone like that ring a bell?" she demanded.

Barbie. My mind supplied the information before the rest of me had completely caught up with the description. I couldn't have said why Barbie's name came to me. There were easily a dozen or so other girls I knew that were blonde and short. But as it stood, Barbie hadn't been far from my mind since I'd first met her a week earlier.

"There are a few people like that at St. Marion's," I answered. "How do you know it's a student from my school?"

Delia's fingers contracted against my windpipe until it became difficult to draw in air. This was getting tedious. I reached up and grasped her wrist, squeezing until her grip loosened. I gently removed her hand and took a step away from the doorway.

"She was young," Delia said. "I didn't recognize her as one of the children from your other parties. I want an address, Torin."

There was no way in hell I would give it to her, but she didn't need to know that. I turned away from Delia towards my sister. "What do you think?" I asked.

Katalin stared out of the window of the third floor study as if lost in thought. The party had ended barely an hour or so ago. The servants and other employees had all been released until the following afternoon. I knew from experience no one would be coming to pick up their cars until closer to noon. The sun was scheduled to be up within the next forty-five minutes though.

"If she used holy water, then I suspect she's a hunter," Katalin finally said.

A figure appeared in the open doorway—Eloise. "I thought Arrius had already taken care of the North American hunters," she said as she made her way over to Delia. "Oh darling, your face is absolutely ruined."

Delia bared her fangs. "I want her dead!" she shrieked.

Eloise grimaced, her arm snapping out so quickly it blurred through the air as she took Delia's delicate neck in her hand and squeezed until Delia's eyes widened in shock. "Do be quiet, dear." Eloise sighed, pursing her lips. "You're liable to give me a headache."

"Vampires don't get headaches," I reminded her.

Eloise squeezed Delia's throat a bit more as she arched her brow, waiting. Delia nodded quickly and was released. "Still," El replied turning away from her pet as she went to Katalin, "it's annoying."

Delia, relatively subdued now that her master had exerted her dominance once more, bit down on what was left of her lower lip and hissed out a breath. "She definitely used holy water," she said. "Otherwise, I'd be healing and I'm not."

"There are those who fall through the cracks of Arrius' plan," Eloise said as she stopped by my sister's side and touched her arm. "You know we have to ensure his will be seen through, darling."

Kat finally looked away from the window. "What do you suggest?"

"I think we should let Torin handle this mess." El sent me a grin. Panic laced my veins and a horrible sinking feeling fell to the pit of my stomach.

"What do you mean by 'handle this mess?'" I demanded.

"Why, find the hunter and put the poor human out of her misery, of course." El smiled. "As Arrius' son, that should be nothing to you. Besides, the hunter won't expect anyone to come for her during the day. It's the perfect plan."

"I don't want the little cunt's death to be short," Delia said. "I want her to suffer. I want to rend the flesh bag limb from limb and saw through her throat with a rusty knife and drain her over a bucket."

"I don't believe you were asked what you wanted, dear," El said.

Delia rounded on her—all earlier fear of her mistress forgotten as her anger came roaring back to life.

"She did this to me!" Delia screamed, gesturing to her face.

"It's more important for the hunter to be dealt with than for you to get your silly revenge." El frowned. "Tormenting the cattle won't return your face to the way it was."

"I'm not saying don't kill her," Delia snapped. "But what harm could there be in torturing her a little?"

"I said nothing about harm or torture," El said. "As long as the hunter is dead, it matters not to me. What about you, dear?" She looked to Kat.

Kat shook her head. "Doesn't matter."

"Then it's settled. Torin will handle this issue." El turned away from Kat and stopped before me on her way out of the room. Her hand lifted, nails scratching down the center of my chest so lightly that it sent shivers of apprehension through me. "I suggest you don't take forever finding the girl and killing her, dear Torin. I'd hate to see what would happen if Delia got to the girl first."

My gaze shot to the side. The warning was accurate. Despite the fact that I'd been relegated to the hunter of the hunter, I had no doubts that Delia would take it upon herself to find whoever had attacked her before me.

Once a vampire was on the path of vengeance it was damn near impossible to sway them away from it.

I hoped like hell that I was wrong about my suspicion, but I didn't believe in coincidences. If Barbie was the hunter, she should have killed Delia when she had the chance. "Give me a week," I said. "And I'll have your hunter." If I had to pay for Barbie to go on the run, then so be it, but it'd take at least a week to gather everything necessary.

"One week." El held up a finger and waved it in front of my face. "Use the time wisely, dear."

EIGHTEEN

MAVERICK

Barbie rested her forehead against my sternum, and though she didn't say so upfront, I knew she was exhausted. I kept my hands light on her spine, not wanting to disturb the spiderweb of bruises I'd seen on her back. It was odd. Less than a full week ago, I'd been ready to have her thrown out on her ass. But now, as her breasts pressed against my abdomen and her soft breaths blew over my side, I was cursing my own stupidity.

What the fuck was I doing? Something wasn't right here, and I didn't just mean Barbie's bruises and cuts. She didn't want to tell me the complete story. Fine. But I would find out. I promised her the weekend, and I'd keep that promise, but as soon as Monday hit, I would find out the rest. If not from her, then from someone else.

Hell, it was Torin's fucking party, and knowing him as long as I had—there was nothing that went on at his parties that he wasn't privy to. Try as he might to act the carefree jackass, I knew him on a far deeper level. I knew his fucking soul, even if I didn't know his secrets. Why he'd suddenly up and quit the football team. Why he'd been with Maryanne. Why he'd walked the fuck away from me.

"You're gonna have to loosen your hold there, crusher, or you might pulverize me." Barbie's dry voice infiltrated my thoughts and I realized that as I'd let my old anger consume me, my fingers had latched onto her and begun to contract. I released her immediately and as she backed out of the circle of my arms, I found I didn't really care to let her go. But I forced my hands to my sides anyway.

I turned and headed for the door. "You should get some sleep," I called back.

"Where are you going?" Her voice hitched slightly.

I paused in the doorway and glanced back. "I'm gonna go watch a game or a movie or something and go to bed myself. I'm not leaving the house," I assured her.

"Don't invite anyone in," she repeated.

I sighed, irritated. "I won't."

With that, I left her bedroom and headed for my own. She didn't have to tell me her secrets. Not yet, but that didn't mean I couldn't use the next two days to do my own digging. I paused as I got to my door and thought better of it, turning instead back towards the longer hallway.

The inside of my parents' bedroom was dark. I closed the door behind me before flipping on the light and heading to my mother's vanity. Pulling out the drawers, I searched through, cursing when I didn't find a damn thing. I left the bedroom and headed for the stairs, moving down and towards the first floor offices. I should have realized, any important files on Barbie or her parents for the adoption would be there. Barbie didn't know it yet, but I knew that my parents were planning on adopting her. She had probably been told they were just fostering her, and they were ... for now. I'd meant it when I told her my parents were well-meaning. They were kind hearted and they viewed her as the daughter they'd never had.

Perhaps it had been initial jealousy to hate her on first glance, but truly I'd been concerned. They didn't know her and they had been willing to open their hearts and their home for her. For all they knew, she could've robbed them blind and disappeared. I didn't regret how I'd treated Barbie, but while I still didn't completely trust that she was being honest, I knew there was more to her now.

I reached my mother's desk and sat in the office chair. On the left hand corner was a picture of me and Dad. On the right, a recently taken photo of Barbie. I picked up the identical frame to my photo and stared down at the blonde-haired, blue-eyed vixen. She wasn't even looking at the camera. She probably didn't even know this picture existed, much less that my mom had already had it printed out and placed here.

I put it down and went to work—digging through the upper drawers and then the lower ones before I found a thick stack of files. Plopping them on the desk surface, I opened one and sucked in a breath. Barbie's background.

It detailed what she'd told me about her family's death. Her parents and brother had been in the house and the house was set on fire. Barbie had been next door —or so she'd told the cops. Foul play was suspected, but the case was closed as a robbery gone wrong. The only issue was that it'd been hard for the investigators to determine what had gone missing after the fire. And everyone assumed that Barbie had been the lucky survivor.

Now, I wondered just how lucky she'd actually been.

NINETEEN

BARBIE

Beth and Jon returned on Sunday evening and by Monday morning, nothing had happened. There was no retaliation. No one banging down the McKnight's door demanding recompense for my nearly killing a local vampire. The longer it went on, the more anxious I grew. I wished they would just get it over with already and try to kill me. The waiting was worse than actual death or attempted murder at the least.

My leg jumped beneath my palm as I tapped out a staccato rhythm with my nails. I chewed on my lower lip, watching the streets go by from the window of Maverick's truck. My nervous fidgeting went on until, finally, Maverick reached over and slapped a hand down over mine. "Stop," he said. "You're driving me crazy."

I sighed and pulled my hand out from underneath his. "Nothing's happened," I said.

"Did you expect something might?" he asked, lifting a brow and half turning his head in my direction.

"Yes? No? I don't know."

"Do you think the people who killed your family recognized you?" he asked and then before I could answer, he went on. "I mean, if all you did was fight with someone at the party, I doubt the cops would come calling over something like that unless there's more you want to tell me."

I stiffened and cursed my stupidity. "Yeah, you're right," I answered weakly. "There's probably nothing to worry about."

Maverick frowned but didn't say anything more as he drove the rest of the way to St. Marion. Since we'd left later than usual due to the fact that Maverick didn't have morning practice, the student parking lot was already half full by the time we arrived. Olivia's white Porsche was parked towards the front and she rested against the back bumper as Maverick and I approached.

Flicking a look his way, she twirled her hair around one slender finger and called out, "hey, Maverick."

Maverick lifted a brow. "Hey?" I bit my lip in amusement as he waited for something else, but it appeared Olivia's brain had short-circuited because she simply stared at him, twirling her hair reflexively over and over again.

I sighed. "See you at lunch," I said, pushing against his spine to get him moving.

Maverick—the boulder—didn't fucking move as he looked back at me. "Are you getting rid of me?"

"Yes, isn't it obvious?"

He pursed his lips, fighting a grin. "You need to work on your people skills, Barbie. I'll see you at lunch."

"My people skills are fine!" I shouted as he strode away.

"Sure they are," he called back.

I growled and watched him go until he disappeared into the school building before turning back to Olivia. She didn't wait for me to say anything. "Oh my GAHD." She sighed dramatically. "Maverick McKnight is like pheromone overload. I couldn't think of anything to fucking say." She collapsed against her car and her hand left her hair. "Jesus, he probably thought I was a ditz."

I thought she was a ditz, but I kept my mouth shut, choosing instead to ask her about something else. "How was your weekend?" I asked.

She groaned and turned, snatching her purse off the ground. "Awful," she confessed. "My parents were pissed about my hangover and I wasn't allowed to go anywhere this weekend. Thanks for taking me home though." She bumped my side as we headed for the doors. "Pretty sure my parents would've taken my Porsche if I'd gotten a DUI or something. By the way, why were my keys in the front seat?"

"Because I took it to the Priest party and I didn't want to wake you up to return them when I dropped it off at your house." We pushed into the main hall and headed through the throng of people that had already gathered.

"You borrowed my Porsche?" She blinked at me. "Well, that explains why my seat was pushed so far up. You're short."

I scowled. "I am not short," I snapped. "I'll have you know five-six is the average height of the American female."

"There is no way you're five-six," she shot back.

"I'm five-five," I said. "I'm average."

"Below average," she insisted.

"I—what the fuck?" Olivia and I stopped in the middle of the front hall as two adults I recognized as Mrs. Echolls from my study hall and a woman who I assumed was another teacher escorted a young girl through the students congregating. The girl, a tall willowy brunette with short spiky hair that I recognized as a girl from my Chemistry class was sobbing openly, her body practically collapsed against Mrs. Echolls.

"I don't know," Olivia said, following the scene with a frown. "Hold on, there's Gabby Dalton. She's bound to know something." I nodded but didn't move as Olivia walked away.

I was nothing more than human, but for some reason, I had a sick feeling curling in the pit of my stomach like some sort of physical premonition reaching deep down inside of me and warning me of impending danger. Over the crowd, I saw the glittering blonde head of Rachel Harris as she, too, watched the proceedings. While everyone around us was quietly murmuring, Rachel watched the girl go with an irritated expression. Compassion was not one of her strong suits apparently. It was obvious to anyone who watched that girl be led off that whatever had caused her outburst had devastated her. Sympathy for whatever had happened—no matter what it was—was the most basic of human emotions.

In the next instant, I was bombarded by Olivia. "Oh my God, you'll never believe it." She latched onto my arm with a cat like grip, her nails digging into my skin.

I flinched as they cut deep, but from the look of utter shock and fear on her face, I didn't think she realized what she was doing. "What?"

"That was Penny Hathaway—she was Derick Gilmore's girlfriend. He's one of the guys on the football team," Olivia explained in a rush.

"Okay?" I lifted my brows as I waited.

Olivia shook her head back and forth, the long strands of her cherry red hair sliding over her shoulders. "He was found dead last night," she confessed.

"What?" I threw her hand away from my arm and grabbed her by her shoulders, shaking her slightly. "How?" I asked. "How did he die?"

Olivia shook in my grip, her face pale. "Gabby's dad is a cop," she said, her voice quavering. "She said that Derick … he … I can't say it, it's too awful."

"Olivia," I snapped.

She crumpled. "His heart…"

I frowned and shook her again. "What about his heart?" I demanded.

"They said it was ripped out. They couldn't find it. Poor Derick. He was nice. And poor Penny! She's probably devastated."

Yeah, she probably was, I agreed silently as I released her.

A loud clap echoed up the hallway, drawing everyone's attention to the front doors where a man in a suit stood with the front office's secretary, Pam Costello. "Alright ladies and gentlemen," the man announced. "I know this is a trying time for all of you, grief counseling will be made available for those who need it, but for now, please head to your homerooms."

And just like that, the bell rang and the remaining students dispersed, many of them chattering with their friends about the events of the morning. Small tidbits of conversation filtered through.

"He was so nice…"

"They found him in his car…"

"Disappeared at the Priest party…"

I admit, I was convinced that a vampire was likely responsible until Olivia had said that his heart was removed. That didn't fit a vampire's MO. *Why would they take the heart?* I headed to my homeroom, leaving Olivia with her other friends as we came upon them and cut across the hallway to head towards my locker on the opposite side. I kept a look out for Torin, but either he was purposefully making himself scarce—which wouldn't surprise me—or he hadn't come to school at all. Not that his absence would stop me. No, Torin Priest didn't realize it, but he was in my sights now, and I would find out what the hell a human was doing with a bunch of vampires.

As the school day had gone by, teachers had tried to console grieving students and flyers for grief counseling had been passed out just like the man in the suit—Principal Sealy, I'd learned later—had announced there would be. Penny never showed up to class.

After school ended, I headed for the football stadium. In the center of the field, Maverick sat with the other players as the coach and his assistant bowed their heads and spoke in low voices. Putting one foot in front of the other, I paced the length of the bleachers, turned and paced back. I had no doubt that the coach and players were mourning the loss of their fallen friend. In the back of my mind, though, I was trying to figure out if it had any connection with Torin Priest.

When several minutes went by and it didn't seem as if Maverick would be set free anytime soon, I plopped down on the top of the bleachers. I pulled out a notebook to scribble out all of the information I'd managed to gain throughout the day, as if by putting it all down on paper, somehow it would help give me some clarity on the fucked up situation.

Derick Gilmore, number 23 defensive lineman for St. Marion's football team, was apparently well loved by his friends and family, and especially his girlfriend, Penny. He was active in school. His grades had been average. All in all, there had been nothing particularly special or extraordinary about Derick Gilmore while he was alive.

That all changed with his death.

I drew a line beneath what I'd written about his life and set to work on what I knew about the man's death.

From what I'd been told, Derick had been at the Priest party on Friday night and after the party ended, he'd never gone home. His parents—who had been out of town like Beth and Jon until Monday—hadn't noticed his absence until they'd returned Sunday morning and found his bed unslept in. His car had been found several miles outside of town at a place called the Peak. I grimaced as I wrote that down.

Olivia had said that the Peak was usually used as a make out area overlooking the valley. It sounded like something from a bad horror movie to me. Derick's cause of death ... I tapped my pen against the page uncertainly before quickly writing in the word "unknown" and sitting back.

Anyone else would likely have said that having his heart removed was probably what had caused his death, but why would someone remove a heart? I went back to where I'd written about the Priest party Derick had been at and underlined Torin's name.

Two years, Olivia had told me. It'd been two years since Torin threw a Priest party and the first time he does after I show up, not only do I discover a vampire living in his house, but a guy from the school ends up dead. I no longer believed in coincidences, but even if I did—this seemed like too much of a sign to convince myself otherwise. The only question: what was the sign trying to tell me? What was the warning?

"What are you doing here?" Maverick's voice jerked me out of my reverie and I glanced up sharply, closing my notebook when I noticed him standing over me. I hadn't even heard him coming up the stairs.

"Nothing," I said. "Waiting on you. Are you done?"

"Yeah, why are you waiting on me?" he asked with a frown. "Olivia could've taken you home."

"I need to take a side trip," I answered, popping up from my seat and stuffing my notebook into my backpack.

"A side trip?"

I rolled my eyes. "Yeah, a side trip. Are you just going to repeat everything I say or are you going to give me a ride?"

Maverick's gaze roved over me. "It depends," he hedged as I made my way down the bleachers and headed for the front of the stadium where the student parking lot was.

"On what?" I called back.

"On if it's illegal."

I smiled, ducking my head as I hurried through the gates. My feet hit pavement and gravel and I turned towards him, pausing. "Not this time," I promised.

He stared at me for a moment more before sighing. "Alright, wait here, I gotta go get my shit out of the locker room. Practice has been canceled for the rest of the week; I'll take you wherever you need to go."

I clasped my hands behind my back and rocked back and forth. "What if I need to go somewhere bad?" I asked teasingly.

Maverick rolled his eyes before arching a brow. "Somewhere bad, like where? Hell?"

"Are you telling me to go to hell?" I asked with a laugh. "Don't worry, I won't ask you to go there. The devil has a restraining order on me."

His brow dropped as his eyes widened and his

mouth popped open. "I … I literally don't know what to say to that," he replied.

I shrugged. "Then don't say anything. Just hurry up and get your shit so we can go."

Giving me one last enigmatic look, Maverick shook his head and headed off.

TWENTY

BARBIE

"You gonna tell me where we're going?" Maverick asked not for the first time since we got into the truck.

"I told you, we're going to church. Gotta save our souls and all that jazz," I replied, following the blue arrow on my phone's GPS. "Turn right up here."

"Uh huh." Maverick put his blinker on and made the turn into the parking lot of the Sunshine Meadow Church of Christ.

Why did they have to put Church of Christ on every single sign? Was there anyone out there who'd ask 'what kind of church is this?' and assume something like 'probably Church of Satan?'

The building was tall and square with white siding wrapping around it from the bottom up to the single church bell dangling above the front section. Maverick parked in the nearly deserted parking lot and shot me a narrowed look. "You get weirder and weirder the more time I spend with you."

"It's called diversity," I said with a shrug. "You might

not get it much at St. Marion, but from where I come from, diversity is a good thing."

"You were homeschooled," he reminded me.

"Semantics," I replied with a huff as I reached for the door handle. "Stay here, I'll be back soon."

"Oh hell no." Maverick's finger slapped the lock button. "You're not going in there without me. I want to find out why you really came here."

"Would you believe to pray for Derick's soul?" I asked.

"I'd be more likely to believe that you came to burn the place down. You didn't even know Derick," he said. "I want the truth, Barbie."

I chewed on my lower lip as I debated. It probably wouldn't hurt to tell him, I decided. He already thought I was weird. "I came to get holy water," I said with a sigh. "There. Happy?"

Rubbing a hand over his head, he grunted and released the locks. "Jesus, just get it and let's go." He unbuckled his seatbelt and laid back, grabbing a folded baseball cap from the console. Placing the cap over his face as I reached for the handle once more, he grunted and settled in to wait. "So fucking weird," I heard him mutter as I closed the truck door behind me.

Yeah, he may have thought I was fucking weird, but he'd still driven me here without much of a fight. It was becoming clear to me that Maverick McKnight wasn't as much of an asshole as I'd originally thought. He was just incredibly protective of the people he cared about.

I headed for the front doors of the church and was

thankful to find them open. Didn't want another repeat of my last uncomfortable church experience. *Maybe I should just figure out how to get ordained myself and make the holy water at home.*

The inside of the church smelled like a mixture of vanilla and floor cleaner. I followed the open entryway into the main chamber of the church and headed down the aisle to the altar. Unlike the last church I'd gone to, however, there was no easy to reach fountain of holy water waiting for me.

"Hello?" I jumped when an older man came around the corner and spotted me. "Can I help you, young lady?"

All in for the weirdness… "Do you have holy water?" I asked.

If he was concerned or confused by the request, the old man didn't show it. Instead, a small gentle smile graced his face as he nodded. "I can give you some, but if you don't mind my asking, why do you need it?"

"Would you believe me if I said I'm hunting vampires?" I laughed awkwardly. *No one ever did.*

The priest stared at me for a moment before he, too, chuckled. "Dear, I'm old, but I'm not senile." He shook his head as he headed for the dais. "I'm Father Birch. Follow me, we'll get you your holy water. I have a feeling this has to do with that poor boy's death."

I stiffened but followed him. "You knew Derick Gilmore?" I asked.

"This isn't a large town," Father Birch replied. "It's not difficult to know most of the residents, but I never forget anyone from my congregation."

"This was his church?" I was kind of surprised by that. From what I knew of the students at St. Marion's —despite the fact that the school had once been a religious institution, I never expected rich people or their kids to be religious.

Father Birch looked back at me with a confused smile. "It was. He will be greatly missed."

"Yeah..." His death really brought home just how short life could be, as if I didn't already know. Some days, the sheer reality of being alive felt like a burden all on its own. If it hadn't been for me, my parents and my brother would've been here with me. I didn't have the luxury of falling apart, though. So, when Father Birch led me further back to a small fountain at the back of his chapel, I pulled out a few water bottles and started to fill up.

"Do you drink it?" he asked, his lips slightly parted as he watched me dunk the mouths of the bottles into the water.

"Sometimes," I said.

"It's just water, you can get that anywhere. Are you—"

"It just makes me feel safer," I interrupted. It made sure that if any vampire decided to take a bite, they'd be in for a world of acidic pain. Father Birch didn't say anything more as I filled up and took a step back from the fountain. "Thank you for showing me where to find it." He nodded, watching me with lowered brows. "I guess I'll ... ah ... be on my way." I turned towards the doors. "Thanks again."

I made it down the dais and halfway down the pews

before his voice echoed from behind me. "I don't know what haunts you, child," he started, making me freeze with my back to him, "but whatever guilt it is that eats at you can't be cured by simple water."

Sucking in a breath, I peeked back over my shoulder at the old man. "Some people believe that holy water has healing capabilities," I replied lightly.

He nodded. "That they do, but in the end, it's just water. Whatever sins you've accumulated will be released in due time. If you're truly sorry and you ask for His forgiveness, He will grant it." I didn't need God to forgive me, but I didn't say as much. He took a step down from the dais but didn't approach me further. "The iniquity of the Father or Mother does not fall upon the son or daughter. Do not allow yourself to be wrapped up in the sins of the dead. They are not your burdens to carry."

I frowned. I had no clue how to decipher that. My parents had no sins that I knew of. I was the sinner here, but there was no way I could tell the priest that. So, I nodded, thanked him, and got the hell out of dodge—letting the church doors slam closed behind me as I hurried across the parking lot to Maverick's quietly idling truck.

"Get what you need?" he asked as I jumped in the cab and clicked the door shut.

"Yeah," I said, subdued as I buckled in. "Let's go."

Shooting me an odd look, he sat his seat up and put the truck in reverse. My eyes strayed to the rearview mirror as we turned out of the lot and as the little white church grew smaller and smaller in the rearview mirror, I couldn't seem to pull my eyes away from it or my mind away from the priest's words.

TWENTY-ONE

TORIN

I WATCHED BARBIE LEAVE THE CHURCH THROUGH THE windshield of my car and get into Maverick's truck. *Did he know?* I wondered. *Did he know about her? Or about me? Did she for that matter?*

Holy water. I knew that's what she had gone in for. The same stuff she'd used on Delia's face. I cursed and cranked the engine before speeding out of the halfway hidden parking spot across the street. My mind reeled as I drove. I couldn't go back to the house yet. Regardless of the fact that Eloise and Delia couldn't control me to get the truth, they would know something was wrong and something was *very* wrong.

Barbie was the hunter.

I slammed my fist against the steering wheel. She had no clue the danger she was in. *Why hadn't she just skipped town?* I wondered. Surely, she knew Delia would come after her. My stomach cramped with hunger, with thirst.

Fuck, when was the last time I'd fed? I cursed and pulled

over on the side of the road, reaching into the backseat for the cooler I'd brought along just in case. Popping open the top, I reached inside and snatched the bag off the top. Opening my mouth and extending my fangs, I popped them into the plastic bag and let them suck down the cold, red fluid. To Katalin and the others, blood was apparently inherently different from person to person, but because I'd only ever drunk from the bag, it was as tasteless as coppery water. When the bag was emptied and the pain in my abdomen had receded, I tossed it back in the cooler and closed the lid.

Resting my head against the leather seat, I let myself come to grips with what I knew. Barbara "Barbie" Steele, was the daughter of Peter and Delvina Steele, and both had been vampire hunters up until six months ago. In the passenger seat of my car sat the whole file on her family. All information I'd gained illegally from a paid hacker and added to the thick folder were my own notes.

Travis and Kent, two of my father's lower ranking minions had been assigned to the Steele family. Six months ago—around the same time Barbie's family had been killed in a supposed robbery and house fire gone wrong—they'd been assigned to kill them. Arrius was intent on wiping out the entirety of vampire hunters on the North American continent. I had no doubt in my mind, though, that it wouldn't be enough for him. Kent and Travis had gone missing after the Steele family's demise.

The image of Barbie's face popped into my mind's eye. She'd probably been responsible for their disappearance. Somehow, she'd managed to defeat not one, but two vampires and escape the assassination attempt with her life. How she'd ended up here—just miles from my house—at the same damn school I attended was all detailed in the folder as well.

Was it just a coincidence? How could it be? Did she know what I was? Katalin had assured me as a child that even if vampire hunters understood that I wasn't completely a vampire, they wouldn't care. They'd strike me down and Barbie certainly hadn't acted as though she cared for me when we'd first met. In fact, she was as surly and aloof as any woman with a grudge.

A dull throb began to form behind my eyes. While El and the like couldn't get headaches, that didn't mean I—half human as I was—couldn't, and the rising feeling of agony pounding at the inside of my skull made it difficult to think straight.

I sighed and put the car into drive once more. I'd give Barbie the rest of the week to get out. If she wasn't gone by Friday, I'd approach her and make sure she knew that leaving was her only option. It was either that or stay and be captured, tortured, and killed by a wrathful vampire with a bad attitude. I could only hope that Barbie was smart enough to use the time I gave her wisely, even if she didn't know she was living on borrowed time and had been since the moment her family had been marked for death.

The front door was open when I returned home. I slowed to a stop, parked the car, and pocketed my keys as I got out. I watched as two men lifted a large trunk and backed out of the doorway as they carried it to a waiting town car. Frowning their way, I headed inside and found my sister and Eloise in the second floor library.

Eloise lounged, as per usual, against one of the reclining couches while Katalin sat in the corner, a book in hand.

"What's going on?" I asked. "Who's leaving?"

Eloise flipped her hair over the curve of her shoulder and looked back at me. "I am, darling," she said. "Arrius has called me to England. He's meeting with the council there to discuss the eradication of the European hunters."

I frowned, but this would make things easier. "Where's Delia?" I asked.

"Still sulking in her room," Eloise replied. "Have you found the hunter responsible yet?"

My spine stiffened. "I'm working on it."

"I would suggest you work faster," Eloise replied. "She's running out of patience and so am I."

"It's only been a few days," I snapped. "And there have been other developments." Such as the death of Derick Gilmore.

"Torin." My sister's voice halted any further conversation as she closed her book and stood up from her chair.

I cast Eloise a dark glare when she snickered and whispered, "Someone's angered their big sister."

Katalin was rarely angry, but when she was, it was catastrophic. I watched her carefully as she strode across the room towards me, her book still in hand. "Father would be disappointed if he were informed that you couldn't track down a single hunter, especially since he's managed to kill almost all of the hunter families in North America," she said quietly. Her gaze lifted, meeting mine.

"I will find the person responsible," I said. It wasn't a lie. I already had found the person responsible. I knew beyond a shadow of a doubt that Barbie was the one responsible. The only issue was, I wasn't willing to let her suffer for her mistake. It would kill something inside of me to see those deep ocean blue eyes paled in physical pain. Anguish was something I knew she felt. Guilt, too. I could see those two things clearly. And when she had accidentally brushed against me that first day as I was leaving the library ... I hadn't shown it then, but I had felt something. A shock of recognition. Katalin had said a vampire mated only once and rarely at that. Many killed their own mates so that they would have no weaknesses. I couldn't imagine killing Barbie. If that was what she was, then all I wanted to do was get her far away from here.

"It would be in your best interests to do so quickly," Katalin said, drawing me from my internal thoughts. "As Eloise has suggested."

I nodded, my tongue thick in my mouth. "Yes, Katalin."

TWENTY-TWO

BARBIE

I TAPPED MY FINGERS IMPATIENTLY AGAINST THE SURFACE of my desk as I waited for the bell to ring. Torin was back. It had taken the entire length of the week and I had a feeling that the only reason there weren't more rumors flying about his unusual disappearance from classes was because everyone was still so focused on Derick's death. The police had no leads and what was worse, neither did I.

But news of Torin's return had popped up in Calculus and as soon as the bell rang, I was out the door and heading for the hallway I knew he'd be coming from. As soon as I saw his head of dark hair towering above the others, I was shoving my way through the crowd of people. He grunted as I slammed into his back and kept going, heading straight for a janitor's closet I'd spotted on my way to him.

Opening the door and pushing him inside, I followed. The door clicked shut and I flipped the lock to keep anyone else from intruding. I had questions and

Torin Priest had answers and it didn't matter what I had to do to get them, but I would. Darkness descended but before I could reach for the light switch, strong fingers wrapped around my wrist and jerked me forward, spinning me and slamming my back into a wall of shelves. I cursed as they dug into my lower spine, making me arch against a wall of hard muscle as Torin's hands moved to my sides.

"What the fuck, Barbie?" I blinked against the darkness—white dots dancing in front of my eyes as I tried to see through the pitch black. What little light there was came from a single line at the bottom of the door. I saw nothing more than the outline of Torin's head as it bowed over mine.

"What the fuck do you mean 'what the fuck?'" I snapped. "That's my fucking line, Torin."

"No, why are you still here?" he demanded.

Shock and confusion rippled through me and I pushed my hands against his chest, trying to put some distance between us. "Let go," I ordered. His hands clamped down harder, even going so far as to slide down beneath my thighs and heft me further up against the wall until my feet dangled along either side of his hips. I froze. "Torin." I had no weapons, my daggers had been lost at the party and with Maverick so close by most of the time, it was difficult to get away long enough to find out where I could get some more.

"I know what you are," he said, leaning forward. "I know *who* you are."

I stiffened. "Torin, let go," I repeated the words, hardening my tone. Inside, I was a fucking wreck. I had to force down the shivers that wanted to escape as I felt his fingers trail up the sides of my arms. He touched my chin, tipping my head up and back.

"I know what happened to your family," he whispered. "What *really* happened to them. Why did you come here, Barbie?"

Ice threaded through my veins. Horror, thick and tantalizing, wove intricate bands through my mind. "You're not a vampire," I said. "Why are you living with them? They're monsters."

"Are you sure *I'm* not a monster?" he asked, pressing his lips against the column of my throat.

I swallowed reflexively. It had been a mistake to push him into the closet. A mistake to approach him on my own. But how could I have asked these questions in front of Maverick? I shook my head, trying to dislodge his attentions. His hand gripped my chin with an unbreakable grasp, holding me immobile. "You can walk in the sunlight." The statement was breathless, my voice coming out light and not at all like I wanted it to.

"I can," he agreed. Those shivers I had been keeping at bay made their way to the surface and raced up and down my back. My whole body went rigid when I felt two points of distinctive sharpness against my neck. "You need to leave town, Barbie. Right now. You can't attack a vampire, leave them alive, and expect to continue on with your life. If you don't leave, you're as good as dead."

I heard him, but I was increasingly focused on the fangs at my jugular. Fangs. Torin Priest had fangs. But he could also walk in the sunlight. He ate human food. I had watched him in the cafeteria. *How was this possible?*

"What *are* you?" I blurted the question even as my hands curled into the fabric of his shirt. My nails sank into the softness of the cotton and then beneath it until he could feel their sharpness in his flesh.

Torin sighed, the puff of air racing over my skin, raising goosebumps in its wake. "What I am doesn't matter," he said. "Are you listening to me? You have to leave town."

"No." I wouldn't leave town just because he said so. Yeah, I knew the vampire was probably going to come for me. I was surprised it had taken her so long. I'd tried to prepare the house as much as possible, but without a viable excuse for Beth and Jon, there was no way I could continue to stay there for much longer unless I handled the situation, and I would rather be staked through my own damn heart before I let them be used against me. I knew from experience vampires had no qualms about hurting innocents to get what they wanted. They'd used me to get my family.

Torin's hands found my arms once more and using his grip on them, he shook me. "Do you have a death wish?" he rasped, anger tightening his voice and sharpening his tone until it felt as though he were trying to cut me with verbal daggers.

"Let's be honest," I replied, reaching out desperately for the one thing that could fucking save me from doing something stupid—sarcasm. "My death will probably be caused by my mouth and not my actions."

Although I couldn't see it, the weight of Torin's

focus burned into me. The sensation of his gaze on my skin was like tiny pinpricks roving over my flesh. "You do have a death wish," he seemed to decide as his hold loosened and he let me drop back down so that my feet touched the ground.

I sighed, but whether or not it was a sigh of relief or disappointment, I wasn't quite sure. "Now that we've gotten that out of the way…" I trailed off. "Time to answer some questions."

"No, I don't think it is," Torin said.

"I disagree." I reached up and latched onto his shirt once more. "You know about my family and I know that you're not quite human."

"So?"

I frowned. "So, answer my fucking questions and I won't—"

"Won't what?" he interrupted and just as quickly as he had released me, I was back in his arms. This time, he turned and shoved me against the door and locked his fingers like manacles around my wrists as he pinned them to the dull, wooden surface. "Tell on me?" he hissed as if the very notion was preposterous. Which, I mean, to give him some credit, it kind of was. No one would believe me and I really didn't need to be locked up at this point in my investigation. I still had to find out why my family had been targeted.

"I'm getting really tired of you manhandling me," I said. "You're lucky I haven't kicked your ass yet."

"You think you could?" he challenged.

"I know I can," I replied. Torin brought his face close to mine and in the darkness, I saw a circle of red begin to glow. No, not a circle—two circles of red. His eyes. They were bleeding red when they had once been a hazel green. I sucked in a breath. Bloodlust. "Your eyes…"

"Don't worry, Barbie," he whispered. "It's not my intention to hurt you. I have enough human in me to give a shit about morality. I think you know that or else you would have tried to kick my ass by now as you've so plainly stated that you could."

Though I suspected he couldn't see me in the dark, I couldn't be sure. He was at least half-vampire after all. I arched a brow at his tone. "You don't believe me?"

The silhouette of his head nodded. "You held your own against Delia, I don't doubt it."

"Delia? The vampire?"

He nodded.

"So, you are with them." It wasn't a question, but a statement. One that left me feeling a deep sinking fear that curdled in the pit of my stomach. I'd known it, but I suppose I had held out some sort of small sliver of hope that he wasn't involved with them.

"They're my family," he answered anyway.

"Your family?" That didn't make any sense. Vampires didn't have families. They had nests, covens. Allies. Enemies. They didn't have—my mind caught up with all of the information I'd been given.

Torin Priest had a vampire family.

Torin Priest could walk in the sunlight.

Torin Priest was human.

But Torin Priest was also a vampire.

"You really need to leave town, Barbie. Please."

"Why?" I couldn't fathom what he was, but the logical side of my brain had already put the pieces of the puzzle together. Torin was half vampire, half human. Even in my parents' teachings, I hadn't known a thing like that could happen. There should be no way he could exist and yet here he stood before me. His eyes glowing the color of rubies in the shadows. I'd felt his fangs as they slid up my throat. And there was no denying his strength as he held me suspended against his body and the door.

"Why?" he repeated my question. "She will kill you, Barbie. Today is your last chance. They put me in charge of finding you. You need to go."

"Do they know it's me?" I asked.

"Not yet, but Delia is on the warpath. Her face still hasn't healed. She's out for vengeance."

"She's not the only one," I whispered. The redness of his eyes faded and silence descended between us. "Vampires killed my family, Torin. I'm not going to run from one."

"Not even if it will save your life?"

"I don't run."

"You need to start," he replied.

I chuckled, the sound of my own sardonic laughter scraping against my ears. "That's not going to happen," I said. "Let her come. I'll handle it."

"With what?" he demanded, his hands squeezing my wrists harder as his tone grew tighter. "I found the daggers you tried to use at the party. They're in my possession. They're useless if you don't have them."

"Then give them back," I suggested.

"And give you another opportunity to get yourself killed?" He barked an unamused laugh. "That's not going to happen."

I shrugged in his grasp. "Then what do you want me to say? I'll deal with it when she comes."

"What about Maverick?" he shot back. I pressed my lips together. Yes, Maverick was still an issue. "Does he know what you know?" Torin asked. "Does he know about me?"

"No," I answered truthfully, not seeing any point in lying. "He knows nothing."

"He will soon if you stick around."

"I'm surprised you didn't tell him yourself," I said. "I heard you two used to be close. Best friends, people say."

"Listening to ancient history?" he inquired and if I could make out the details of his expression, I would have bet that his lips were curled as he said it.

"Gaining information," I hedged. "You're an interesting subject. They call you two the Kings of St. Marion. I wonder what they would think if they knew the truth."

"I wonder what they would do if they knew what you did with your spare time," he replied. "You're playing a dangerous game, Barbie, and no matter what you may think of me or my family, I don't want to see you dead."

Dead. Like Derick Gilmore. The reminder ricocheted through me. "Speaking of," I said. "What do you know about Derick Gilmore's death?"

His head leaned back as if he were surprised by the

question. I waited for an answer. "What about it?" he asked.

"His heart was ripped out," I said. "It's still missing. That doesn't sound like a vampire, but it also doesn't sound like something a human would do."

"Doesn't it though?" Torin sighed, and his hands fell away from my wrists, but he didn't release me completely. His head bowed until his lips pressed against my neck and despite how used to his nearness I had grown over the last few minutes, I stiffened once more as he opened his mouth and his fangs scratched up the line of my throat.

"I drink holy water," I said quickly. "Frequently."

He chuckled darkly. "And?" he asked.

"If you bite me, my blood is infused with it. It'll rot you from the inside out," I warned.

Torin trailed his lips to the side and closed his mouth over the juncture between my neck and my shoulder, sucking sharply until I winced. "No, all it would do is give me a stomachache," he replied. "I'm not fully vampire, remember?"

A bolt of fear shot through my body. That was right. A creature with all of the strengths of a vampire, but none of its weaknesses. He shouldn't exist. It wasn't right.

"Humans are far more dangerous than many vampires," he said, distracting me. "But you're right, Derick's death is not because of a vampire."

"So, you're saying you know nothing about it?" I asked.

"No, I don't but I intend to find out. Just as soon as

you leave town." He released me completely and nudged me to the side so he could go to the lock on the door and flip it. "I suggest you do so before it's too late."

The door cracked open, releasing all the light from the hallway. Gasping, I shielded my eyes with one hand as they went from near blindness to an overload of stimulation. When I lowered my arm once more, Torin Priest was gone.

TWENTY-THREE

MAVERICK

I DUCKED MY HEAD AND HEADED ACROSS THE HALL WITH my gym bag slung over my shoulder. Anger pulsed red-fucking-hot under my skin. I headed past people calling my name, making a beeline for my truck. Popping open the backdoor, I stuffed my duffle into the backseat before grabbing a baseball cap out of the side pocket and slapped it over my head, yanking the bill down low over my eyes to shield my gaze from the sun.

I was so fucking stupid. It was a damn hard pill to swallow, but it was the truth. *I'd been fucking played.* I paused and leaned my forearms on the leather seat as I bowed my head. Barbie fucking Steele. She was a fucking curse on my goddamn life. And she was a liar. I should never have believed that bullshit about her fucking family. She'd probably gotten into a fight with Torin that night. He'd been so quick to come to her aid, or at least to stop me from being alone with her. The image of the two of them leaving the janitor's closet was burned into the back of my skull. She was just like Maryanne.

"Maverick!" I gritted my teeth and silently cursed my hesitation. I backed out of the backseat, slammed the door, and headed around to the driver's side. "Maverick! Hey! Wait up!" I opened the door as Barbie hurdled herself forward, barely skating into the side of my truck before I managed to set even one foot inside the cab. She turned and leaned against the vehicle, panting with exertion. She was barely two feet away from me, her scent lingering on the air, lifting to my nostrils. I clenched my fists and shook my head, trying to focus my thoughts back on my anger.

"What?" I snapped.

Out of the corner of my eye, I saw her pull back, eyes widening. "What the fuck is with the attitude?" she asked, cocking her head to the side.

"I don't know, Barbie." I slammed my door closed and turned on her. "You tell me."

"As much as I'd love the ability to read a man's mind, I'm afraid all I'd find would be pornography and a list of the best boobs in class, so I'm gonna take a hard pass," she replied. "You're a big boy, if you have a fucking problem maybe you should use your words and say something rather than getting all moody about it."

The mouth on this girl made me want to fucking shove her against my truck and dive my hand beneath the waistband of her pants. I bet if I got my fingers in that sweetness of hers, and gave her an orgasm, she wouldn't be so—shit!—I shook my head. No. I didn't need to get distracted. She'd already done that enough. I'd been so fucking stupid, letting myself be drawn in by her. "I saw you," I said after a beat. "With *Priest.*" I spat his name, biting fury itching at my skin.

Barbie's face froze for just a moment, but a moment was all I needed. I nodded my head as I scoffed. "Of course. You fucking went to him, didn't you?"

"It's not like that." But her eyes veered to the side. The sign of a liar.

"Not like what? I didn't say it was like anything specific, so if you're saying it's not like *that*, then there must be something you think it *is* like."

Barbie cut her gaze back to me and huffed. "What exactly did you see?"

"I saw the two of you coming out of the janitor's closet." I'd been coming back from the gymnasium when I had spotted the two of them. Torin—who'd been absent all fucking week—and then Barbie, both emerging from the closet.

"That's all you saw?" She arched one brow and pursed her lips.

"You're not going to deny it?" I asked.

She shook her head. "Of course not."

"Then maybe you'll be willing to tell me what the fuck you were doing with him?" I moved closer to her, backing her up against my truck.

She looked up at me but didn't seem too concerned by my nearness. Maybe I didn't affect her the same way she affected me. Whenever she was nearby, it felt like my insides were vibrating with the need to tear her open and sink inside. She, on the other hand, had a poker face made of steel.

"What I was doing with Torin is none of your business, Maverick," she said slowly. "That's not why I came to you."

"No?" I laughed, the sound dry and raw as it scraped out of my throat. *Fuck her*, I thought. And yet … I couldn't back away. Instead, I felt myself leaning farther down until I had eradicated any last piece of personal space she might have had. My chest to hers. My arms settled against metal warmed by the sun as I bowed over her smaller frame. And finally—fucking finally—that external casing of hers cracked.

Her breath grew shallow as she looked up at me. Light pink blossomed on the tops of her cheeks. Still, she kept her lips pressed together as if refusing to answer me.

I slid forward until my mouth was right next to her ear. "You're keeping secrets," I whispered. "They have to do with Torin Priest and if you want me to trust you at all, you're going to fucking tell me what they are."

Small hands found their way to my chest and I closed my eyes against how good they felt. But then they pushed ever so lightly and the image was ruined. I should've known better. Barbie wasn't one to be cowed by threats. I backed up a step, letting a wave of impassiveness fall over my expression.

"I can't tell you, Maverick," she said. "I wish I could, but it's just too dangerous. Trust me, I would if I could."

I glared down at her—at those big blue eyes beseeching me. "What is it about him?" I wondered aloud. "That makes every bitch lose her fucking mind."

"I already told you it's not like that," she said. She hadn't even flinched. No, of course not. Not Barbie fucking Steele. Hell, I was saying that enough that a curse should probably be her middle name. God knew she was a curse on me.

"Yeah, whatever, Barbie." I pushed away from the truck and away from her. "Fuck you."

"Maverick." I ignored her call as I moved to the driver's side door, opened it and got in. "Maverick!" I cranked the engine and revved before I put the truck in drive and left her standing there, in the student parking lot staring after me.

I didn't want to admit how much it hurt to know she couldn't be trusted, but if I was being honest with myself, I knew it from the start. I hadn't trusted her when she had shown up and I certainly shouldn't have let myself be swayed. I slammed a fist against the steering wheel.

Fuck her.

Fuck him.

Fuck them both.

TWENTY-FOUR

BARBIE

I WAS ONE-HUNDRED PERCENT OUT OF MY DEPTH AND MY emotion manifested itself in physical frustration. I slammed my fist into the punching bag in the McKnight mansion's at-home gym for the hundredth time and this time, my fist went right through the plastic-y fabric and sank into the sand filler. I groaned and jerked my hand out of the hole I'd made and turned away, kicking at the sack on the floor. Useless. I was so completely useless.

Sweat coated my upper lip and ran down the sides of my face. Exercise was always a routine my dad had ingrained in my brother and me. We'd used our irritation with our parents to beat the shit out of each other. I'd never been able to beat my dad in a fair fight, but somehow I'd managed to kill not one, but two vampires. Maybe it was just a damn stroke of luck.

The muscles in my legs bunched and jumped as I strode across the gym and then paced back. I was naked without my daggers. I should've taken more weapons from the house before I left, but there'd been no way I could hide it from DSS when they'd come for me. It was a miracle I'd managed to hide the daggers I'd had.

I stomped across the room to the sink and counter against the wall and snatched up a towel, blotting my face with it. Insecurity ate away at my insides. *Was I just a little girl pretending at being a hunter?* I shook my head. No. I threw the towel into the laundry basket by the door as I strode out. I was a hunter made a survivor. I'd find out why my family was attacked. I'd find the vampire responsible and when I did, I'd rip his head from his fucking shoulders and make sure that any and all vampires who thought to come after me again would think twice.

I'd put the fucker's head on a pike and send a message to the night crawlers. Come for Barbie Steele and she will return the favor ten-fold.

The doorbell below rang and I looked back over my shoulder, confused. Jon and Beth had gone out to dinner hours before and had warned Maverick and I that they would be out late. I pulled my phone out of my pocket and checked the time, my eyes widening. I hadn't realized how late it'd grown. I moved towards the top of the stairs and what I saw had the phone slipping from my grip.

"Maverick, don't open the door!" I snapped. Maverick shot me a look over his shoulder and headed for the front door anyway. *No.* "Maverick!" I screamed his name, but his hand was already on the doorknob. I wasn't going to make it. I tried nonetheless. My hands gripped the stairwell railing as I leveraged myself up and over. My feet hit the floor below, slamming down with a loud echo that ricocheted up the walls.

"Barbie? What the fuck—" I reached for him. *Too late.* The realization rattled around in my skull. A nail in his coffin. No, I couldn't let this happen again. The door was open and Maverick's comment was cut off as a hand reached in and seized him by the throat, tugging him forward as her fingers began to smoke, long tendrils of gray lifting from her flesh as it sizzled and popped. Delia's lips—her face deformed as it now was—smiled.

"Invite me in," she hissed.

"Maverick don't—"

"Come in."

Delia dropped him unceremoniously and shot forward, bowling him over as she slammed into my front, shoving me to my back as she crouched down over me. "Hello dear." Her nails sank into my upper arms until beads of blood rose forth. I winced at the pain. "I wanted to stop by and thank you for the gift you gave me."

Kicking out, I slammed the bottom of my sneakered foot into her abdomen. Her nails receded, but as she was shoved back, they scratched down my arms in deep grooves until blood ran in rivulets down my forearms. Rolling backwards, I jumped to my feet and kicked again. Delia avoided it easily enough, flexing her nails as she looked at me.

"Fuck, you're ugly," I said with a laugh. "Did I do that?"

Her scowl made the scarred half of her face twist and pull tight against what was left of it. Vampire eyes flashed red and she dove for me just as I expected she would. I dodged and lunged for Maverick, who was blinking and sitting up from where he'd been thrown to the ground. "Maverick, you have to get out of—" My head was snatched back, cutting me off mid-warning as Delia used her hold on my hair to toss me across the room.

My body slammed into a mirror on the wall and shock coursed through me as I fell and landed amidst the shattered pieces. The shards cut past my clothes and into my flesh, each new wound burning with pain. I cursed and scrambled out of the way as she came flying at me again.

"I'm going to enjoy torturing you," she hissed as I yanked a particularly sharp piece of glass out of my leg with a grunt.

"You have to catch me first," I said through gritted teeth.

Sharp canines lengthened and I watched as she licked a drop of blood—my blood—that had hit her cheek. "Oh, you've already been caught little hunter, you have no clue, do you? There's no escaping now."

I spread my arms wide. "Does it look like I'm trying to escape?" I countered.

"You look like a pinned butterfly struggling against the inevitable." I didn't even see the punch coming, and truthfully, coming from a vampire, I hadn't expected one. My abdomen tensed and rippled with the blow and I landed hard on my knees as the breath was knocked from my chest. "Or maybe..." I looked up sharply, grinding my jaw as agony lanced through me. Delia had left me and moved to Maverick, her claws around his throat as she lifted his much bigger body as though it weighed nothing. "Maybe I can torture you another way."

"Stop!" My fingers wrapped around a jagged piece of the destroyed mirror, the sharp edges cutting into my palm.

Maverick's eyes widened as his feet left the ground and he struggled against her hold. It was useless. Leveraging up to my feet, I slammed against the wall as my balance went off kilter. Gasping, I closed my eyes and centered my thoughts. The world slowed down to the beat of my heart as it pulsed—rich with life—in my veins. Wet blood oozed from my cuts, sliding over my pale skin and dripped across the wood floor, leaving smudges as I moved forward.

"Release him," I commanded. "He's not the one you want."

"He has to die nonetheless," Delia said with a smile. She reached up and I knew her intent—vampires were ruthless and it seemed she was done playing with me. Or at the very least, using him to play with me. She meant to snap his neck. I sucked in a breath and let the mirror shard fly. It left my fingertips as I threw it and in the next instant, Delia froze. I blinked as I stared.

"Holy shit..." I didn't know what I'd expected, but damn I must have been practicing with those daggers enough because holy fucking shit, I had just sliced off three of her fingers from the hand she had raised.

She didn't cry out in agony or pain, but her eyes flared a dangerous red once more and she dropped

Maverick to the ground. He coughed and choked, rolling to the side as he struggled to get up again.

Glass and debris from the fight crunched under her heels. Distantly, in my head, I wondered who the fuck wore heels to a fight? Evidently, she did.

I moved back, slamming into the wall as I watched Maverick get to his feet. "Get the water bottles from my room!" I screamed at him. "Go!" He looked at me as if I were crazy. I could imagine, but we didn't have time. "Maverick if you don't grab them, she'll kill us both. GO!"

With a gritted curse, he darted up the stairs and whether or not he came back with the holy water in time, I hoped he would at least be smart enough to try and escape. Because if I couldn't kill this bitch, we were both as good as dead.

"I've had enough playing around," Delia said conversationally as she bent down and grabbed the same piece of mirror that had sliced off three of her fingers with the hand that was still whole. She held it up so that it reflected in the light and I winced when it blinded me. But that had been her intention.

Moving faster than the human eye could see, she flew across the room and slammed the sharp fragment into my side, knocking the wind once more from my chest. Gasping for breath, I fell over and she followed me down, twisting the glass into my side. I couldn't help it, I screamed. "Fuck!"

Evil was a smile covered in blood. Delia leaned down and licked the side of my face, her tongue coming away wet with more of my blood. I coughed as I tried to breathe through the pain. "Are you gonna want this back?" I panted reaching down as she released the glass and yanked it out of my skin on my own. "Or can I keep it?"

Before I could use it to stab her back, she caught my hand and slammed it against the floor. Once, twice, three times until I finally let the fucking thing go.

Black dots danced in my vision. A figure appeared at the stairwell. I rolled as Maverick vaulted over the railing in much the same manner as I had. Unfortunately, he landed on a table against the wall and the piece of flimsy wood buckled beneath his weight. I winced as the splintering wood shattered, the legs shooting out on either side and Maverick grunted. The water bottle in his fist went flying, bouncing against the ground until it rolled to a slow stop at the edge of the couch.

Long manicured fingers wrapped around my throat and I choked. Delia's face was before mine again. I coughed and kicked, struggling to get out but she merely compressed my windpipe until no air passed through. My breath stuttered to a squeaking stop as I wheezed and fought against her grip.

The light grew dim. The room around me blurred out. Then, all at once, her hand released me and it all came screaming back. Maverick stood over the two of us with two handles of a wooden chair in his grip, blinking down at us in shock and confusion.

Delia stood up and grabbed him by the front of his shirt, flinging him across the room—right through the doorway leading into the kitchen. The piercing shrill of breaking glass and dishes shot through my aching head as I turned and crawled the few feet to reach the bottle of holy water.

"Oh, no, no, no you don't." A hand wrapped around my ankle and dragged me back, flipping me over once more. I uncapped the bottled water and threw half the contents into her face the second she had me on my back. "You bitch!" Her pained scream was garbled by the water as it ate away at her undead flesh. Staggering to my feet, I stumbled over to one of the broken legs from the table Maverick had landed on. Upending the rest of the bottle, I poured the rest of the holy water onto the makeshift stake—I didn't care if it was a waste.

"You made a big fucking mistake coming after me," I managed to say as I lurched back to her as she rolled on the floor, her hands half covering her damaged face and neck. Her flesh cracked and flaked away. She looked like a half-dead burn victim. It must have been agonizing. I didn't give one single shit as I held the sharp broken end of the table leg over her. "Rest in pieces, *bitch*."

She shrieked as I brought the pointed end down and slammed it into her chest. I winced as the wood cut into my palm. My blood dripped along the outside of her dress as the stake was driven through her chest cavity. I knew the moment that it hit her heart because as soon as it pierced through, she gurgled one last time and then her vacant eyes went to the ceiling, clouding over as her whole body disintegrated into ash.

I looked over my shoulder, panting hard as Mav stumbled back in. He leaned heavily on the frame of the doorway, his hand holding onto his side as he gaped at the carnage left behind in the fight. The ripped curtains and blood splattered floor and walls and the piles of ashes beneath me on the living room floor.

"What the fuck was that?" he asked, panting.

"That," I said weakly, "was a vampire."

I leaned back onto the balls of my feet and looked down at the cuts and bruises forming on my skin. My blood had slowed to a small trickle in many of the wounds but was running freely from others. I pointed the end of my makeshift stake, still somewhat slick with holy water and ashes sticking to the wet parts, at him. "Next time I say 'don't answer the door,' don't answer the *fucking* door."

"This ... Barbie?"

I wavered on my feet, the stake dropping from my hand as I went down amidst the pile of ashes. "Fuck..." I swallowed against a dry throat. The room was spinning.

"Barbie can you hear me?" Warm hands found my upper arms and drew me back against a solid chest. I looked up into Maverick's brown gaze. His frown pulled the corners of his mouth down as he passed a hand over my forehead, wiping away blood from my skin. "Shit, you're really hurt, Barbie. I have to get you to the hospital. Can you tell me where—"

"No," I choked out. "No hospital."

How would we be able to explain this? Answer: we wouldn't. There would be cops called. Social services. I'd be taken away and Maverick and his family would be left vulnerable.

"What the fuck do you mean 'no?'" Maverick

demanded, looking down at me as his frown turned into a deepening scowl. "You're fucking bleeding out."

"No hospital," I repeated.

"You've got to be fucking kidding me." He stared down at me, his jaw working as he ground his teeth. I reached up and clenched my fingers in the fabric of his shirt.

"Please," I rasped. "No hospital."

He glared at me. "If you fucking die, I'm going to spank your fucking ass."

I couldn't help but chuckle at that. It came out frail and weak and I hated every bit of it, especially when laughing made my chest burn hotter in agony. I shook my head. "Just … no hospital," I repeated once more as I closed my eyes.

The warmth and gentleness of his fingers smoothed over my cheeks and down to my neck. Darkness closed over me behind my eyelids and soft hair whispered against my skin as Maverick's lips found the corner of my mouth. "You're going to be the death of me," he whispered.

I hated that I couldn't reply. I was already falling into oblivion. If I had been able to speak, though, I would've told him that he wasn't going to die. Not if I could help it.

TWENTY-FIVE

MAVERICK

VAMPIRES ... I GLANCED OVER TO THE PASSENGER SEAT, worry tightening my grip on the steering wheel. *What the fuck was happening? Fucking vampires?* Still reeling, I took the back roads to the only place I could think to take Barbie.

The vision of her covered in blood stabbed me deep. Her head rested against the glass window, but not at all due to her willingness. She was unconscious and after she'd closed her eyes back at the house, I hadn't been able to wake her up again. If it weren't for the ever so slight rise and fall of her chest, I'd think she was dead. But no, she was still breathing. For now.

I turned back to the front, pressing the gas pedal to the floor as I sped into the night. No fucking hospital. She'd extracted that fucking promise from me right as she'd passed out. I wasn't even sure if she'd heard it, but already I was regretting making it. If she died because she didn't want to go to a hospital...

I ground my jaw as I turned my truck down a familiar road. I hoped I wasn't making a horrible mistake. The façade of Torin's estate came into view, my headlights washing over the tan stone steps as I ground the truck to a halt.

Shutting off the engine, I got out of the vehicle and dashed around to the side. Behind me, the front doors opened. I popped the passenger door open gently and reached inside, stopping her from starting to lean out as she sagged to the side. I unbuckled Barbie and lifted her into my arms before I turned.

"Maverick?" Torin stopped when he saw the girl in my arms. His eyes went first to her blood covered face and then to me before back to Barbie. I watched as his expression hardened. He turned back to the house.

I snapped. "Torin!"

"Not here," he said. "Meet me at the farthest guest house. You know the way."

"She needs medical attention," I said.

Torin stopped in the doorway and looked over his shoulder. "I can see that. I'll be there soon with what we might need. Get her into the guest house. Clean her up. I won't be long."

I wanted to fucking punch him in his emotionless face. There wasn't even a hint of concern past his initial confusion. One moment he'd been completely human and the next, a cold block of ice. Perhaps this had been a bad fucking decision, but where else could I have gone? *Nowhere*, I decided a split second later as I put Barbie back in the truck and buckled her in once more.

Jumping back into the driver's seat, I sped out of the driveway and swung down the long narrow road, leading towards the back portion of the Priest property, glancing over every so often. But Barbie didn't even stir.

I pulled up outside of the last guest house—the very one where Torin and I had ended our friendship. As I got out of the truck and moved around to get Barbie a second time, my mind whirled with memories from that night two years ago.

Two years prior...

I'm sorry, Maverick, but I just don't think things will work out between us anymore... Maryanne's last words cut through me as I whipped the truck into Torin's driveway and drove right past the front of his house. Maybe I shouldn't have been driving this angry. I'd just gotten my fucking truck along with my license the week before, but fuck if I was going to wait for composure before I had it out with the bastard.

Fucking betrayed by my own girlfriend, but even worse was the feeling of being betrayed by my best friend. The man I fucking treated like a goddamn brother. I stopped the truck and was out of the vehicle before I'd even shut it off, taking the stairs up to the front door of the guest house two at a time. The door opened. I didn't wait for an explanation or for any sort of apology. I threw the first punch and suddenly, I couldn't stop throwing them.

Torin went down under my fist, but then just as quickly he blocked the next one and the next one. Until it felt like I was trying to hit a dodging monkey. "Maverick!"

"No!" I yelled, punching out again and this time, I caught him by surprise on his jaw. *Fuck!* It felt like my knuckles hit pure rock. They split apart, blood oozing from the wounds. I paused, panting, my shoulders shaking with the effort as I tried to hold myself back. "You don't get to call my name. You don't have that fucking privilege. You destroyed it."

"The fuck are you talking about?" Torin stepped back and stared at me, his mouth twisted. He reached up and rubbed lightly at his chin where I'd landed the last blow. *Good,* I thought, I hoped I'd hurt him. "Maverick, talk to me, what the hell are you talking about?"

"Maryanne." Her name changed the atmosphere. Torin's back went ramrod straight. He swallowed reflexively.

"Maverick—"

"Stop saying my fucking name." My fists clenched again, my knuckles stinging. I didn't give a shit. I'd break off my fingers if it meant hurting him. After everything, I wanted him to know just how badly he had fucked up. "First the silent treatment, and then Maryanne," I said. "If you wanted to fuck up our friendship, you've done a spectacular job." I spread my arms wide. "But the thing I don't fucking get is why? Is it your dad?"

Torin just stood there, his eyes cold. He released his fists and crossed his arms over his chest, looking away. I waited. Still, he didn't talk. I groaned and shoved my knuckles—blood and all—into my eye sockets, pressing back until I felt the pounding in my skull recede just a bit.

"This is so fucked up," I said. "What the fuck happened to us?"

"Maryanne's leaving because her dad was offered a better position in Germany," Torin said.

I dropped my arms and took a deep breath. "Did you sleep with her?" There it was, an opening. A chance for him to tell me no. For Torin to tell me he'd never pull this kind of shit. But he just remained silent. Those cold green eyes staring at me. *What the fuck was wrong with him?*

My feet ate up the small distance between us and my hands went out and grabbed him by the front of his shirt as I lifted him up. "Fucking say something," I demanded.

"What do you want me to say?" he asked quietly.

"That you didn't fucking do it," I said. "What else do you think I want you to say?"

"I can't say it."

I released him just as abruptly as if he had sucker punched me in the gut.

"No." I shook my head. *Please, fucking no.* It might have hurt less had he stabbed me in the face. "You—"

"I think you should go, Mav."

I stumbled back and just stopped and stared at him. This was the man I'd grown up with. The man who'd gone through all of the ups and downs I'd had with Maryanne with me. The one who'd let me wreck his sister's Impala and took all of the blame when we were thirteen.

"Why?" That's all I needed. A good excuse. I was

sure he had one. He had to. "Give me a fucking reason why you would do this?" I demanded. "You have to have one. You can't just throw this away. Maryanne's not fucking worth it. I've known you longer. You're my fucking brother, Tor." My breath rasped in and out of my chest. "Please, for fuck's sake, give me something."

Torin just shook his head, turned around and headed back into the guest house without saying another damn word. The door closed behind him with a resounding click. The end of an era, of a friendship, of a brotherhood. I whirled away, my mind reeling as I staggered down the steps and back to my truck.

My anger had transcended my body until I wasn't angry anymore. What I felt wasn't rage or the fucking hot burn of betrayal. Instead, as I got into the driver's seat and cranked the engine, my chest ached with something else. Grief. Loss. He hadn't offered a single excuse. He hadn't given me any indication that he cared. I'd poured my fucking soul out and practically begged him and still, he'd just walked away.

That told me all I needed to know even if I wasn't ready to fucking hear it.

So, I drove. I drove back to my house, raided my dad's liquor cabinet and hours later, when the blaze of alcohol had incinerated all of my inhibitions, I finally allowed myself to grieve. Blind fucking drunk and still I missed him. But at least he'd taught me a valuable lesson. No one outside family could be fucking trusted. I took another gulp of Hennessy, hating the taste but loving the feeling of sinking deeper into oblivion. Somewhere far away. Where no one could ever fucking get inside and damage me. Where I could lock myself away and throw away the key.

"Yeah..." I slurred aloud. That's exactly what I needed. To be alone. To not give a fuck.

So, I drank until I reached that place and it didn't hurt quite so much anymore.

TWENTY-SIX

TORIN

Present Day...

SHE HADN'T LEFT. THE LITTLE FOOL.

I hurried to collect what I thought I'd need. Bandages, a suture kit that had never been opened, antiseptic. All things Katalin had purchased when I'd been brought to live here as a child. She had never had a hand in raising any children, much less a half human, half vampire child. She didn't know if I'd be more vampire than human or if I'd need the first aid supplies. I never had until now.

I hurried through the main house and as soon as I hit the back patio, I put on a burst of speed and made it to the last guest house within a few minutes. It would have taken a regular human closer to half an hour to get there, but I didn't have time for that or to grab a car. I took the stairs at a leap and slammed through the front door just as Maverick was putting Barbie down on a long, elegant table.

"I didn't know if I should put her on the couch," he said. "She's bleeding pretty badly."

"This is fine." I dumped my supplies on the table alongside her. I handed him a pair of scissors. "Start cutting off her clothes," I ordered.

"What the fuck?" He took the scissors and just held them. "Why the hell would I—"

"We have to get her clothes off so I can assess the damage," I snapped. "Do you want to sit there and keep asking me questions or are you going to help?"

Maverick scowled at me, his eyes burning a hole into me as I set to work on her shirt, ripping it down the front until I revealed her abdomen and bra covered breasts. I stood back and swallowed as a wave of thirst rose up. *All that blood …* I swallowed against the moisture in my mouth and focused downward.

I prodded against her side around what looked like a particularly deep wound. Grabbing tweezers, I used the sharp tips to open the cut and winced. Glass. I began the process of removing the small slivers that were still embedded in her skin. Moving from one wound to the next. So many cuts were still bleeding. I didn't know if there were internal injuries. I stood back and debated my options as Maverick found the suture kit and tore it open.

"You're not going to ask me any fucking questions?" he asked.

I shook my head. "No."

He frowned. "Why?"

"Because I know what happened."

Maverick froze before he turned on me just as quickly. He jerked me away from the table and slammed me against a wall, the tweezers fell from my grip. I'd had enough of this. I grabbed him by his shoulders, spun and had his spine against the wall and my forearm at his throat before he could blink. He stared down at me, the scent of shock and fear permeating my nostrils. Not that he'd ever let it show. No, not Maverick.

"How the fuck did you know something like this would happen?" he demanded. "Do you know who that bitch was?"

"Her name was Delia," I said. Of course, Maverick wouldn't know her. Delia hadn't shown up until after we'd cut our ties. "And I knew something like this would happen because I warned her if she didn't leave town after what she did that it would," I said. "She chose to stay, so yes, I expected this to happen."

He struggled against my hold. "Did you have anything to do with it?"

I shook my head. "Do you really think that?" I asked harshly. I knew Maverick hated me, but I hadn't expected a small comment like that to hurt so badly. Before I knew what I was doing, I shoved him up until his feet left the floor and his eyes widened. We'd been best friends once, he and I, but that was in the past. This was the present. I shoved down my pain and leveled him with a dark look. I needed to show him that I wasn't to be messed with. "The answer is no. I didn't. Anything else you'd like to ask?" Maverick simply glared at me, unspeaking. "Great," I deadpanned, "then here's how this is going to go. We have work to do if we want to save her life. You're going to put your grudge against me away for the time being and we'll fix her up. Then you and I are going to have a talk. There's a lot that needs to be explained. It won't make up for anything I've done, but it might make some things clear. I have a feeling there's no avoiding that now." I waited a beat. "Nod if you understand."

He didn't nod. Instead, choosing to choke out the words. "I understand."

I sighed and released him. Maverick's feet hit the floor and in the next instant, his knuckles hit my temple. Stars danced in front of my vision, but I couldn't say that I hadn't expected some sort of retaliation. Thankfully, however, that was the end of his reprisal. Maverick shoved past me and returned to Barbie's side to finish cutting away her work out pants.

I picked up the tweezers and went to work. A human might have needed a magnifying glass to see all of the little bits that had made their way into her flesh, but not me. I managed to get every single one out. Plopping them into a bowl I'd retrieved from the guest house kitchen. They'd have to be burned later to get rid of the scent of her blood. Even if we burned everything she touched in this state, the scent would still linger at least for a few days. My nose twitched, my inner beast coming to the forefront as I felt my canines shifting in my mouth. I bit down on my tongue, tasting the coppery tinge of my own blood.

"What next?" Maverick asked, looking over Barbie

with a haggard expression. He sagged against the table, his palms holding him up.

"We could sew her up," I said, gesturing to the suture kit he'd opened just for that purpose. "But she's lost a lot of blood. It won't stop while we're doing it."

"Then what do you suggest?" he bit out.

"Why did you bring her here?" I asked by way of answer.

He sighed. "She said not to take her to a hospital. I didn't know where else to go."

I nodded. That didn't surprise me. Though she was just a girl, Barbie was smarter than the average teenager. Wiser beyond her years probably, due in large part to what had happened to her six months ago.

"We have two options," I said with a resigned sigh. Only one would give us the results we needed, though. "We can try to stitch up every cut and hope she doesn't have any internal injuries…"

"Or?" Maverick prompted after a moment of silence.

I gritted my teeth. "I can give her some of my blood and let that heal her." She wouldn't agree. But the great thing about her being unconscious is that she wouldn't have a choice in the matter. It'd heal her. She'd come out just fine. Even if she would hate me for it.

"Your blood?" Maverick stared at me. "What…" He grew pale as he took a step back. I detested the look he gave me, like he was going to be sick. "You're one of them?"

"If you're asking if I'm a vampire, the answer is a bit more complicated than that."

"Is that why you … with Maryanne? With me? You—"

I shook my head and cut him off. "I'll tell you everything after we help Barbie, but we have to make a decision soon. I can't make it for her and she's not exactly conscious right now. What's it going to be, Mav?"

"Will it turn her into one of you?" He swallowed and clenched his fists as he returned to the table.

I hid my smirk. "No."

"You're sure?"

"Yes."

Maverick looked down to Barbie's pale face. His fingers trembled as he lifted them and smoothed two down her cheek. The blood had already grown dark, brown against her flesh as it crusted in the dry air. That didn't make this any easier. We hadn't done much to clean her—only cut away her clothes to assess the damage. And it was bad. Delia had obviously not gone down easily. I paused, a thought occurring to me.

"The woman who did this," I said, "is she still alive?"

Maverick shook his head. "No, Barbie killed the bitch."

As relieved as that left me, it also raised a few other problems. It was lucky that Eloise had left earlier that week. Katalin didn't notice Delia enough to care if she was missing.

"Okay," I said, nodding. "That's good. Now, what's your answer, Mav? What are we doing?"

He grimaced. "Can't we wait until she wakes up and ask her?"

I shook my head. "If she stays this way, she might not wake up at all."

"Fuck." He looked down again, his hand smoothing her matted hair from her face and I had to admit, I got it. She was a beautiful girl, but more than that, there was something about her that was special. Her blood called to me, made me thirst when all others had been dull scents by comparison. I'd never had human blood fresh from the vein before, but she made me want to take a bite. She made me willing to do all I could to protect her —lie, cheat, steal. Betray the very people who'd raised me. All for her. If she wasn't my vampire's mate, then she was certainly something above ordinary. "Fine," Maverick said, his tone heavy with regret and irritation as he stepped back. "Do it."

I had my wrist to my mouth before he could change his mind. I bit down and released, letting the blood pool and flow out of the twin holes I'd made as I reached for her with my free hand. Sliding a palm beneath her skull, I cradled and lifted it up and pressed my wet wrist to her mouth. The blood painted her plump bottom lip red as it trickled inside.

"How much does she need?" Maverick asked as he watched.

I shook my head. "I don't know, but I can't give her too much. We're playing it by ear. I'll give her just a bit now and see if it makes a difference and if it doesn't, I'll give her a little more."

"What if we're already too late?"

I didn't want to think of that. So, I refused to answer as I gently eased her head back to the table and licked my wound closed. Maverick looked at her. We both held our collective breaths, waiting for something—*anything*—to show us that we hadn't been wrong, that we'd made the right decision.

Slowly, but noticeably, her color began to ripen. A sigh of relief slid from between my lips and I nearly sagged against the table. I'd never given my blood to another before. I hadn't wanted to show it, but I'd been just as unsure as Maverick. Now, though, I saw the evidence of my blood healing her right before my eyes. Her wounds closed, the skin stitching back together. Her bruises—which had been popping up all over her body as we'd worked at cutting off her clothes—began to fade. Her cheeks, so pale before, were growing pink with vitality, with health.

"Yes." Maverick's whispered praise echoed my own sentiments as I reached for her face, touching her cheek. His head turned, his eyes sought out my hand and paused. I knew he wanted to ask, but he didn't.

I took a breath. "Let's get her cleaned up and changed and then we can talk," I said, stepping back.

He nodded and straightened. I left the room and retrieved a bowl of warm water and some washcloths. When I returned, Maverick had moved all of the supplies I'd originally brought out of the way, stacking them together in the corner of the room. I handed him the bowl and a washcloth. Together we worked in silence to clean the cracked and crusting blood from Barbie's skin.

When she was as clean as we could get her without actually dumping her into a soapy tub full of scalding hot water, I left Maverick to remove the last of her clothes while I darted to one of the bedrooms and returned with a long flannel t-shirt. He didn't say a word as we worked together to get it on her and then moved her into the bedroom.

"Torin." I stopped as I reached the hallway, turning back as Maverick looked up from her bedside.

"Yeah?"

"Are you going to answer my questions this time?" he asked.

I hesitated. There was no point in keeping the truth from him now, I acknowledged. But after all the years I'd kept my secrets, it didn't make me feel any more comfortable knowing that I was about to reveal all of them, even if it was to him. I scrubbed a hand down my face.

"Yeah," I finally said. "Yeah, I am."

He stared at me as if trying to determine the truth of my answer. He must have found what he was looking for because instead of responding, he looked back to Barbie and bent down, kissing her brow before joining me in the hallway and shutting the door behind him.

I couldn't say what seeing him kiss her did to me. It was a confusing experience. A mixture of jealousy, anger, understanding, and lust. Maverick looked at me and frowned.

"Let's go." He strode past me, back to the living room, but I remained behind, my attention locked on the door housing the person that had brought him back to me. Two years ago, I'd let him go to protect him and now he'd been brought back. We were together not because he gave a single shit about me, but because of the girl beyond that door.

Whatever Barbie was to me, she was also something to Maverick. What would happen if neither of us could let go?

TWENTY-SEVEN

MAVERICK

I STRODE INTO THE GUEST HOUSE'S LIVING ROOM AND then straight past it as I headed for the kitchen. Or more aptly, the liquor cabinet. Pulling open the frosted glass doors, I snagged a handle of whiskey and another of brandy before slamming them closed once more with my knuckles as I clutched the bottles.

I met Torin in the living room again, setting the brandy down in front of him while I popped the cap on the unopened whiskey and took a drink. The liquor burned down my throat, but it also relaxed my fucking muscles, calming me enough so that I could look at him without wanting to throw him through a goddamn window—or puke.

"I think you should sit down if we're going to talk about this." He gestured to a chair across from him. I didn't even fight or tell him where he could shove his suggestion as I usually might have. I was too fucking tired for that. I sat.

I took another drink and wiped my fingers across my mouth. "Talk," I said. "What are you?"

"I'm a dhampire," he said. Silence stretched between us.

"You're gonna have to give me more than that," I snapped. "I don't know what that fucking means."

He sighed. "Maybe you should—"

"No." I shook my head, cutting him off. "Let's just get this over with. Rip it off like a big fucking Band-Aid, asshole. Tell me what that means and then tell me what the fuck you were doing in the janitor's closet with Barbie." His eyes widened. "Yeah," I said. "I fucking know." I put the mouth of the bottle to my lips and tipped it up. Fire licked a path over my tongue and down my throat. I couldn't quite bring myself to give a fuck if getting drunk was a good idea or not.

Torin took a breath and released it. "Okay," he said, watching me carefully. "A dhampire is the product of a human and a vampire mating. I'm—" He paused and grimaced before continuing. "As far as I know, I'm the only one in existence, at least right now, I am."

"Why?" I set the bottle down on the coffee table between us, nearly losing my grip on it and sending it crashing to the floor before I caught it and nudged it back onto the hardwood.

Torin watched the entire scene without comment. "How much do you know?" he asked.

I shook my head from side to side, stopping when the room grew fuzzy in the corners of my vision. "Nothing," I managed to say. "I didn't even know they existed until Barbie said it after she'd finished staking that bitch through the heart. And if I hadn't seen the psychotic cunt turn to ash right before…" I stopped, realizing that I was slurring my words. I nudged the whiskey bottle another inch or so away before continuing. "Right before my eyes, I wouldn't have believed it."

"That makes things … well, I'm not sure if that makes this simpler or more complicated," Torin admitted.

I spread my arms out and sat back. "Just treat me like a beginner," I suggested.

He shot me a look. A Torin look. One I hadn't seen since before we had ended our friendship. The one that told me I was being a smartass and he didn't appreciate it. I didn't realize how much I'd missed it until that moment. I lowered my arms back to my sides and watched him.

"Vampires were created by the mating between a minor blood god and humans when the creature escaped from hell thousands of years ago," he started. "It was more of a powerful demon than an actual god, but vampire ancestors are particular about the difference between gods and demons. Those children were the original vampires and they found that, once born, they couldn't procreate. The only way they could create lasting families was to turn already existing humans."

My fingers itched to reach for the whiskey, but this was important. "So, how did you come to be born?" I asked.

Torin's eyes held mine as he continued talking. "The word 'dhampire' originates from the Albanian language, meaning 'to drink through one's teeth'," he explained.

"My existence is not an anomaly. I wasn't an accident, but the product of centuries of research. When my father was turned in the early eleventh century—"

"Wait." I stopped him with a raised palm. He frowned as I reached for the whiskey, but fuck that, learning that your best friend's—ex-best friend, I reminded myself—dad was older than the founding of the United States of America tended to need a little something extra. I swallowed down another gulp of the amber liquid before taking a shaky breath. "Your dad is…" I tried to work out just how old we were talking here.

"Old," Torin said. "He's very old."

"What about your sister?"

"She…" Torin took a breath. "I do think of her as my sister, but I guess she's kind of my niece?"

My eyebrows shot into my hairline. "What the fuck?"

"Katalin was turned closer to the mid fifteenth century. When my father was turned, he left behind a wife and a son. His first son, my brother, went on to live a perfectly normal human life. Met and married a woman, they had children. Their children had children and so on until Katalin." Torin waves a hand absently. "I don't know how many generations down she went, but my father met her in Egypt around the time of her twenty-fifth birthday, realized the relation and turned her."

So much information. "Why?" I couldn't possibly imagine that Katalin would have wanted that. As quiet as she was, at least when I'd known her, she had seemed to enjoy simplistic surroundings and uncomplicated relationships. Finding out your great-great-however many greats-grandfather wasn't just alive, but was a fucking vampire? I just didn't see her jumping head first into a life with him.

Torin shrugged. "She's never said," he admitted. "Not in all of the years she's raised me. I don't think it was something she had much of a choice in, though. Things were different then."

My fingers played against the bottle in my grip. It was lighter now, half empty. I set it down once more. "Continue," I said.

Torin looked up and focused on me. "My father enjoyed the powers of being a vampire for several centuries. The speed, the control he had over humans, the strength. Immortality agreed with him, but with the immortality of being a vampire, there also came weaknesses."

"Garlic?" I asked.

He snorted. "No, garlic simply has a pungent smell. It has no effect on us. Holy water, however, does."

"Why?"

He shrugged. "I suppose because it would have had an effect on the creature from which vampires were created. Waters and weapons blessed by those favored by God don't necessarily agree with creatures from the pits of hell."

"So, God's real then?"

Torin leaned back and scratched the underside of his jaw. "I guess," he replied. "I don't really know, but if vampires are real then why not?"

I sucked in a shaky breath. "Okay." I nodded more to myself than him. "Okay," I repeated. Then, after a beat, "What about bats?"

"What?" He frowned my way.

"Do you turn into a bat? Because that would be fucked up if you did." God, I couldn't fucking imagine it. Or—actually, I could, and it creeped me the fuck out. Winged little rats. A shudder worked its way through me.

"Do I look like a bat to you?" Torin deadpanned before shaking his head. "No, and before you ask—mirrors are fine too. It was the silver behind them that had any sort of effect."

"So, weaknesses include silver and holy water?" I clarified.

"For vampires, yes," he replied. "Suffice it to say—silver, holy water, and blessed weapons are the main weaknesses. Vampires can't enter a home inhabited by humans without receiving permission—"

"That's why Barbie told me not to answer the door," I surmised. "I wasn't planning on giving her permission —the vampire—but when she commanded me to, I just … couldn't stop myself."

He nodded. "Simple mind-control is something most vampires can do after they've grown older than a hundred or so," he said. "It wasn't your fault. You couldn't have known."

I heard what he said, but it still didn't forgive what I'd done. I'd let the bitch in. I was the reason Barbie had nearly fucking died. I hunched over, my stomach churning as I sank my head into my hands.

"I shouldn't have opened the fucking door," I said. "She told me not to. I didn't—"

"Mav." Fingers gripped my wrists and pulled my hands away. I jerked. I hadn't even heard him move. Torin didn't step away though once he had my attention. "It's not your fault, man. Don't start thinking like that." He eyed me. "If you start that shit now, you'll never stop."

I gritted my teeth against the urge to tell him he didn't know what the fuck I was feeling. Now was not the fucking time. I closed my eyes and breathed through my nose. In. Out. In. Out. Until the urge to pound my head into the nearest hard surface receded and I was ready to hear the rest.

"Finish this," I said, gesturing for him to return to his seat. "I want to know everything. Anything to help her."

He released my wrists and stepped back. "You'll need more than just knowledge to help her, Mav."

I stared up at him. "Then give me what I need to help her."

Torin met my gaze and something passed between us then. An understanding. Something we hadn't had in two fucking years. But before we could address it, I needed the information he had. Torin took his seat once more, steepling his fingers as he resumed his explanation.

"I don't know why I was born," he said. "But I do know that my father contracted a black witch from one of the Eastern continents. I don't know specifics, but I do know that my father's intention was to create something that had all of a vampire's strengths and none of its weaknesses. I can walk in sunlight. I can eat. Holy water gives me a mild allergic reaction, but other than that, I can drink it or bathe in it just fine. I have the speed, night vision, and healing capabilities of a vampire. With that, however, I also have to drink blood to survive and if I don't feed both sides, food and blood —I'll lose control of the vampire."

I nodded. That made sense—or whatever kind of fucked up sense this shit was supposed to make. "So, what about Barbie then?" I asked. "Why did that bitch come after her?"

Torin grunted, a sound of irritation in his throat as he released his hands and stood up, pacing across the room to the windows. "Because she's a fucking fool," he snapped.

I grinned. "Smart mouth?" I asked. He nodded. "Doesn't listen to a fucking word you say?" Once again, he nodded. "Drives you crazy, doesn't it?"

"Like you wouldn't believe," he replied. "She attacked Delia—the vampire who attacked you—at the party last Friday. One thing about many vampires, you need to know, is that they are a vile, spiteful bunch. They hold grudges for eternity—literally." He shook his head and turned away from the window, staring at me from across the room. "Barbie comes from a family of vampire hunters. They were killed six months ago by vampires. She hasn't given up the fight."

"She told me that she recognized someone at the party," I admitted. "She told me about her family; she just left the part about them being killed by fucking vampires out of it."

Torin tilted his head. "Can you really blame her?"

No, I supposed I couldn't. "What now?" I asked. "She killed the bitch, but does that mean it's over?"

Torin's eyes filled with cold steel. "No," he said. "It's not over." He looked me over. "Are you still going to insist on helping her?"

I stood up. My knees bumped against the coffee table, so I moved away from it. "Of course I fucking am," I replied.

He nodded and then strode across the room until he came to a chest against the wall. Bending down, he flicked open the locks and reached inside. "Then you're going to need to learn how to use one of these." He turned and held out a gun.

I stared at it and then at him. "You're fucking serious?"

There was no hesitation in his expression. It was stone cold determination. I reached out, my fingers closing over the black metal. He held on and my eyes flashed back to his. "You take this, there's no turning back, Mav." The warning was clear.

I didn't have to think. I finished closing my fingers over the gun and took it from him. I held it up and examined it. "Did you sleep with Maryanne?" The question barreled out of my mouth out of nowhere, but once it was out, there was no taking it back. I kept my gaze fixated on the weapon in my fist as I waited for an answer.

Torin's breath was loud in the nearly silent room. "No," he finally said. "I didn't."

My eyes flashed up to his. "Then why did you let me believe you did?"

His shoulders were wound tight, his jaw clenched. "It was easier," he admitted.

"For what? For who?" My hand squeezed around the gun as I lowered it to the side, keeping my finger from the trigger. It probably wasn't even loaded, not that I would use it on him.

"For me, for you, both of us, I guess." Torin's breath shuddered inside his chest, shaking his whole body. "You were in danger and it was the easiest way to get you away from me."

"Your father?" I guessed.

He nodded.

"What's changed then?"

Torin met my eyes. A beat of silence slithered through the air and then he answered. I didn't know it then, that his answer would change the rest of our relationship. "Barbie."

TWENTY-EIGHT

BARBIE

Blood. It covered me from head to toe. Soaking into my skin, far beneath my flesh until it couldn't be removed. The only issue was—it wasn't mine. This was someone else's blood. There was something different about it. I was somewhere I'd never been before. Curling into a ball, I closed my eyes and tried to find my memories.

The fight. Delia. The house—destroyed. Maverick. Then ... nothing. Where was I?

"You're sleeping." The voice wasn't mine. It was deeper, darker. Masculine. Gravelly with a hint of an animalistic growl beneath the surface.

My eyes popped open and the image of Torin appeared before me. I blinked and straightened. "What are you doing here?"

He took a step forward and I scrambled to my feet, backing away. "I came for you," he said. "I saved you."

"You—w-what?" I didn't understand. Spinning in a circle, I sought out an exit, but there wasn't one. In fact, there were no doors or windows. There was only white. For eons and eons, it stretched

into the vast distance. There was only white, and him and me. And the blood.

Torin waded through it, his bare feet turning red the closer he got to me. I looked down at it all. I didn't know how long had passed since I'd passed out, but I knew I hadn't been wearing the white shift currently covering me. And while I was grateful that I wasn't naked, I also didn't care for it.

"Did you dress me in this?" I asked. "Seems a bit sacrificial virgin to me, don't ya think?"

He chuckled, that rich voice of his vibrating through the air until it hit me square in my nether regions. Holy mother of fuck. *I clenched my thighs against the urge to attack him as he stopped in front of me. Lust bolted through my core, wrapping thick long fingers around my throat and squeezing until it was difficult to breathe without the desire to jump him.*

"W-what's happening?" I gasped out. I urged my feet to move away from him—to take me far from the creature that was currently the only thing I could focus on. He was the source of my newfound hunger. My libido was charging at him, though, and while she and my will to back away collided, neither won the fight and I stayed right where I was.

Red eyes met my gaze and I gasped again as he reached out and stroked my face down to my neck. My breath stuttered in my chest, stopping altogether when his hand moved down to where my heart beat a doubled rhythm. I couldn't have slowed it had I tried. Shit. Shit. Shit.

"You're not Torin," I said, the realization coming as his ruby colored eyes darted back up to my face.

"No, I'm not."

"Who are you? Why do you look like him?"

"Because I am part of him."

I frowned. "You just said——"

"I am not him, not fully," he interrupted, flipping his hand over and sliding it back up until he gripped my jaw in his palm and tilted my face up. "I am his other half."

I scowled and jerked my chin from his grip. "Don't touch me," I hissed.

He didn't act offended. To the contrary, he grinned, revealing sharp fangs. "Such brazenness. No wonder he's taken by you."

"What are you talking about?" I still couldn't move. My feet were rooted to the ground.

Plop. Plop. Plop. *I closed my eyes against the sound of droplets of blood as they hit the ground at my feet.*

Vampire-Torin's eyes flared bright. "You were damaged, you had to be healed. We allowed you to drink our blood."

"What!" Shock rippled through me. No, he wouldn't have. Not without my permission. Maverick wouldn't have let… My thoughts trailed off as I released the futility of my denial. Maverick wouldn't have known my wishes. Maverick wouldn't know how abhorrent I would have found the idea of drinking vampire blood, even if Torin wasn't a complete monster. I would have refused. But that didn't matter. The choice had been taken from me.

Soft fingertips feathered against my cheek and I jerked back automatically. Vampire-Torin caught me, sliding a hand around my waist and pulling me into his body with a rush of speed before I could fight back. With my hands against his chest, I leaned away from him. My legs went weak as his breath fanned against my skin and he bent his head to lick at my skin, cleaning the blood away.

The muscles of my stomach tightened, and as much as I wished it were in revulsion, I knew better than to lie to myself. I was attracted to him. To this … creature. I panted as he slid his lips over my shoulder, pushing the strap of my dress down as he scraped the roughness of his tongue against me.

"Is there a reason for this?" I asked dryly. "Or are you just trying to make a point here?"

Vampire-Torin chuckled, the sound sifting through my ears and causing a shiver to run up my spine as he pulled back and looked down at me. "Are you saying you don't enjoy being in my arms?" he inquired, lifting a brow.

"I'd rather eat glass than be in your arms," I lied. In actuality, I wanted to climb him like a fucking tree. I wanted to wrap my legs around him and slide down until his cock pressed inside and relieved me of this horrible, god-awful ache that was swelling up in my core.

"You already did, in a manner of speaking," he said. "Torin had to remove glass fragments from your skin."

I frowned. I thought I'd managed to pick out all of the larger pieces mid-fight. I hadn't felt anymore, but then again, I'd been kind of woozy at the end and growing numb to the all consuming pain. I hadn't exactly just laid down and decided to take a nap of my own accord. My body had simply failed to stay awake.

"What happened?" I asked.

Vampire-Torin drew me farther into the curve of his arms despite my fragile resistance. He gently urged my head into the crook of his neck and the scent that hit me bowled me over until I couldn't refuse his nearness. I pressed my nose to the column of his throat and inhaled. My mouth watered.

"You sustained multiple injuries, Barbie," he answered. "You were not well. Unless you had made it to the hospital there was nothing else that could have been done. I am certain now that I've been inside you—"

"Been inside me?" I interrupted, my mind fogged over as I licked my lips and stared at the pulse of his throat.

"Blood, Barbie. You were given my blood to heal your wounds."

"That's why you're here?" I asked before adding, just to make sure, "in my dream?"

He nodded. "Yes. Now that you've had some of my blood, I will remain in you until you are healed completely."

"Will I continue to have dreams about you?" I grimaced at the idea.

A puff of air slid over the top of my head as his chest vibrated with a quiet laugh. I liked that feeling. My hands moved to his sides of their own accord, my fingers squeezing against his skin as they slid beneath his shirt and over the small of his back. I groaned and closed my eyes, pressing my forehead against his sternum.

He rumbled. "Yes, you may continue to see me in your dreams," he answered. "Now, do you want to hear what happened or are you too overcome by the bloodlust?"

"Bloodlust?" My eyes popped open and I leaned back to look up at his face.

His eyes glowed with desire. My teeth clenched at the expression on his face—the tightening of his features, the fullness of his lips drew me in. My gaze zeroed in on them. He broke the spell when he shook his head.

"You drank vampire blood, there are certain … side effects that have taken hold of you."

Holy shit. My crazy, out of control libido. He meant my lust for him and … his blood? I struggled weakly, trying to fight my way out of his arms. With a sigh, he merely settled me more firmly against him.

"*Do not be afraid, Barbie. I will not let you do something you would regret,*" he said. "*Not yet.*"

"*Yeah,*" I said. "*That makes me feel* loads *better.*"

"*Regardless, you need to listen,*" he said. "*I am certain that without my blood, you would have died. You suffered internal damage in your battle with Delia.*"

"*I killed her,*" I said.

His hand came up to the back of my head and stroked through the strands of my hair. "*Yes, I'm aware.*"

I swallowed against a suddenly parched throat. "*What is that going to mean?*" I asked. "*There are others—your coven—will I have to leave?*"

"*You weren't willing to before,*" he said with a huff. "*Would you truly be willing to now?*"

I thought about it for a moment. "*No, probably not.*"

"*Why does that not surprise me?*" He shook his head as his fingers continued to move and stroke, lulling me into quiet serenity. "*You needed a blood transfusion,*" he continued, bypassing the rhetorical question he'd asked and moving onto the heart of the matter. The fact that I now had semi-vampire blood running through my system. "*Without a hospital, that wasn't possible. You cannot be angry with Maverick for making the decision for you.*"

I didn't like it, but he was right. "*I know.*" I sighed. "*I'm not angry with him.*"

"*Good.*" He nodded, his chin bumping the top of my head.

"*Where does that leave me, though?*" I asked. "*I'm not leaving.*"

"*You're lucky. The vampire you killed—Delia—her absence won't be noticed for a while. I'll come up with a story. Something believable that will explain her death. I'll claim that I killed the hunter responsible, but not in time to save Delia.*"

"Okay."

"That means you have to stop hunting, though."

"No!" I shoved at his chest. Any sense of security fell away with that announcement. I glared at him, but his expression didn't budge an inch.

"This is not up for discussion, Barbie. You will need to stop hunting or they won't believe the lie."

"I have to find out who killed my family," I said. *"I'm not going to stop until I find the vampire responsible and put him in the ground."*

"You will get yourself killed, is that what you want?"

"If that's what it takes," I replied.

"Even if it gets Maverick killed in the crossfire?"

I froze. "What do you mean?"

"He knows now. About me. About you. About the whole ordeal. Vampires. Everything. Do you really think he'll stand back and let you do this alone?"

"I'm going to give him a choice," I said.

"You're not leaving, but you're going to demand that he not intrude if you're in trouble. Do you really think he'll listen?"

"He will if he wants to protect his family," I bit out. But even I wasn't convinced. He would want to protect his family, but something had changed in the time since Maverick and I had come to know one another. He'd want to protect me too.

"You're part of his family now, Barbie," Vampire-Torin said softly. *"He's not going to leave you alone to face death."*

"I can't…" I couldn't just let go of my vengeance. It still burned red-hot inside of me. My parents had given their lives for me; they'd died because of me. As did Brandon. Guilt was a living, breathing monster inside of me.

What right did I have to keep living if I didn't avenge them?

"I will help you," he said.

I jerked my head up, shocked by the offer. "You will?"

He nodded. "If—and only if—you listen to me. I will help you in your vengeance, but not at the cost of your life and not at the cost of his. Do you understand?"

Hope blossomed. I shouldn't trust him—I knew. He wasn't completely human, but what other choice did I have? And he had saved my life. I bit my lip as I stared back at him and then I nodded. "Alright," I said. "Yes, if you'll help me, then I'll listen."

He waited a bit, watching me, his eyes hooded. Then he stalked forward, a predatory shadow against the white of the rest of the dream world. "W-what are you doing?" I asked as I backed up.

"Sealing the vow," he said as he grasped my arms and pulled me to him. His head came down over mine, his mouth slanting against my lips in a quick—almost too fast—movement.

Electricity raced through my veins. My eyes slid closed as the desire I'd been fighting all along broke free from its chains. My hands sank into his hair, yanking at the locks as I plastered myself against his front. The kiss was a wave of torment rippling through me, devouring every logical thought I had ever had or ever would have. The rest of the world fell away. The white. Reality. Nothing could compare to this.

No kiss I'd ever been given had been as all consuming. The one time I'd drowned my sorrow in alcohol and mistakenly given up my virginity to a fumbling foster kid from the same Youth Home paled by comparison. That was a murky night to this clear galaxy. The kiss stretched onward, vast and enthralling.

"Barbie." Vampire-Torin gasped my name as he drew away. He chuckled, the sound thick and bountiful with his lust. "I think that's enough for now, though I appreciate your enthusiasm."

"No…" I locked my fingers at the back of his neck and drew

him back down, ignoring his surprised expression. "It's not enough." I took his mouth this time. Diving in deep and thrusting my tongue against his. Acute passion swelled within me, driving me to clutch him closer, hold him harder. I rubbed my breasts against his chest until my nipples prickled with the sensation.

Lips against lips. Tongue to tongue. I let myself drink from his taste, loving the shockwaves of fire trembling along my nerves. I craved him.

My muscles clenched as I drew closer. I jumped. He caught me. Blood—still wet—slid between us, marking his white skin, marking mine. I didn't care. Nothing else existed but him and me. My thighs burned with the friction of how hard I was squeezing them against his sides.

Gasping, my mouth broke free and slid down to his throat. My lips parted. My teeth scraped against his cold flesh. A hard hand sank into my hair and gripped, jerking me away.

"Barbie, no!"

"I want it!" I screamed. I needed it.

Barbie ... you have to stop. It's time to wake up. Wake up, Barbie.

"No!" My body cramped with the desire to sink my teeth into him. The kiss had ignited something darker inside me, a hunger I hadn't known before.

I'm sorry, Barbie. So sorry. Open your eyes, sweetheart. Open your eyes. You'll thank me later.

"No, I won't. I want it. Please, Torin. Please…"

I'm protecting you from yourself, Barbie. And from me. Now. Open. Your. Eyes.

TWENTY-NINE

BARBIE

My eyes bolted open and I blinked at the bright room. Sunlight poured in from the windows alongside the bed. I squirmed beneath the fluffy comforter covering me, feeling my bare thighs rub together. Fingers grasping at the edges, I lifted the blankets away to look down my body and sighed with relief when I realized I was somewhat covered, just missing pants.

Where the hell were my fucking pants?

"We had to cut them off," came the answer from the doorway.

I looked up, my eyebrows shooting into my hairline as Torin—real, actual Torin—rested against the frame. Looking exhausted and haggard, Maverick ambled up behind him and rested against the opposite side.

"I didn't say that aloud," I pointed out. It wasn't a question, but he wasn't stupid. He knew what I was getting at.

"A result of drinking my blood," he said. "Don't worry, it'll fade."

So, it hadn't been a dream after all. I supposed I knew that, deep down, but as the memory of my last reaction to Torin—or rather, Vampire-Torin—surfaced, I blushed and wished it had been.

"What level of Hell is this?" I asked to distract him from the thoughts rolling through my mind. Flashes of Torin's skin under my nails made me ball my hands into fists.

"It's not Hell, Barbie, you're alive," Maverick said as he moved past the doorway and headed for my bedside. "We're in one of Torin's guest houses."

I sucked in a breath and threw off the covers. "We need to leave," I said. "We can't be here. I can't be here and you certainly can't be seen with me."

"Slow down there, killer." Torin flashed to my bedside and without thinking, I punched him in the face. Everyone froze.

With a grimace, I apologized. "Sorry," I said. "Habit."

"Vampire speed set it off?" He inquired as he lifted his hand to his now bleeding nose. Red droplets dripped past his upper lip and for some reason, I found my eyes drawn to them. I was fascinated by the way they glittered against the sunlight, shining a bright ruby color. My mouth watered.

I clamped a hand over my mouth and stared at him in horror. "What have you done to me?" My question was muffled by my fingers, but they heard.

Maverick sighed, grabbing tissues from the bedside table and handing them to Torin. "I asked him to save you," Maverick said.

"That's not what I mean." Slowly, I let my hand return to my side. "What are these feelings?"

Maverick frowned and looked to Torin who took the tissues and wiped the blood from his upper lip and nose. "They will fade as well," Torin said.

"That doesn't explain what they are," I snapped. "You haven't answered my question."

He grimaced. "Because you won't like the answer." I waited. He sighed. "When you consume a vampire's blood and you aren't turned, you will experience some…" His jaw locked and he looked away as he crumpled the remains of the tissues in his fist. "You may experience some attachments," he finished.

"Why didn't you fucking say anything last night?" Maverick growled.

"We still wouldn't have had a choice," Torin said.

"What kind of attachments?" I asked before they could get into it.

Torin turned back to me. "Dreams. Cravings. Projecting your thoughts to me. It will fade," he said. "It's not forever."

I shook my head. "You shouldn't have done it." I pushed away Maverick's arm as my feet reached the floor. The flannel shirt I was wearing fell to my upper thighs.

"We didn't have much of a choice," Maverick said. "You were dying."

"Had you left when I told you to, none of this would have been an issue," Torin reminded me.

I shot him a dark look. "Why don't you row row row your boat quickly the fuck away from me, hmmmm?" I stomped past the two of them and into the hallway.

"Is that any way to thank someone for saving your life?" Torin called back.

I ignored him. "Maverick, come on, we have to go," I snapped.

"Barbie, wait, hold on." I didn't wait. I didn't hold on. I strode to the front door of the guest house, but as I reached for the handle, I was snatched up from behind and catapulted across the room. My back landed against the couch and I rolled as Torin came down on top of me, narrowly missing me as I slid to the floor and popped back up on my feet.

I swung. He blocked. Fingers circling my wrists as he yanked me to him and bound me against him with a forearm against my back. "Let. Go!" I struggled in his hold.

"Not until you calm down," Torin barked. "You're being unreasonable."

"*I'm* being unreasonable?" I pulled my head back and slammed it against his nose.

Torin clamped his arms harder against me until moving made me wheeze. "I just healed that," he said with a huff.

"Serves you fucking right." The more I fought, the less my struggles seemed to make any difference. Finally, I slumped against him, panting, sweating, and worn out.

"Are you done?" he asked.

"Fuck you!"

He sighed. "You really need someone to help you adjust that attitude problem of yours."

"I don't have an attitude problem," I replied. "If you have an issue with my attitude then that's your problem, not mine."

Maverick chose that moment to come around the couch, arms folded as he glared at the two of us. "He's right, Barbie," he said. "You're being unreasonable."

"Not you, too. I thought you hated him?"

Maverick and Torin exchanged a look. Whatever had happened last night had obviously changed some things and while Maverick watched Torin with caution, he wasn't outwardly antagonistic.

Well, fuck.

Torin snorted. "Stay out of my head," I snapped.

"Stop projecting," he retaliated.

"Okay, enough." Maverick reached down. Surprisingly, Torin released his hold on me as Maverick took my arms and pulled me away from him. "Torin and I talked last night, and he told me everything."

I eyed him and then Torin. "Everything?" I repeated, nonplussed.

Maverick nodded. "But we've got more important things to worry about right now."

"We do?"

Torin stood up behind me and I stiffened when he moved past, disappearing into another room. Maverick smoothed a hand down my back and urged me to sit on the couch. "You've been out all weekend," Maverick said.

"All weekend?" I frowned. "What day is it?"

"It's Sunday afternoon," he answered.

I groaned. "What about Jon and Beth?" I hated to ask, but with how the house must have been left…

"They think we had a break in. I told them you were really shook up and weren't comfortable staying there until everything was put back together. Mom came over to see you."

"So, they know we're staying here?" I sucked in a breath.

Maverick nodded. "Yeah, I told them you were shaken up so you took some sleeping meds. Mom's worried about you, she's been calling me nonstop."

Unusual warmth flooded my chest. "Okay," I said, swallowing roughly. "Then that takes care of your parents, what else was there?"

Torin came back into the room. He pitched a water bottle first at Maverick and then a second at me. I fumbled as I caught it and set the ice-cold bottle in my lap, over the fabric of my borrowed shirt. "The morning paper," Torin said, pulling a thick wad of grayish papers from under his other arm and tossing that at me too. "Look at the front cover."

I frowned, pushing the water bottle to the side as I lifted the paper to my face and read the headline. "St. Marion Murderer strikes again," I read aloud. "What the hell?"

"Another student's been killed," Torin said.

"Same situation as Derick," Maverick replied.

"Heart removed?" I asked. They both nodded. Shit.

After a beat, Torin stepped forward. "It's not a vampire," he said. "At least if it is, it's not one involved with my family. You killed Delia, Eloise left days ago, and my sister…" He paused and took a breath. "It's not her."

"You don't have any other vampire's in your coven?" I asked, narrowing my eyes on him.

"No."

I searched my mind for the memories from my parents' teachings. Despite the fact that I'd thought they were crazy, they had made my brother and I study extensively. We'd covered all of the weak spots of vampire physiology. The throat. The heart. The head. We'd learned the history of vampires, about their powers, where they'd supposedly come from—a malformed deity that had crawled from the mouth of hell and mated with humans had somehow been responsible for the creatures that now slunk through the night and drank human blood.

I darted a glance to Torin. Well, almost all of them anyway.

"It could be a human," Maverick offered. "That's not under Barbie's purview."

"Technically, nothing is under Barbie's purview except herself," Torin said.

"Excuse me?" I pushed the paper to the couch and stood up, crossing my arms over my chest.

"You could've died the other night," Torin snapped. "I told you to leave and you didn't. You have no business hunting vampires. You're young. You can start over a new life somewhere. You don't have to end up like your family."

"You said you'd help me," I snapped. Even past the embarrassment over how I'd reacted to our kiss, I knew that the dream had been real. And in the dream, he'd sworn he would help me in avenging my family. Now he was telling me to quit? I didn't get it.

"What?" Torin looked at me like I'd lost my ever-loving mind. "What the fuck are you talking about? I never said I'd help you. I certainly won't help you kill yourself and that's what this is, suicide."

"You—" I stopped. No, it hadn't been him. It'd been his vampire. Did Torin really not recall the dream?

"I what?"

I shook my head. I didn't know what to say, if I should have told him about what his other half promised me. I thought Torin and Vampire-Torin were one and the same, but he didn't seem to remember ... so maybe they weren't.

"Regardless of whose responsibility it is," Maverick said, drawing the attention back to him. "Something has to be done, right?"

"There've only been two murders, right?" I asked.

Maverick grimaced. "Finish reading the article," he said nodding to the paper. "There were two more. Three all together. This is a serial killer."

"I lost my daggers here, Torin," I said. "I need them back."

He shook his head. "They won't do you much good," he replied. I growled, my back tightening as I prepared to lay into him, but he held up a hand and stopped me. "But I know you won't back down," he conceded. I eyed him suspiciously. "I've already sent something over that'll help you protect yourself." He sighed. "It'll be far more useful than those little pricks you called daggers."

"I'll show you a little prick," I grumbled.

He lifted a brow but didn't respond. Instead, he turned to Maverick. "I expect you to keep practicing at the gun range. I've ordered a few more boxes of ammo. Practice with normal bullets, only take the silver and holy water bullets with you if you're going with her."

I looked between the two of them. "I'm sorry, what?"

Maverick smirked. "You didn't think after Friday night, you were going to do this on your own did you?" he asked. Confusion and a sick, uneasy feeling bloomed in my chest. He couldn't mean what I thought he did. Maverick reached behind himself and pulled a Glock from a holster at the small of his back. "That's right, Princess, you've got yourself a partner."

Fuck. A fucking. Duck.

THIRTY

BARBIE

"I'M SO SORRY WE WEREN'T HERE, BARBIE." BETH'S bosom squished against my cheek as she clutched me to her, fretting in a way that was more uncomfortable than the hug. I allowed it, even though it made my back itch and my hands sweat. Beth was a good person, and she cared. Pulling away would hurt her feelings.

"I told you, it's fine," I said when she finally released me. "You couldn't have known."

"It was so messy. There was so much blood." She sniffled. "I thought someone had died."

Someone *had* died, but she didn't need to know that.

I shrugged and knocked my skull with my knuckles. "Head wounds bleed a lot," I said. A lie by misdirection. Torin's blood had healed all of my major cuts and wounds. I felt better, stronger, and faster—all of which he told me would fade back to normal levels within a day or two.

"I'm so surprised no one got seriously hurt from all of the glass," she said, shaking her head. "We were so

247

lucky it was just a few cuts and bruises." She squeezed me against her again and this time, I couldn't help but sidle away, evading her touching grasp.

Huh, I hadn't felt like this with Torin or his vampire, I thought.

"Mom," Maverick interrupted, "come on, she's fine. I'm fine. We're all fine. We're going to be late for school."

"You got back so late last night," Beth said. "Why don't you stay in today? I don't know if I'm comfortable with you two going to school right now."

"We already missed yesterday," I reminded her. Despite my insistence that we leave, Maverick and I had remained with Torin Sunday night and Monday only returning after midnight the night before.

"Mom, just because they called him the St. Marion Murderer doesn't mean he's actually targeting St. Marion students. We're going." Strong fingers wrapped around my upper arm and tugged me away from Beth. "We'll see you later!" Maverick called over his shoulder.

"Text me when you leave school," Beth ordered from the kitchen.

I shook my head as Maverick led me outside and towards his truck. He released me and we both got in. "Here." Maverick reached into the backseat and pulled out a long box wrapped in pink ribbon. "I grabbed it before my parents could get a look inside. It's from Torin."

I pulled against a string and unwrapped the ribbon from the long box as he cranked the engine and backed out of the driveway. My jaw dropped as I removed the lid from the box. Two short swords glimmered in the early morning sunlight. The handles were made of soft leather and thick silver. I lifted first one and then the other. Strong. The blade was slender, but not so small that it would break easily. Perfectly balanced. These were the most beautiful weapons I'd ever held. I loved them, and a part of me hated myself for it.

"Damn, never thought I'd see that look in your eye." I shoved the lid back over the box and returned it to the backseat.

"What look?" I asked.

"The kind girls usually reserve for diamonds and Louis Vuitton purses."

"I'm not that kind of girl," I said with a harrumph.

He arched a brow, burnt autumn eyes watching me curiously. "Oh? Then what kind of girl are you?"

I shrugged. "I'm like a flower. I look beautiful and sweet, but I've got a fuck ton of thorns and if you fuck with me, I will stab you."

He laughed, shaking his head as he focused forward once more. The scenery flew by outside the window, a small distraction to my thoughts. Halfway to the school, I spoke. "So, I didn't say this before," I started quietly, "but I know this weekend was probably a shock to you and you ... um ... I wanted to thank you." I leaned to the side and cracked my neck, avoiding his gaze as I saw his head turn my way.

"For what?" he asked.

I sighed. "You saved my life, Maverick," I said.

He slowed to a stop at a red light and when the light turned green and he still hadn't moved, I looked over.

Maverick's eyes were on me, serious and fierce. "You should have told me," he said.

A car honking behind us interrupted my reply and Maverick cursed, pressing down on the gas and whipping the truck into the nearest empty parking lot before he shut off the engine and flipped back to me.

"You wouldn't have believed me," I said before he could speak. "Vampires, Maverick. Think about it." I jerked my hands away automatically when he reached for me and he froze. Sucking in a calming breath, I shook my head. "I'm sorry."

His eyes were twin pools of molten whiskey, burning in the sun as he stared down at where I'd drawn my hands back. "Why do you do that?" he asked, looking up at my face. "Why do you pull away?"

My throat dried up. My tongue swelled. Hands on my shoulders. Holding me back as my family's blood flowed across the scarred wood floor and old carpet. "It's not you," I said, hearing my voice as if it was coming from down a long dark tunnel. "When my family—I was held back," I answered. "When they were killed. It doesn't happen all the time, just when I feel…" I trailed off not sure how to explain that when my emotions overflowed, my senses drew away and so, too, did I.

"Barbie." Maverick's face bobbed in front of me, his fingers gently reaching up to touch my face. "You're not alone. You don't have to thank me for saving your life. You did the same thing for me."

"What?" I frowned, confused. *When had I—?*

"The vampire?" he prompted with a raised brow. "If

you hadn't been there, she definitely would have killed me."

"If I hadn't been there, you wouldn't have been in danger at all," I pointed out.

He shook his head. "Doesn't matter now." His fingertips trailed down my jaw and I tightened all over. Not pulling away, not drawing back, not moving at all. But my whole body clenched with awareness as my gaze went immediately to his lips. His lips were full, masculine jaw hard. I swallowed. "Will you tell me if you need my help again?" he asked.

My lips parted, but no sound emerged. I closed them, thinking. Finally, I came to a decision. "Practice with the gun Torin gave you," I said. "Spar with me. Train and I ... *maybe* I'll tell you if I need help."

Maverick chuckled. "Of course," he said, his hand falling away from my face as he sat back with a thump against the leather seat. He laughed and shook his head, reaching for the key in the ignition. As the engine revved back to life he shot me a look. "You've got yourself a partner, now, Barbie," he warned as he put the truck in drive. "I'll practice. I'll spar with you. I'll train. There's no getting away now."

For some reason, that announcement felt like a mixture of an assurance and a threat. I shook my head and said nothing more, though I turned the conversation over in my mind while he drove the rest of the way to school. More than that, I tried to work through why I had focused so intently on his mouth and why his fingers against my skin had made me want to pull him closer.

With how everything was going though, it came as

no surprise that when we arrived, the student parking lot was more scarce than usual. While Maverick and I weren't afraid to come, that bravery didn't extend to the rest of the population. I spotted Olivia's white Porsche, though, so at least I knew I could have her fill me in on anything I might have missed.

"Barbie!" And there she was, standing by the doors, her arms up and waving.

"See ya later," I said, starting across the asphalt. Not two seconds later, Torin's motorcycle revved into the parking lot. I stopped at the sidewalk and looked over my shoulder as he parked alongside Maverick's truck.

"Oh my God." A red flurry of hair slammed into my chest. I winced as Olivia's nails dug into my arms, her eyes glued to the two guys beyond my shoulder. "Are Maverick McKnight and Torin Priest actually talking to each other again?"

"Olivia." I removed her claws from my skin. "They're just people." Well, one of them was an odd half-vampire with a penchant for forgetting promises made by his other half, but still…

Olivia looked up at me as if she hadn't realized she'd nearly bulldozed me in her shock. She narrowed her gaze on me. "You did this, didn't you?"

I rolled my eyes and headed for the doors. "I don't know what you mean."

"Bullshit," she snapped, her nails latching onto my arm once again as we reached the main hall, drawing me to a halt. "You have something to do with those two, I just know it."

"Do you really want to talk about Torin and Maverick, or do you want to tell me what the hell happened this weekend?" I asked, diverting her attention away from whatever connection I might have had with the rekindling of Maverick's old friendship.

"You heard about Mack and Charlie, didn't you?" she asked.

"It's all over the papers," I replied.

With a sigh, she hooked her arm in mine and led us down the hall towards her locker—her purse dangling between us, smacking my side every step of the way. "They went to a party on the outskirts of town. One of the guys from the wrestling team was throwing it. They got a little wild. Everyone was drinking and doing drugs, I heard."

"You heard?" I asked. "You weren't there?"

She winced and released my arm as we got to her locker. "Still grounded," she grumbled, reaching up to put in her lock combination. "Though I never thought I'd be grateful to be grounded. Otherwise, I would've been there."

I rested my spine against the cool metal of the lockers and frowned. "Who else was there?"

"Pretty much everyone," she said. "From the football players and cheerleaders to the debate team. It was a huge party. Though I heard Maverick and Torin never showed." She shot me a meaningful look as she retrieved her books and put her purse up. "Wonder where they could've been?"

I shrugged and looked away. "No clue," I lied.

"Well, wherever they were, they must have been really tied up." Olivia snapped her locker shut and turned to me. "Heard they didn't answer anyone's texts or calls. Rachel's furious. Maverick's been ignoring her lately."

"Were they dating?" I asked. He had never mentioned the possibility, but I hadn't missed the way Rachel had talked about him when she'd approached me before. The possessiveness in her tone was telling.

"Not for lack of her trying," Olivia admitted. "She's been pretty pissed about you showing up."

"Me?" I yawned and pushed away from the lockers before we continued on down the hall towards our classes. "It's been a few weeks, surely she's gotten over it by now."

"Ha, you don't know anything about high school girls, do you?"

"I was homeschooled before this year," I replied. "Didn't really need to know anything about them."

"Homecoming is coming up and she's determined to get Maverick to take her," Olivia confessed. "She's terrified he's going to ask you."

"Terrified?" I let my doubt fill my tone. The only thing that seemed to scare that girl was being knocked down a peg or two, which was too bad because that was rather easy to do. At least, it was for me.

"It's her senior year," Olivia said. "She's gunning for top spot. Homecoming Queen—the whole shebang."

I hummed, the sound vibrating my throat. Homecoming. I'd only ever seen Homecoming in movies and on TV. I grimaced. I had a feeling that if things continued to escalate the way they were, Homecoming would be more like the movie *Carrie* than fluffy dresses and ribbons and tiaras.

"When is it?" I asked. Olivia stopped. It took me a few more steps to realize that I'd left her behind. I paused and glanced over my shoulder. She stared at me as if I'd grown a second head. "What?"

"Tell me you're joking," she commanded.

"Uhhh." I floundered. "About what?"

She gestured to me. "Homecoming!"

"No?"

"Look around you," she said. "The flyers and decorations have been up since you got here."

I blinked and turned my attention to the rest of the hallway, my lips parting in surprise. She was right. Flyers were posted on the walls. Banners hanging from the ceilings, covered in dark navy blue glitter.

"It's next week!" Olivia cried.

"Oh." I grimaced.

"Oh? That's all you have to say?" Olivia strode forward with purpose. She grabbed my arm and whirled me to face her fully. "You haven't even gotten a dress, have you?"

"I wasn't exactly planning on going…"

"Oh you're going," she said with a shake of her head. "If I have to drag you there myself, you're going."

"I don't think—"

"I think that's a great idea." I stiffened as a thickly muscled arm settled over my shoulder. Sparks danced down my back. Olivia's face reddened until she looked like an over-ripened tomato.

I closed my eyes, begging the universe for patience.

"I don't think I want to know your reasoning for that ludicrous idea," I said, waiting a beat before I reopened my eyes.

Torin smiled, his teeth white and perfect. It made me want to punch him in the face. Again. Or kiss him. *No, I definitely don't want that,* I thought, cursing myself when he tilted his head at me curiously. He'd obviously heard that last little tidbit.

"Because you're going with me," he said.

"Oh, look at that," I said. "I was right. I really didn't want to know."

"Y-you're going with Torin?" Olivia's eyes were the widest they'd ever been as she looked between us.

"No."

"Yes."

I glared at him. "Torin," I snapped. "I am not going to Homecoming with you."

"I'll … erm … let you two talk this out alone," Olivia squeaked.

"There's nothing to talk about," I said, but she was already backing away, her books clutched to her chest.

"I'll … ah … talk to you in class, Barbie."

"Wait—" She turned away and practically sprinted down the hall, leaving me in the arms of the monster. I snarled and jerked out of his grasp, facing off with the handsome beast. "What the fuck was that?" I demanded.

"Homecoming, we're going," he said, his tone turning serious. I gaped at him. This had to be a fucking joke. *Oh, please be a fucking joke.* He shook his head. "No joke."

I growled and snapped my hand out, grabbing him by the front of his shirt. "Stay. Out. Of. My. Fucking. Head."

"Wear something sexy," he replied, pulling my fingers from the fabric one by one. "Or else I might not put out."

My hand itched to slap him, but by the time I decided it was a risk worth taking in the middle of the school's hallway, he was gone. My anger raged.

THIRTY-ONE

BARBIE

I slid into the cafeteria seat next to Maverick and glared. "So, tell me why we're going to Homecoming," I ordered. Several eyebrows shot up around me.

Maverick sighed. "Torin told you," he guessed.

"If by told, you mean, he said I'm going with him and then disappeared then yes, he 'told me' this morning," I answered.

"You and Torin are talking again?" one of the guys sitting across the lunch table asked.

Maverick cracked his neck. "We worked things out," he said, purposefully keeping his answer vague. He couldn't exactly say that he had to come to grips with the fact that his ex-best friend was part vampire and he needed his help to save my life.

"Is he joining the football team again?" the same guy asked. He wasn't the only one who seemed interested in the answer, I noticed as I looked around and saw that every single guy in the nearby seats were leaning towards the two of us, waiting on the edges of their seats for the answer.

Maverick scowled. "I don't fucking know, man, why don't you ask him?" He stood up from his seat and stomped away with a deep scowl.

"Sorry," I said, glancing back to the guys. "He's on his *man*stral cycle."

"His what?" someone asked, confused.

"You know," I hedged. "Guy PMS?" I shook my head when they still stared at me with unblinking eyes. The joke went right over them. "Never mind." I popped out of the seat and headed after Maverick, finding him as he dumped his lunch into a trash can and cut across the cafeteria towards the courtyard.

"Mav—" I lifted my arm to call out but came to a careening halt as an apple went sailing past my head, smacking the wall and dropping to the ground. Slowly, as if my head were turning on a pike, I looked towards the direction it'd come from and saw none other than Rachel fucking Harris, official pain in my ass.

"Oh, sorry," she said with a yawn as she brought up her nails and examined her cuticles while her friends—two bottle-blondes along either side of her—giggled. "My hand slipped." I looked down at my feet as the apple rolled to a stop against my shoe. "Maybe you should eat that," she said, her friends' laughter getting louder in my head. "An apple a day keeps the doctor away and all that."

I reached down and picked it up, clenching my fingers around the red skin of the fruit. "An apple a day can keep anyone away," I said softly. "It all depends on how hard you throw it." I let it loose, but instead of aiming for Rachel, I let it sail right past her, slamming into the girl on her left's cheek. The apple bounced off her cheek and smacked the girl's eye. That was going to leave a bruise. Rachel didn't bat an eyelash, even as her friend cried out and hit the ground. My lips twisted.

"I'd be careful if I were you," she said. Her eyes shone with some sort of strange light—as if the light pouring in from the windows was being reflected against a glassy surface.

"You'll have to forgive me if I don't take safety advice from a bitch with a death wish," I snapped, turning away and heading out the door. The muscles of my back tightened with the weight of her gaze.

I WAITED FOR MAVERICK BY HIS TRUCK AS USUAL, BUT AT half an hour past the end of school, he still hadn't shown up. I sighed and snatched my backpack up, swinging it over my shoulder as I started towards the football field. I had thought that with two more deaths, football practice would have been called off again. That obviously didn't seem to be the case.

I hadn't made it more than ten feet away from the truck when Torin's figure emerged from the school building. I stopped in the middle of the parking lot as he lifted his head and met my gaze. I glared at him as he approached.

"Waiting for Mav?" he asked.

"I still haven't forgiven you from this morning," I snapped.

He looked towards the football field. "Come on, he'll be a while yet. Let me take you home."

"Not until you tell me what the fuck that Homecoming bullshit was about," I ordered.

"I was never planning on keeping it a secret," Torin said.

"Then why didn't you tell me right off the bat?" I crossed my arms over my chest.

He smirked and I hated how much it made him look like Mav. Bright. Normal. *Human*. His smirk disappeared. "I am human, Barbie."

My scowl deepened. "What have I told you about staying out of my head," I snapped.

Torin spread his fingers wide. "I can't fucking do anything if you're practically yelling it at me."

"You can tell me how to stop," I shot back.

"What would be the point?" he asked. "It'll go away in another day or two."

I glared at him, crossing my arms over my chest defensively. "What do you want?"

"I want you to come with me," he said. "To practice."

"Practice?" I repeated.

"You got those swords I left you?"

I shifted on my feet. "Yeah. I got them."

He fished into his pocket and pulled out a set of keys. "We're gonna go see if you can handle them."

"They're locked in Mav's truck," I pointed out as he circled the truck and headed for his motorcycle.

"I've got similar ones back at the guest house. I wanna see what you can do with those first." He reached into his saddlebag and retrieved a helmet, tossing it to me. I caught it with two hands and then just held it as I watched him swing one thickly muscled thigh over the bike.

"I thought you didn't approve," I said. "I thought you weren't going to help?" *Did he remember?*

He frowned as he looked over at me. "Remember what?"

I frowned but didn't chastise him for listening to my thoughts this time. "When I was unconscious," I started. "I had a dream."

He looked at me over the handlebars of his motorcycle. "About what?" he asked.

"You," I said. "Well, vampire you. And vampire you promised to help me, but then when I woke up you…" I trailed off, but I figured he could pick up the rest.

Silence filled the air for a beat. When he spoke, his voice was gruff. "Barbie." He turned the engine over, the bike roaring to life. "Get on the bike," he called.

I didn't know how to take that, but instead of arguing for a change, I slipped the helmet on and buckled it before I made sure my backpack was on all the way and securely zipped shut before I approached. My hands found his shoulders, nails biting down into them as I swung my leg over the seat behind him. My feet left the ground and found the footholds. My front melded to his back, my breasts against his spine as the vehicle rumbled with a low hum beneath me. I inhaled sharply, my core tightening when he reached back and snagged my hand drawing me even closer until I was practically plastered against him. I didn't know how we could get closer.

"Hold on," he ordered just before he took off.

My hands tightened automatically, fisting into his shirt as he sped out of the parking lot. Minutes later, as we drove past the Priest estate, I leaned back and stared up at the closed curtains of the upstairs bedrooms and the very window I'd crashed out of in an attempt to get away from a furious vampire. A lot had changed since the night I'd snuck out of my parents' house to go to a party. The supernatural reality of my life had finally come to light. Death. Moving. Sex. *I* had changed. I was no longer the naive girl who thought her parents were crazy and paranoid. I was a hunter, and I couldn't forget what that meant.

My hands squeezed against Torin as we rounded the side of the driveway and headed down a long, dark, and narrow road. Every so often, a smaller driveway would appear on our right, but we didn't stop until we came to the very last one. He pulled up to the front door and shut off the engine, and in the silence that followed, I realized just how hard my heart was beating.

Slipping off the back of the motorcycle, I stood to the side as he nudged the kickstand down with the toe of his boot and swung his leg over the seat. "Come on," he said, "I'll grab the gear."

Torin had me drop my stuff off inside the door as he led me further inside, stopping to grab a long duffle bag out of a chest in the living room before we headed for the backyard. Unzipping the duffle on the porch, he withdrew a pair of swords similar to the ones I'd received.

"How well trained are you?" he asked, handing me one.

I took it and hefted it in my fist, twisting first one way and then another. "I can handle myself," I hedged.

He looked at me and then took a stance. "If you can land a hit on me using the flat of your sword, I'll promise to help you with your task."

I stiffened, lowering the weapon in my grip. "You already promised to do that," I reminded him.

He shook his head. "My vampire can't make any decisions like that without me," he said.

"Oh?" I tilted my chin as I watched him. "Why don't you remember the conversation we had?" I asked. "With your vampire, I mean."

He swallowed, lowering his weapon as well. "I suppress my vampire, Barbie," he answered solemnly.

"You don't have complete control when you sleep, though," I guessed.

He nodded. "I believe that you drinking my blood to heal opened a door for him to enter your dreams, for which, I am sorry."

I shrugged. At least he didn't know about the kiss. My eyes went to his lips and my face heated. I sucked in a breath. "Let's do this," I said, raising the sword again.

He lifted his sword as well. "One hit," he reminded me. I struck.

Over an hour later, I was sweating and cursing as he managed to dodge another attack. I hit the ground, rolling and popping back up onto my feet as I circled him. My breath sawed in my chest as I flipped the sword to my left hand to give my right wrist a break. The weight grew heavier the longer I gripped the hilt.

"You sure you want my help?" he taunted.

I growled and surged forward. Swords clashed. Sparks flew down the metal as it shrieked along Torin's blade. I cursed and ducked as they released and Torin spun. I barely managed to dive out of his reach before his sword sang by overhead.

"You're focusing too hard on my sword," he said. "Focus on my movements. Where my body goes."

"I am!" I shouted. I wasn't. It went against everything my dad had ever taught me, but every time I looked at his body I was reminded of vampire-Torin. How he'd surged around me, his hands gripping me, the pulse of his blood beneath his throat. My mouth watered. "Stop!" I screamed as he reached me, his blade flashing in the air. He froze and I went low, smacking the flat of my blade against his thigh as I slid beneath the reach of his arms and tumbled across the ground, panting and sweating. I stopped and looked back over my shoulder. "I win."

"You do not," he snapped. "You cheated."

"All is far in vampires and war," I said with a shrug, tossing the sword to the ground as I sagged against the porch. "I won. Now you're obligated to keep your promise."

Lights flashed from the front of the house as tires crunched over gravel. "Maverick's here," Torin growled, reaching down to scoop up the sword as he passed by. "Go home."

"Don't be a sore loser," I said.

He stopped at the back door and looked back, his shoulders loosening as he shifted so that one hand held both hilts. "I'm not," he said. "But I would suggest that you keep up your training. You were right to cheat. You wouldn't win a fair fight with a vampire, but you kept up with my vampire speed well."

"Then why do you seem angry?" I asked as a car door slammed around front.

"I don't like you in danger, Barbie."

"If that were true, then why did you bring me here to train?" I asked.

"Because danger seems to follow you where you go," he said.

I frowned. "You never told me why you and Maverick decided that we were going to Homecoming," I said, changing subjects.

He sighed and reached for the door handle. "We're pretty sure that whoever's been killing students will be there and we're going to find them one way or another."

"You trust me to help?" My foot hit the bottom step of the back porch as I looked up at his back.

"I trust that you're not one to back down from a challenge. Now, go home and take a shower, you reek of human sweat."

He slammed into the house as both of my brows shot up towards my hairline. *What a fucking asshole,* I thought, and I hoped he heard it too.

THIRTY-TWO

BARBIE

Blood red silk sifted against my skin, smooth and cool. I sucked in a breath as a familiar hand curled against the fabric and dragged it away from my naked body. Ruby red eyes shone in the darkness as Vampire-Torin moved against me.

I groaned. "Can't you leave me alone?" I grumbled against the pillows, trying to ignore the fact that I wasn't wearing a stitch of clothing and neither was he.

"Now, why would I want to do that?" he asked as he settled his chest against my spine. Deft fingers danced along my side, moving across my skin and making me squirm against him. "We have so few hours together as it is."

"Maybe because I'd like to get some sleep," I said.

"You are sleeping," he reminded me, pressing an open mouthed kiss against my shoulder.

I stiffened and tried to scoot away. It didn't do any good. He turned me so that I faced him. Yanking me close so that my bare breasts were shoved against his chest, he looked down at me and smiled, revealing razor sharp canines. I blinked dully.

"Is there a point to your visit?" I asked, trying to hide my

reaction to him. It was useless, though. He slid his hand between my thighs, strong fingers digging into one as he hefted it up, sliding his own into the space created until my core was pressed down against his muscular leg. I tightened unconsciously.

"He's agreed to help you with your vengeance," Vampire-Torin said as he bent low and blew across the space between my neck and shoulder.

I shivered in his arms and leaned away. "It would have been nice to know that he wouldn't recall the promise you swore to me." I growled low in my throat as his touch wandered over the curve of my ass.

He chuckled, the sound vibrating through my nipples until they grew tight and pebble-hard. "Are you angry with me?" he asked, sliding those devious lips of his across my skin.

Without even meaning to, my head tilted back to give him better access. What the hell was wrong with me? Why did I let him do this here? Why didn't I pull away? Was it because none of this was real? "Furious," I said, gasping when he bit down lightly against the column of my throat, but not deep enough to sink his fangs in or draw blood. It was just enough to curl my toes and make my nerves stretch tautly until they were on the knife's edge of too tight and ready to shatter.

The action brought me closer to a blinding white orgasm. With it, I managed to work up the energy to struggle against him. "Shh-hh." Vampire-Torin held me still, rolling so that he was on top of me fully, his body coming down hard over mine. "I won't hurt you, dear mate."

"W-what?" I stuttered as he spread my thighs and settled between them. "What the hell is that supposed to mean?"

"What do you know about vampire mates, Barbie?" he asked.

"Nothing," I answered. *"It's not exactly something I need to know in order to kill a vampire."*

"Au contraire, sweetheart." He leaned down and whispered the words against my ear. *"Vampire mates are a huge weakness to exploit."*

"Okay?" I squirmed in his grip, my thighs growing wetter as he brought his cock closer to my core and rubbed the underside of it instinctively against my folds. I gasped and shoved my hands up against his chest to stop him. *"Don't."* As difficult as it was in that moment, I managed to grit the word out between clenched teeth.

"You want me," he said lightly. It wasn't said with any sort of arrogance, but with simple confidence. A statement of fact.

I shook my head. *"And yet, I'm still saying no."*

He pulled back, those unnatural red eyes of his roving over me curiously. *"Why?"* he asked.

At this moment? I had no fucking clue. But I knew if I gave in like this, I'd regret it. Instead of answering, I asked another question. *"Why are you here?"*

The muscles of his upper arms tightened as he continued to hold himself above me, observing me with those uncanny eyes of his. *"You're in danger, Barbie."*

I thought about that. It seemed Torin was right, danger was never far from me and I was never far from it. *"From what this time?"* I asked.

"I wish I could say," he answered, lowering his chest back over me. His hands went to my outer thighs as he drew them over his hips. *"Shhhh."* He hushed me again when I would have protested. *"I will not test your breaking point tonight. I just want to make you feel good."*

"*Tell me what you meant,*" I ordered. "*When you said I was in danger.*"

He hummed, the sound moving across my skin in an invisible wave, leaving a trail of goosebumps all along the flesh of my back. Instead of answering, he directed my attention to the heat building between us—and the hardening cock between my legs. "*I won't push you, dear mate,*" he said again. "*But if you don't give me this then I'm afraid Torin might suffer.*"

I froze, letting him maneuver my limbs as he liked until I felt the head of his cock brush against my pussy once more, more firmly. Only then did I reach up and snap my hand around his neck, squeezing to get his attention. "*Do. Not. Push. Me.*" The warning was a dangerous growl.

He looked down at me, an ever present smirk gracing his beautiful lips. It was difficult for me to see Torin's face without Torin there. His vampire was nothing like his human. Where the human side of Torin was serious—only sardonic in small intervals—his vampire shoved insistently against boundaries, laughed at my resistance, and tempted me far beyond what I was comfortable with. I tightened my grip on his throat.

"*What the fuck do you mean Torin might suffer?*" I demanded.

"*You shared his blood, Barbie,*" he said simply. "*My blood, or do you not recall?*"

"*What does that have to do with anything?*"

"*Torin resists me almost as much as you do, sweetheart,*" he answered, dipping his head despite my threat and licking up the center of my chest. My grasp on his throat weakened as his tongue darted a path past my chin and sank into my mouth. He kissed me like he was plundering a battlefield full of warriors—aggressively, dangerously. The kiss was full of blood pumping fervor and feroc-

ity. When he finally released me, I was left gasping, my hand having fallen away from the column of his neck. He nudged my head to the side with the length of his nose and pressed the tip of it beneath my ear, inhaling sharply. "You smell like fire and chocolate. Blessed dark god, I want to feast on you."

"Y-you haven't answered my questions," I reminded him shakily.

He sighed, the puff of air sliding over my flesh. I reached up and sank my nails into his shoulders. Something—anything—to keep me grounded when I felt like I was at risk of floating away into the pit of lust he was creating. "Torin is more human than vampire most days," he said quietly, the explanation rolling over my ears as his hips rolled against the softness of my flesh below. I groaned, low and needy. "Unless he lets his emotions overtake him —anger, hatred, excitement*—" he hissed the last word against my pulse, demonstrating just what kind of excitement he was refer- ring to, "he can maintain control. Giving you our blood, however, has raised certain side effects—"*

"These dreams?" I asked breathlessly as he reached down and gripped my thigh, leveraging it up higher on his hips as his fingers danced further between my legs, sliding through wetness to my clit. I sucked in air, but it never reached my lungs.

"Yes, dear mate," he agreed. "The side effects include an increased level of attraction to the one whose blood you consumed."

I shook my head as his hand teased at my clit and then he sank his fingers down until one wiggled into my entrance. My back arched and I clawed at the broad expanse of his back. "It's not real," I snapped, squeezing my eyes shut. That fucking hurt, but if what he said was true, then all of this desire, the lust, it wasn't real. It was all fake. I was being manipulated.

"Not exactly." Vampire-Torin thrust his finger into my core,

withdrawing and driving in again until the movement had my hips wiggling and arching towards him on every forward thrust. "Drinking my blood cannot create attraction when there was none to begin with, dear mate. Fear not, everything you're feeling—all of the pleasure I give—is real."

I moaned as he pulled back, moving down my body until his mouth brushed against my stomach, tongue circling my belly button lightly before blazing a path straight for where his finger had moved in and out of my body. "I told you—" I started, the threat and warning clear despite my hoarse voice.

"Do not worry," he said, a soft chuckle blowing across my sensitive, wet skin. "I told you I would not push you, and I won't. But unless you allow me to give you some sort of pleasure and relieve this pressure inside both of us, then I'll simply keep coming back."

I closed my eyes, biting down hard on my lip as his words filtered through my head. Give in now or later? Those seemed to be my only options. What was I supposed to do?

"Barbie." My name on his lips had me opening my eyes and looking down. That red gaze threw shadows across the pale flesh of my stomach, like lines of blood glowing unnaturally in the darkness of the shared dream. His tongue flicked out and licked against my clit. My lips parted and my hands shot down to his head, fingers threading through the dark locks of his hair. "Let me…" The whispered plea rocketed through me.

"Will he remember?" I asked. I didn't know if I could do this and then go back to normal if Torin would remember everything his vampire had done to me in this dream.

Vampire-Torin tilted his head and looked up at me. "It will be in the back of his mind," he admitted. "He will never be sure. It will seem like a dream to him. He is with me, always. He may see us as two different people, but he and I are one and the same. My desires are his. His are mine. I—the vampire—may be in control, but he is at least somewhat aware of what we're doing here as I am when his human side is in control."

"He didn't remember the promise you made me," I pointed out, my nails scraping against his scalp.

"He did and he didn't," Vampire-Torin replied vaguely. "He was unwilling to admit it, but there is a reason why he took you to train with him and challenged you for the assistance you demanded. He felt obligated."

"So, he will remember this then?" My breath sawed in and out of my chest. My lungs burning and knees shaking as I repressed my body's desires.

"He will be aware and he will remember the desire and even, perhaps, pieces of this, but it is a dream to him. Nothing more," Vampire-Torin said. "He does not realize that this is more than an average dream." He grinned, his fangs sharp in the shadows. "Rest assured, he will remain ignorant of our deal should you wish to keep it to yourself." I sighed, releasing all of the burning air in my lungs with a sound of relief. "Now, what is your decision?" he demanded.

I had only one choice. I couldn't hold back anymore. My resistance was worn too thin. I had a sexy, naked vampire between my thighs, and so long as the repercussions of this decision remained trapped in the confines of this dream world, there was nothing left stopping me from taking advantage.

Leveraging my head up, as I sank my fingers further into his hair, I stared down at the twin red-dotted eyes. "Eat me." The words were a harshly whispered double entendre. A shaky consent.

"Fear not, dear mate, I will devour you." He stopped and licked his lips. "In the best way possible." His breath slithered over

the heated wet flesh of my pussy. "I will take until you have no more cream left to give and when you call out my name, I will know you are screaming your desire for me."

Vampire-Torin's eyes brightened, practically flaming into an illuminating raging fire as he descended. Lips touched my core. His tongue darted out, stroking back up to my clit as his fingers sank inside. First one and then two. My back arched. A cry of pleasure escaped my throat, no more words possible.

My thighs tightened. Vampire-Torin set his hands on either one and spread them wide as he sucked my clit between his lips and drove me half-mad. It was too much. It wasn't enough. It was everything.

I screamed as my orgasm ripped through me, tearing my mind open and leaving me blown apart. My fingers clutched at his head. Warm liquid spilled over my palms. A sharp pain brought my head up as a new scream erupted from my throat. I jerked my gaze down and cursed as I saw his fangs against my skin, piercing the soft vulnerable section of my inner thigh. He released me almost as quickly as he'd bitten, licking up the blood he'd spilled.

That image was the last thing left as the shadows of the dream encroached on my vision, and I was left spiraling into oblivion.

THIRTY-THREE

BARBIE

"ARE YOU SURE YOU'RE OKAY?" MAVERICK'S QUESTION echoed up the hallway as we headed towards the indoor shooting range. I gulped down the rest of the coffee in my plastic throwaway cup and tossed it in the nearest trashcan and shook my head.

"I'm fine," I repeated for the tenth time.

"You look like you got run over by a semi," he commented dryly.

I sighed and looked back at him over my shoulder. "Just what a girl wants to hear."

He shrugged. "You look like shit. I'm just saying maybe you should sit this one out."

"Who's going to teach you how to use that thing properly?" I asked, gesturing to the Glock in his hand. I was more than exhausted. I was jittery and on edge. The dream from the night before played over and over in my head, like a fucking film on eternal rotation. Vampire-Torin's red eyes moving over me, his lips, his tongue, his fangs on my skin. I shivered as we hit the entrance to a larger room and strode down the line of sectioned off tables where a few others were up early enough to try their own hand at some practice shots.

A yawn overtook me as we found our section and I stepped up to the table previously set up. "I can manage," Maverick said behind me. "Torin brought me here earlier this week."

I didn't doubt that, but I wanted to see his progress on my own. "Step up to the line," I ordered, reaching into the bag I carried and withdrew a clip. "These are your average lead bullets," I said. "Other than at practice, you'll be carrying special bullets made of silver or soaked in holy water."

"I know." Maverick took the clip, his fingers brushing against mine. I ignored the zing of sensation that traveled up my arm.

"Alright." I took a step back and gestured for him to move into position as he inserted the clip and double checked the weapon, flicking the safety off. I lifted two pairs of noise reduction ear muffs and handed him one. "Show me what you got," I called as I settled them firmly in place on my head.

Maverick raised both arms, took aim, and pulled the trigger. The resounding echo of the gunshot was loud in my ears even with protection, but a few seconds later, someone else responded with their own barrage of bullets. I stared out at the target and frowned when Maverick lowered his arms and glanced at me.

"You're all over the place," I said with a sigh.

"What? But I hit the target."

"I want you to focus on one place and try to hit that one place repeatedly, as many times as you can."

Maverick scowled. "I can't hit the same place multiple times."

"You can," I pressed, handing him another clip. After he inserted it, I took the Glock from him, dropped the bag, and stepped up alongside him. I aimed the barrel at the target several yards away and pulled the trigger. Holding my finger down, a quick succession of bullets left the chamber. I lowered the gun and stepped back. "Look."

Maverick's head lifted and he squinted down the way. "I can't see that far."

I reached down and pressed a button beneath the table, causing the person shaped target to move forward until it was much closer. Right there, in the center of the outline of the person's skull, were several shots circling the cross in the forehead, and then one right over where the cross met.

"I've been shooting since before I could drive a car," I said, handing his gun back to him. Maverick was silent for a moment and I waited to see what he would say or do. He stared down at the gun in his grip, his hand squeezing it as his knuckles turned white. "Mav?" Hesitantly, I reached for him, placing my hand on his arm. "It's not your fault. You just started. More practice will help." Guilt ate at my chest, but at the same time, he needed to know that this wasn't just a game. He knew about vampires now and that put him at risk. He needed to be able to protect himself.

"Am I a danger to you?" His voice was so quiet, I almost didn't hear the question.

I looked up. "What?"

Maverick set the gun down on the table in front of us and turned to me, pulling off his ear protection. "Am I putting you in more danger?" he asked.

I shook my head, taking mine off as well. "Don't worry about that," I said. "Don't worry about whether or not I'm in danger. Focus on protecting yourself first."

"I can't do that." My eyes widened as he stepped forward and without thinking, my legs went back and I smacked into the cubicle wall.

"You have to," I snapped. His head dipped and he sighed as his forehead pressed against mine, his eyes closing. "Mav? Are you okay?"

He cupped my cheek and I froze, startled. *What the fuck?* "I don't want to get you hurt," he said gruffly, his eyes sliding open again. They pierced me through, a blade sliding between my ribs. *Fuck.*

I cleared my throat and sidled out from between him and the wall. "You're not going to get me hurt," I said. "Just keep practicing." I looked away as I snatched up the bag and took out all of the clips I'd brought, setting them on the table. "Stay here and keep hitting that target."

"Barbie, where are you going?"

I yanked out my cell and backed out of the cubicle.

"I'm … ah … I forgot I had plans with Olivia," I lied, avoiding his eyes as I took another step back, my heart in my throat. *Shit, fuck. I really needed to get the fuck out of here.* "I have to go get a dress for Homecoming. It's next weekend."

"You—"

"I'll see you back at home." I bolted. There was no other word for it. I ran like a bat out of fucking hell and slammed through the thick double metal doors at the end of the room, pressing the call button on my phone almost as soon as I was out of his sight. Beth had told me that my car would be delayed for several more weeks, unfortunately, and I had no other way out. I needed a rescue.

"Barbie?" Olivia's cheery voice echoed in my ears.

"Can you give me a ride?" I blurted as I hit the sidewalk outside of the shooting range building.

"Uh, yeah sure?" she said, her voice rising in pitch with her confusion.

I sighed, already hating what I was sure would be several hours of pure, unadulterated torment, but it was either this or staying behind in close proximity with Maverick. And after what I'd allowed myself to do with Vampire-Torin, I didn't trust myself anymore. "I need a dress for Homecoming," I said weakly.

There was a breath of silence and then a quick intake of air as she squealed in my ear. "I knew you were going!" she screamed. "Oh my God, I'll be right there. Don't move a muscle. I know just the place and they do alterations too."

The sound of stuff being thrown, keys being jangled, and the soft, but quick patter of heels on hardwood floors echoed in my ears a split second before a car door closed on the other end of the line and the phone went dead. I pursed my lips. She hadn't even waited for me to tell her where I was. I typed out a quick text with the address of the shooting range and leaned back on my heels, looking up at the gray clouds churning overhead. A wind whipped down the street, tearing through the light jacket I had on.

Rain was coming.

OLIVIA'S PORSCHE SHRIEKED TO A HALT AND I GOT INTO the passenger seat, pulling the door closed as she gunned the engine. "The door wasn't closed!" I snapped. I reached for the seatbelt and yanked it across my chest as she swerved into traffic, taking a turn too fast.

"Sorry," she said, "but we have to hurry or we'll be late."

"Late?" I echoed as I finagled the buckle into its clip and clutched the damn belt to my chest as she roared through a yellow light.

"Blondie Boutique," she explained. "It's the only place you can get the perfect dress." She flipped her hair over one shoulder and sent me a reproachful look. "Really, you should've just confessed that you were going earlier. You're lucky I've spent like a fortune there every year since I started high school. I called on the way to get you and they said they had a cancellation and could squeeze you in, but we've only got like five minutes to get there."

I reached for the 'oh shit' handle and clutched onto

it for dear life as she took another turn. I swore I felt the vehicle rear up on its side. "I'd like to get there alive!"

"Psh, we're fine. I know my car." She swung into the parking lot of a strip mall and screeched to a stop at the end, snagging a parking spot in the corner and jerking the small car into it just as another car was leaving. I didn't want to know how close she'd come to hitting them, and they obviously didn't care because they kept going. She shut off the car and popped her door open with a sigh of relief. "Oh thank goodness, two minutes to spare." I looked down at my hands, still clutching the seat belt against my chest and took a breath. "Come on!" Olivia called, her heels clicking against the pavement as she hurried away from the car towards the front doors of the boutique.

Prying my hands from the belt, I unbuckled and slid out of the car, snapping a hand against the roof to steady myself before wobbling after her. I was already regretting this.

Inside the Blondie Boutique, two young women dressed in all black approached us and welcomed Olivia like a long-lost friend, crying and throwing their arms around her in excitement. The girls chattered away as they led us further back to a secluded area with a small room curtained off in front of a luxurious suede couch.

"This is my friend, Barbie," Olivia introduced. "We're looking for a *to-die-for* gown for Homecoming."

One of the women, a reed thin brunette with a sharp nose and petite slanted eyes, approached and looked me up and down. "Good figure," she said. "I think we have a few options off the rack."

"That's fine—" I began.

"The rack?" Olivia interjected. "Don't you have anything from the Deloris Collection?"

"Off the rack is fine," I said.

"No." Olivia looked at me like I was crazy, her lips pursed in disapproval. "This is Homecoming. Senior year. You're going with Torin Priest. Off the rack is *not* acceptable."

"I don't care—"

"Torin Priest?" the second woman echoed, her eyes widening as she stared at me.

Olivia grinned. "Oh yeah, I heard him ask her myself."

"He didn't really ask," I pointed out. "He just told me we were going."

"Hey, you accepted, no complaining," Olivia shot back.

I grimaced, but it wasn't like I could simply say that I accepted more because we suspected the St. Marion murderer would be at Homecoming and we were pretty sure that whoever was killing male students and ripping out their hearts was a supernatural creature. Vampire or not, they needed to be stopped.

Olivia and the women congregated together and whisper-hissed a few words before they nodded and disappeared back into the main section of the boutique. Olivia went to the couch and reclined on it with a sigh. A moment later, a young man carrying a bottle of Champagne entered and presented the bottle along with two crystal glasses and a bucket of ice to her.

"We're underage," I reminded her tersely as she allowed the man to pour her a glass.

Olivia laughed. "Not here, hon. Take a seat."

I frowned her way but saw no point in standing around, so I did as she suggested and sank down onto the couch cushions next to her. Holy fuck, it was comfortable. I groaned as I laid back. A girl could fall asleep on something this plush.

Olivia snickered. It took more effort than I cared to admit to lift my head. "What?" I asked.

"You," she said, sipping at her champagne as the man disappeared out the door.

"What about me?"

"Anyone else would be lording it over everyone that they were going with Torin Priest to Homecoming," she said.

I shrugged. "So?"

She shook her head. "You're just an odd duck."

I stared up at the ceiling, my mind whirling. Torin Priest. Half-vampire. King of St. Marion. Red eyes on my naked flesh penetrated my thoughts. My thigh throbbed.

"He's just a man," I said.

She snorted. "Sure he is," she replied.

"He is," I insisted. The thing was, I wasn't sure if it was her I was trying to convince or myself.

Torin Priest *was* just a man, but so was Maverick McKnight. One, dangerous and deadly. The other, safe and pure fucking human.

THIRTY-FOUR

MAVERICK

I FROZE, RIVETED AS BARBIE TOOK OFF. MY CHEST tightened as she backed away, turned, and fled. And whether or not she wanted to admit it, that's exactly what she was doing—running away. The dark circles beneath her eyes worried me. I set the Glock on the table and pulled my phone out of my pocket, dialing the number I'd seemed to never have forgotten.

"Yeah?" Torin's voice on the other end calmed me, but only marginally.

"It's me." But before I could say anything more, one of the other shooting range attendees started firing. "Hold on." I headed for the closest door and kept walking until the sound of shooting was muted enough that I could hear myself think.

"What's up?" Torin asked. "Are you at the shooting range?"

"Yeah, but that's not why I called. It's about Barbie." Silence. "She doesn't look good," I admitted. More silence. "Torin?"

"I—ah—listen, I gotta go."

"What the fuck, man?" I clutched the phone to my ear and frowned. "I call you to tell you something's up with Barbie and you blow me off?"

"It's not that," Torin said. "I just have to—" he grunted, cutting himself off. A moment later he was back. "Are you sure she's not just tired or something?"

"She just bolted from me," I said. "She was watching me practice and I just…" What had I done? What had I been thinking? I'd just wanted to know if she thought I was a danger to her. I wasn't skilled at this shit. Sure, my dad had taken me shooting before. I'd been hunting, but not for a few years. I was strong. Football kept me fast, but this— vampires? This was something new for me. I'd watched the way Barbie had taken out that vampire bitch. She'd been thrown clear across the room. The damn cunt had even lifted me up without batting an eyelash. I was facing something completely new here.

"What did you do?" Torin asked.

"I…" Maybe it had been a mistake to call him. "Never mind," I said. "It doesn't matter."

"Mav." Torin's sharp bark stopped me from hanging up. My fist clenched around the phone. Irritation swelled inside me, ballooning in my gut until I found myself eyeing the wall across from where I'd stopped, wondering how many times I could hit it without breaking anything. "Listen to me," Torin said, bringing my attention back. "Worrying about whether or not you're good enough is more likely to get you killed. If it were up to me, you never would have found out about any of this shit."

I scowled. "You would've kept me in the fucking dark?" I snapped.

"Yeah," he replied, no remorse in his tone. "Of course I fucking would have." The sharp sound of his breath on the other end grated against my nerves. That wall was looking better and better. "I didn't want any of this out in the open. I didn't want you anywhere near it."

"I don't need your fucking protection," I growled.

"Shut up and listen, will you?" Torin's voice deepened. "I have to fight a part of myself every day. I drink human blood." I had known that, but hearing it aloud felt like a sucker punch to the gut. I leaned back, the crown of my skull smacking into the wall at my back. "I'm not completely human," he continued. "As much as I wish I wasn't, a part of me is a monster. I wanted to protect you from that reality and so does Barbie. I'm sure she doesn't want you anywhere near the creatures who took her family from her."

"It's more than that," I said. "I…" *How the fuck did I say it?* "I don't want to lose *her*." I couldn't quell that fear inside. "I keep seeing her covered in blood," I admitted through clenched teeth. "And I keep thinking what if I hadn't gone to you? What if it'd been too late? What if I get her killed later on down the road?" Torin didn't respond for several long moments. So long, in fact, that I pulled the phone back and looked down to see if the call had dropped or something. I put it back to my ear. "Tor?"

"I'm ... here." He sounded odd. His voice hoarse as he spoke. "It's ... this is something you'll have to live with," he said. "Worrying about 'what ifs' won't do anyone any good. So, pick up the fucking gun I gave you. Practice. Shoot. Get good. Protect her." A growl echoed through the phone. "Now, I have to go."

I blinked and looked down in shock as the line went dead.

THIRTY-FIVE

TORIN

THE PHONE IN MY FIST CRACKED, A FISSURE SLITHERING across the glass face as my hand contracted on it. Hard. The small object left my hand before I knew what I was doing. I watched as it sailed through the air and slammed into the wall, the screen shattering upon impact into a hundred tiny little cracks, glass particles raining down as it hit the floor.

So possessive...

I growled as the voice intruded. "Shut up."

You really don't like the fact that he likes her, do you? Red hot fury boiled within me. No. I fucking did not.

My hands curled into fists and I turned away from the mess I'd made. "I said, shut up."

Just admit it—your feelings for her.

"What would that do?" I snapped. "She's human."

So are you, in part.

I groaned, rocking back on my heels as I lifted my arms and shoved my knuckles into my eye sockets, grinding down until black and white dots danced in front of my vision.

"Have you heard?"

I jerked in surprise, dropping my arms as my gaze shot to the doorway. Katalin stood there, one slender eyebrow lifted as she looked from me to the remains of the phone. I cleared my throat. "Heard what?"

Tilting her head to the side, she examined me, cool hazel eyes traveling down and then back up. "There's been another killing."

I paused, watching her carefully. "Another student?" I inquired.

She shook her head. "An employee from the Harris estate. Male."

I waited, but whether or not she had more information, it seemed that was all she was willing to part with at the moment. I couldn't let it be. "What do you think?" I asked.

"What do you mean?"

"Do you think they're human? The murderer?" I asked.

As I expected, she didn't betray any of her inner thoughts. "I think you should find out on your own, yes?"

I frowned. "Don't you want to know?"

"I already know." My muscles tightened. She knew. That meant it wasn't a human. It couldn't be. Unless it was and she just ... didn't care? Katalin's perceptive gaze never wavered.

"I suggest you use caution," she said quietly.

"What does that mean?" *Did she know what I was already planning? What Barbie, Maverick, and I were planning?*

"It means that this is a test and you should do everything in your power to pass it," she replied.

"A test?" Did that mean—*what* did that mean? She couldn't be saying that Arrius was behind the murders, could she? I gritted my teeth, feeling the sharp edge of my vampire as it rose to the surface. He'd been closer as of late. A fact that I usually wasn't so pleased with, but in these matters, the more power I had the better. "Tell me, Kat, did *he* have anything to do with this?" I demanded.

"You know I can't answer that." She shook her head and sighed.

"Then what can you answer?" I knew my eyes were glowing red. I could feel the heat beneath my skin, the anger that I so often worked to keep under control spreading throughout my limbs.

"I'm not the one you need to seek answers from."

"Then who the fuck am I supposed to—"

"Your vampire knows who you're looking for," she interrupted, her voice dipping into a warning growl. "Do not make the mistake of irritating me, Torin. I have been kind enough to turn my cheek in recent days. Do not think I don't know about your new human friends."

I stiffened. If she knew that I was seeing Maverick again, if she knew about Barbie—there was nothing stopping her from telling Arrius. And after the ultimatum Arrius had given me two years ago, I didn't want to know what he might do if he found out. I stared at her, wanting to ask, but at the same time, this changed things. Katalin turned and strode away. Her comment wasn't a threat, but a warning. The murderer wasn't human and on top of that, it had more than likely been sent by my father. Katalin knew about Mav and Barbie. It was only a matter of time before he did too.

I didn't like this. Not one fucking bit.

THIRTY-SIX

BARBIE

"Trust me."

"You know what else says that?" I asked. "Vodka. And yet, the trust issues I have with vodka still aren't resolved." I could practically picture Olivia's responsive eye roll as I grumbled under my breath. The five-hundred dollar piece of fucking shit.

"Try this one." A mass of white and black came through the curtain, Olivia's arm wiggling as she shook the damn thing at me. I snatched it out of her grasp.

"I swear to fuck, if you—"

"Just put it on," she interrupted.

I rolled my eyes and finished stepping out of the previous disaster. "You know I don't actually care what I wear," I commented as I pulled the dress up my legs and slid my arms through the straps, the fabric thin. They fell right down my arms. I gritted my teeth and slid them back up as I reached behind me and zipped up the dress. Annnnd down the straps went.

"Are you fucking kidding me?" I growled and shoved

them back up, but there was too much slack. Everywhere else on me the dress fit perfectly. Turning, I snapped the curtain to the side and stepped out. "The damn straps keep falling," I complained.

Back on the couch and taking another refill on her champagne, Olivia turned to me. "It's supposed to be like that," she said as her drink was topped off. "They're just for decoration."

"Aren't they supposed to hold the dress up?" I asked, moving my arms up and down. I felt like a fucking windmill.

"Do you feel like it's going to fall down?" she replied.

"Well, no..." I turned in a circle. The dress fit me pretty well and other than the straps, it was great for movement. The tulle skirt flared out just under my waist, staying closer to my body until it hit my hips where the skirts were much thicker. The bottom didn't even touch my knees, the hem hitting just above them. I frowned down at the fabric, reaching for the layer of white beneath the black lace of the bodice and lifting it up to look at it closer. It wasn't actually white at all, but a very light pink.

"I love it, it's perfect," Olivia said.

"How much is—"

"Don't worry about that," she interrupted again. She was getting rather comfortable at that. I glared at her. With a sigh, she downed the rest of her drink and got up from the couch, circling me. "I already called Mrs. McKnight, she gave her card number over the phone."

"What?" I blinked at her in shock.

Olivia continued circling me. "I think this is it. This is the dress. Torin's mouth is going to hit the floor."

His mouth had already hit somewhere... As soon as the thought slipped into my mind, I felt my eyes widen. The memory rushed at me, unbidden, like it had just been waiting for a slip up to remind me what I'd done.

Torin's red eyes all over me. His tongue in my pussy. His fangs piercing my flesh. I should have been disgusted. I should have hated every part of it, but I didn't. It had been hot. Boiling hot. Volcanic. And I wanted it to happen again.

My mind reeled as Olivia pushed me back into the curtained off changing room and commanded me to strip. I didn't even argue. I pulled the dress off and shoved it out the curtain into her waiting hands. My mind drifted back to my dream and I wondered if I would have another tonight. It was wrong. I had to focus on other things, like the murderer, like training Maverick.

Maverick...

"Alright! It's all done and paid for." Olivia's cheery voice startled me as she came back—what must have been minutes later—and slid the curtain out of the way. I looked down, thankful that I had seemed to get redressed by rote memory. "Let's go grab some coffee."

I didn't pull away as she yanked me out of the dressing room and led me out of the boutique, calling goodbye to the girls who had helped us over the last few hours. We got into her Porsche and I clipped my seatbelt, still muddled by my thoughts. I didn't even notice her bad driving.

"Ugh, I have been dying for this all day," Olivia whined as we arrived at the coffee shop and got out. "I mean, I don't mind that you called so early, but—hey, is that Rachel?"

I frowned and looked over in the same direction she was staring. Across the street, Rachel's dirty blonde hair swayed with the movements of her ponytail as she pumped her arms and legs on the treadmill at the front window of the gym.

"Hmmm. Weird," Olivia commented, turning away with a shrug.

I followed. "What's weird?"

"Rachel hates working out," Olivia said, pushing through the door into the coffee shop. A bell jingled above our heads announcing our arrival, followed by a few 'welcomes' from the staff.

"So?"

Olivia moved to the counter and placed her order before turning to me. "She's a cheerleader, she doesn't need to do anymore working out. Cheerleading is an actual sport, like gymnastics and all that." She waved her hand as if that encompassed everything else she was trying to explain about it before continuing. "Rachel basically tells everyone who works out that they're just lazy. If they wanted to be in shape, they should've been born with a metabolism—one that she's definitely got in spades. I've seen that girl put away pizza at a slumber party before, she's—"

I sighed and snapped my fingers in front of her face. "Liv," I said sharply, "stay on task. Why is it weird for her to be working out?" I repeated the question.

"She doesn't believe in it," Olivia said simply. "She thinks people who work out in a gym are stupid. Her parents are weird with their whole fresh farm to table, vegan, no unnecessary technology stuff. Her dad's the owner of a huge vegan grocery store chain. They think people should run cardio in the 'real world.'" She lifted her fingers and curled two on each hand as she air-quoted 'real world' with a roll of her eyes. "And that a treadmill or anything in a gym is a waste of money and resources. They're super weird about it."

I thought it over as our orders were called and we picked them up at the end of the counter. When we headed back out to the car, my eyes sought out the window of the gym across the street but either Rachel was done, or she'd moved on to a new machine.

"Maybe she's just trying to lose weight for Homecoming," Olivia suggested as we got into the car. "She was pretty pissed when she heard that Torin was taking you."

"When did she hear that?" I asked. "Only you and —" My eyes widened as she gave me a guilty grin. "You didn't."

Biting down on her lower lip, she buckled her seat belt. "Gabby was asking why he was hanging out with Maverick and everyone knows that you're hanging out with both of them, so I just…" She trailed off. "It's just gossip," she tried to assure me as I groaned and sank back into my seat. "It'll blow over soon."

"Why did you have to say *anything*?" I snapped.

She shrugged as she backed out of her parking spot.

"The longer they wonder, the longer it'll go on. Just date one of them and people will stop talking."

"*Date* one of them?" I stared at her in horror. "You've got to be fucking kidding me!"

"Why do you make it sound like that?" She shot me a confused look, lips pursed, both brows raised. "They're hot."

"I'm living with Maverick," I reminded her. I couldn't date him. Not to mention the fact that I was still planning on finding the vampire who killed my family and making them pay. I couldn't date Maverick. He was human, one who was quite new to all of this. He was in danger. All I could do was teach him how to protect himself and get the hell out of his life. That's what he deserved. He deserved some vestige of safety and as long as I was around, it wasn't going to happen.

"But not Torin," Olivia pointed out. "And he is the one taking you to Homecoming, right?"

I shook my head. "They're best friends."

"*Ex*-best friends," she said.

That was right. They weren't friends anymore. The only reason that they'd been forced to see each other again was because of me. I had forgotten. But … maybe when I left they'd reconcile. If that was going to be the case, then I should just stop now while I was ahead.

"No." I shook my head from side to side again. "Absolutely not."

Olivia's mouth popped open as she rolled to a stop sign and looked over at me. "You're the strangest girl I've ever met, Barbie Steele."

"I'll take that as a compliment."

"It's not." I shrugged. I didn't really give a shit what she thought. She didn't know me. Not the real me. "Anyone else would *kill* to have either of those two. From where I'm sitting, it looks like you could have both."

"Both?" I looked at her. "Are you certifiable?"

She shrugged and turned the corner, one hand over the other on the steering wheel as she returned her gaze to the windshield. "Maybe, but at least I admit it."

"I—"

She stopped me before I could say anything else. "I don't know what you're scared of, but whatever it is, you better get over it soon. No matter what happens, life goes on. Make sure you're living it before you're too old or too dead to enjoy it."

I gaped at her. Was I really getting life advice from a preppy cheerleader knock off? Apparently, I was. What the fuck would I say to her if she was right?

THIRTY-SEVEN

BARBIE

I panted, sweat dripping into my eyes. Metal flashed and I ducked and rolled across the grass, sliding as I dodged Torin's attack. I weaved and spun, narrowly missing another downward swing of his sword. Within seconds, my back slapped the ground and he came down hard over me, his chest slamming against my breasts as the flat part of his blade touched my throat.

"Is this what your father taught you?" he asked, his face flushed with color. I looked at him closely, noting how dilated his pupils were. In the center of the green irises, red bled out into the rest of the color. "I'm surprised you managed to kill not one, but two vampires on your own."

My chest rose and fell, pressing my breasts against him as I tried to catch my breath. I gritted my teeth against the insult. "Hey!" Maverick's call caught both of our attentions. As Torin's head turned, I hooked one foot behind his knee and shoved against the opposite side of his chest, rolling us so that I was on top and his

299

blade fell away from my throat. I rose up and jerked the blunt—but still deadly—end of my own sword down.

The edge thrust into the soil next to his head and I leaned down, my lips right by his ear as I spoke. "How's that for fucking training?"

"Enough fucking around, I've got some information to share," Maverick said from the back porch of Torin's guest house. He watched us—his eyes both curious and something else. I couldn't quite place the emotion that lit his face, but it was intense. His gaze focused on where my groin was pressed against Torin. I huffed and jerked off of him, standing up and holding a hand out.

Torin didn't take it, instead choosing to get up on his own and stormed past me. I threw both arms up. "Fine, be an asshole," I snapped. "As if I give a shit."

"Inside," Maverick barked, turning and stomping back into the house. Torin shot me a look and followed him.

Great, I thought. *Just my luck, I get stuck working with two fucking assholes with manstrual cycles out their fucking twatholes.* A part of me wished Torin could hear that, but in the days that had passed since I'd taken some of his blood, his prediction that the side effects would fade was correct. Well, mostly. My attraction to him was a completely different matter. One I wasn't quite ready to face just yet.

I left my sword in the ground and took the steps two at a time until I hit the backdoor and strode inside. Lifting the hem of my shirt to mop up some of the sweat dripping down the front of my face and neck, I closed my eyes and rubbed the fabric between my brows.

Almost as soon as I hit the living room, I slammed into a broad expanse of back muscle.

"Jesus—fuck!" I stumbled and released my hem, nearly falling down as my legs gave out from under me. Maverick turned and grabbed me just before I hit the floor. Our eyes connected and a dull, low heat rose to the surface of my cheeks. I pulled away just as quickly, muttering a quiet "thanks" as I rounded him and headed for the couch.

I collapsed back on the cushions as Torin came in through the kitchen, tossing me a water bottle and taking his own seat. "What's this about?" he asked, turning his focus to the man standing in the doorway.

"The last vic," Maverick started, "was an employee working a large business gathering at the Harris estate."

"Yeah?" Torin popped the cap on his bottled water and downed half of it in one go. I couldn't help but stare at the long lines of his throat and how it worked as he swallowed. Sweat droplets collected on his collarbone and slid sideways until they reached a point where they could slide further down between his pecs, disappearing into the neckline of his workout shirt. My throat went dry.

"Every victim so far has been present at a large gathering or party," he said. "This guy was the only one who isn't involved with St. Marion. So, whoever the murderer is must be using parties as his hunting ground."

"So, the likelihood that they'll be at Homecoming increased?" I guessed.

Maverick nodded. "Exponentially."

Torin finished off the majority of his water and sucked in a lungful of air before leaning over and pouring the remainder over the back of his head, wetting the long dark locks and making them stick to his forehead as he braced his elbows on his knees and looked up. Water ran down his face, dropping haphazardly on the floor. The red in his eyes had receded completely, but he kept his focus on Maverick as he spoke. "I have some information, too," he said with a grimace.

Maverick noticed and crossed his arms. "What did you find out?" he demanded.

Another breath. A moment of silence. And then… "I have no doubt that my father is behind the murders."

Shock was a silent scream in the room. "I'm sorry, what?" I stood up abruptly. "Your father is in town and you didn't think to fucking tell us?"

Torin shook his head. "No, it's not—he's not here."

"Then how can he be responsible for the murders?" Maverick asked, his tone deepening as his brows puckered.

"I don't know exactly, but Katalin said something the other night—something about testing me. He's a bastard, I know that. He's corrupt and as a vampire, he's pretty fucking ruthless. Killing is nothing to him. Simply a means to an end."

Killing as a means to an end. I was quiet for a moment as something hit me. I wasn't dissimilar.

"Where does that leave us then?" Maverick's question pulled me back to the conversation at hand. I shook my head and refocused.

"It's not human, that much I do know," Torin imparted.

"Do you know what it is?" I asked.

He stiffened and shook his head. "No."

"Then we don't necessarily know how to kill it." Shit. That wasn't good.

"Bring your gun and holy water anyway," Torin said. "There's nowhere for Barbie to hide the swords so I'll be giving these back to you." Torin stood up and reached for the chest in the corner of the living room, pulling out two familiar looking daggers. He handed them over to me and released them just as quickly, pulling his hands back before my fingers brushed his. My brows lowered and my mouth tightened, but I didn't comment.

"Do you think we have a chance?" Maverick asked. I looked up in time to see him unfold his arms and step farther into the room, his gaze seeking Torin out, worry creasing the corners of his eyes.

"We have as good of a chance as we're going to get. You've been practicing with that gun I gave you?"

"Every day," Maverick said with a nod. "Barbie's been trying to teach me some self-defense at home, too."

"Good, keep it up," Torin replied. "It shouldn't be bad, whatever it is, and I'll be there. And if worse comes to worse, I'll unleash the vampire."

"Is *that* a good idea?" I asked, my hands tightening on the dagger handles.

"He and I have an ... understanding," Torin said without looking my way. I just fucking bet they did.

I sighed, shoulders slumping. "Okay then," I hedged.

Maverick looked my way and then at Torin before seeming to come to a decision. "Let's head out then." He turned towards the front door, pausing as he glanced to Torin one last time. "See you at the game tomorrow?"

Torin shook his head. "I probably won't be at the game, but I'll be at the dance."

"Because you're taking *me*." I couldn't help the upper curl of my lip as I said it. "Are you sure we have to go through the whole charade?"

Torin turned and lifted a brow my way. "Why, are you scared?" he asked.

I jerked my head back, a scowl overtaking my expression as I stormed around him and headed for Maverick's side. "I'm not fucking afraid of shit," I said. "I'll be at Homecoming."

"In a fucking dress," Maverick commented, shaking his head as he headed out the door.

"In a fucking dress," I agreed.

"We'll see, sweetheart." Torin's words echoed in my ears as I trailed after Maverick.

Sweetheart. That was what his vampire had called me. Along with … mate.

THIRTY-EIGHT

BARBIE

THE DAY OF HOMECOMING ARRIVED. I DIDN'T KNOW what to expect, and it seemed that everyone had forgotten the fact that, up until a few months ago, I hadn't even been put into a classroom with other students. Homeschool really did cut out a lot, even if I had managed to learn a lot of things no one else my age knew. Like how to fight. How to survive. How to shoot a gun. I eyed Maverick as he came stomping down the stairs.

Beth was so overjoyed that I would be taking part in Homecoming that she took it upon herself to tell me everything I would need to expect. I stood dutifully as she helped me zip up the dress I'd bought with Olivia into its protective bag.

"Every school has their own Homecoming traditions," Beth explained. "For St. Marion, it's the afternoon football game with one of the local rivals and then the dance. Lots of schools parade the Homecoming

Court at halftime, but they won't announce who won king and queen until the dance."

"Why are they on the same night?" I asked. "Won't the players be tired?"

"More like wired." Beth chuckled as she shot her son a look as he grunted and took the dress bag from her before moving out the front door. Rich, warm sunlight poured over the front porch as we followed behind him, stopping on the top step. "Homecoming is a wonderful tradition any young man or woman would want to be a part of," she said. "I'm sure you'll have loads of fun. Please, just do me one favor."

"What?" I looked at her, curious.

Biting down on her lower lip, Beth's hands shook as she reached out and took one of mine in both hers. I stiffened, the contact awkward and uncomfortable. Yet something kept me from pulling away. "Be safe," she whispered. "They still haven't caught the man responsible for those killings." She shook her head, her eyes misting. "If I could, I'd hide both you and Maverick in the house and not let you out, but I doubt my son would ever forgive me if I did that."

"I doubt Jon would either," I commented lightly with a forced smile.

"You're right." She huffed, letting my hands go. "He's more into football than Maverick sometimes." She shook her head. "I certainly don't understand it."

"We'll be fine," I assured her. "I'll be with Olivia during the game. Afterwards, we're going to her place to get changed and ready for the dance."

"Torin's picking you up there?" she asked, a frown

on her face. I nodded. "Oh ... well, get photos for me? You don't want to forget your first high school dance."

As I expected the dance to be the piéce de résistance of the entire night, I highly doubted I would be forgetting it anytime soon. Something told me that Torin's predictions that something would happen tonight was accurate. As it stood, all of the other victims had been killed during large parties—even the man who'd been attacked earlier that week.

"Pictures," I said, smiling up at her as Maverick slammed the truck door, signaling that he was ready to go. "Will do. Thanks for the info. Gotta go!"

Beth smiled and waved from the front steps as I shot down the porch and headed for the passenger side of Mav's truck, popping the door open and reaching for the handle to leverage my short legs into the cab.

"Could you talk any longer?" he grumbled putting the truck in drive as I buckled in.

"She's worried," I reminded him. "With good reason." He grunted, keeping his eyes forward. I sighed. "Maverick?"

"What?"

"Are you okay?"

"Why wouldn't I be?"

"You just seem, I don't know, off. Are you sure you're—"

"I'm fine, Barbie."

I huffed out a breath and turned my head back to the window. "Fine." Seconds stretched into minutes. It wasn't until we were pulling into the student parking lot outside of the football stadium that he finally broke the awkward tension in the air.

"I'm sorry," he said.

I stiffened, keeping my eyes on the window. "What for?"

"For … everything, I guess."

Startled and confused, I finally looked back at him. "What do you mean?"

Maverick's hands gripped the steering wheel like a lifeline, and even though we were parked and were about to get out, I had a feeling that he wanted nothing more than to throw the truck in reverse and leave. His body practically vibrated with energy.

Was it fear? I wondered. I could understand that. The first time I had come face to face with real vampires, I'd been torn between disbelief and a shit ton of fear. So much fear that I hadn't even managed to do anything until it was too late.

"If you want to go home, no one would blame you," I said quietly.

His head snapped to the side. "What?"

"I said—"

"I heard what you fucking said," he growled, unlatching his hands from the steering wheel. He shoved one over the short strands of his buzz cut. "You're fucking telling me that if I can't handle it, I should go home?"

"That's not what I meant," I said, shaking my head. I reached for my belt buckle and pressed the button to release it. "I just mean that I wouldn't blame you, no one would, if—"

"I'm not fucking scared," he barked.

"It's okay to be scared."

"I'm not—"

"I was scared." I said the words so sharply that they stopped him from saying anything further. He looked at me. I mean, *really* looked at me. His eyes soaked me in, drifting down to my hands in my lap to my face. "The first vampire I ever met was a guy I had a crush on at a party," I admitted on a whisper. And just like that, the whole story seemed to pour out of me before I could stop it. "My parents were paranoid about vampires. They didn't let Brandon or me out after dark, ever. We were homeschooled. Neither of us had any friends. Well, I know Brandon didn't. We were each other's best friends, but there were things that he couldn't get from me and things I couldn't get from him. Our neighbors had a daughter around my age. I met her a few times when I was in the backyard training or fucking around with Brandon—I don't remember. He had the biggest crush on her." My lips twitched with amusement. Sometimes, I thought that he only liked Hannah because she was the one girl around his age that he could talk to that he wasn't related to.

"Hannah told me about a party some friends from her school were having. She invited me and Brandon, but when Brandon learned that she had a boyfriend and he'd be taking us, so he turned her offer down. I knew he really wanted to go, but he was already backing away. He didn't want to be hurt. I was selfish. I didn't stay with him that night, but I went with Hannah. And there was a guy there—Travis. He was so beautiful—vampires are like that, I guess. Beautiful. Otherworldly. They're like movie stars. I think it's to lure their prey. My mom had that theory on it anyway. But I met Travis there and he followed me home. He forced me to invite him in and the rest is..." I swallowed and glanced at Maverick. "He had a friend," I said. "Two vampires followed me home, broke in and killed my family, all while I watched. I was frozen in fear. The fear in me allowed me to let my family get killed. I wouldn't judge you if you were scared."

He was quiet as he watched me. Eyes burning like coals, rich and hot. "What freaks me out the most isn't even the supernatural part," he said.

I tilted my head. "What is it?"

"It's you." My lips parted in surprise. "You admitted that you think your fear killed your family, but that's not true. Your bravery saved your life."

"At the cost of theirs," I reminded him sharply. Maverick shook his head. I sucked in a breath and spun towards the door, my brows drawn low as I reached for the handle.

I heard him move, but it was too late. Maverick had his seat belt off and had slapped the lock button before I finished curling my fingers around the handle. I yanked on it uselessly. "I want out, Maverick," I growled.

"No." His voice sounded right next to my head. I held myself excruciatingly still. "I'm not done talking, Barbie. You started this conversation. You can't just run away because you don't like what I have to say."

"Then say what you want and let me out," I said.

His breath whispered over my ear. *Don't react, don't*

react, don't you dare fucking react. I chanted the words in my mind, but the mantra did nothing for the wave of warmth that threatened to overwhelm me.

"You fucking took on that vampire that came to the house to kill us without a thought. Jumped a fucking railing. Stabbed her. The wounds you took—when she threw you into the mirror and all of those shards came down, I thought..." Slowly, with incredible restraint, I pivoted my head to take in his expression. The apocalypse could have happened right then and there and I wouldn't have been able to look away. His gaze rooted me to the spot. "I lied," he whispered. "I *am* afraid. I'm fucking terrified. I feel like everything that fucked up my life two years ago—Torin's distance, the secretiveness—it's all finally making some semblance of sense. You walked into my life and shattered it apart. I hated you when I first saw you. I wanted you gone. I don't know how, but in some way, I knew your arrival meant something big was on the horizon. I couldn't have predicted *this*." He laughed without humor. "Vampires. Demons. Murders. Yet, I wouldn't trade it to go back."

"You wouldn't?" That, more than anything else, baffled me. If I could go back in time and trade back everything I'd been given—Torin, Maverick, the McKnights—if it meant I could have my family back, would I? I didn't know.

Maverick shook his head in answer to my question. "I wouldn't. But I also don't want to see you like that again. Hurt. Bleeding. It made me feel useless. I still feel useless. I'm not the worst with a gun. God knows I've put in more hours than I have anything else in the last few weeks, but a few weeks of gun training will not make a difference when we're fighting something that doesn't play by the rules. Shooting at targets is nothing like shooting at a living creature trying to kill you."

"No, it's not," I agreed.

"But I'll be fucking damned if I let you go without backup," he said. "I'd honestly rather you took my truck and drove as far from here as possible."

"I'm not leaving," I said.

He sighed, the air leaving his lips on a rush with a small chuckle following it. "I know," he said. "I knew you wouldn't even consider it, but after this…" He reached up, his fingers grazing my cheek. "After this is all over, you and I, we're gonna have a talk."

"A talk?" I squeaked. "About what?"

He eyed me, unresponding. His hand fell away from my face once more and he backed up, hitting the lock button again before giving me one final look and getting out of the truck and walking away.

My heart stuttered in my chest, a sinking feeling filling my gut. If anyone had bothered to ask me what I preferred: talking or dying? I would have answered dying without a single fucking ounce of hesitation.

THIRTY-NINE

TORIN

I can smell it ... brimstone and sex. "Brimstone and sex?" I repeated, the words a confused whisper as I passed through the crowd of cheering fans.

Yes. It's here. My gaze darted around, but nothing out of the ordinary stood out. There were no strangers, no one I didn't recognize. The people who had all come out for the Homecoming game were my classmates, my teachers, and parents. Their faces passed by in a sea of color. Sweat permeated my senses. Not brimstone and sex. Then it was there—sulfur wafting off someone's skin. A demon. The creature was a demon. I whirled around, trying to catch the direction but it was gone almost as if it had never been there to begin with. As if I'd imagined it.

You did not, my vampire assured me.

I growled, startling a girl near me. She looked back, her eyes widening when she saw me standing behind her, squeaked, and scrambled away. I clenched my teeth to keep from going after her. Running away from me when I was so close to my vampire was never a good idea. *When was the last time I had blood?*

"Wow, that sure is a scary expression." The dry comment was both a blessing and a curse. I turned as Barbie and her friend strode closer. I eyed the second human as she stared up at me, her eyes wide and round. "Penny for your thoughts?" Barbie crossed her arms and lifted a brow when I still hadn't spoken.

"I'm in a mood," I gritted out.

She unfolded her arms and turned to her friend, leaning over and saying something in a low voice. I followed her movements with a lasered focus. The friend bobbed her head, red curls hurdling over her shoulders as she stepped back and turned and left.

"Come on." A small hand gripped my wrist and tugged me forward. I let it happen. Barbie's skin on mine had my mind in an uproar. My fangs itched to descend.

Barbie pulled me through the throng of people in the stands, watching the football game, watching Maverick. Did she want to stay behind and watch him? My muscles tightened in refusal. Heat boiled behind my eyes. *No, I couldn't do this here.* I shut my eyes, knowing full well that they were blood red, and let Barbie lead me.

We didn't stop for several minutes. Gradually, people moved around us less and less and then the sounds of the cheering crowd were muted. "You can open your eyes now," she said. "We're alone." Slowly, I raised my lids and looked down on her. The hunger must have been etched into my expression because she frowned. "When was the last time you fed?" she demanded. I shook my head. I didn't know. I couldn't recall. "Shit." She hissed out the expletive, turning from me and pacing away before pacing straight back. "Do you have any blood on you?"

My lips parted. Shit, I could already feel my fangs protruding. "Car," I rasped. "In cooler. Backseat."

She nodded. "Okay, give me your keys. I'll run and grab a bag." She eyed me silently before she looked away and muttered, "maybe a few bags."

"I need it now," I lisped, my fangs fully descending. Once they were down, I couldn't get them back up. Hunger pulsed inside my veins. I zeroed in on her throat where her heart beat a steady rhythm. The sound of blood rushed in my ears like water being poured from a glass. I didn't even realize I'd taken a step closer until I could feel her stiff body against my chest.

Barbie looked up at me, her mouth set in a grim, determined line. "Take a step back, Torin," she ordered. "Or I'll shove a dagger in your chest."

Gulping down the urge to shove her against the wall and rip her pants from her legs as I sank both my body and my fangs into her, I took a shaky step back. "Sorry, I'm—" I cut myself off, covering my eyes with one hand as I tried to regain control.

"You're right," she said. "You need it now. Let's go."

Once again, she latched onto my wrist and dragged me with her, leading me to the parking lot, towards the SUV I'd borrowed from my sister. She took the keys from me, and using the insignia on the fob, she tracked down the right car and pressed the unlock button, waiting for the lights to flash before she yanked me after her. Popping the backdoor open, she spotted the cooler, turned and shoved me inside, climbing in after me.

"Alright, let's do this." Reaching into the white and blue container, I felt my fangs fucking *throb* as she lifted out a bag of blood. "Do you need me to slice it open or—"

I snatched the bag out of her hand without letting her finish, snarling as I popped the plastic with my teeth. Barbie sat there, her eyes darting between her now empty hand and the quickly deflating bag in my grip.

"Well, damn, someone's hangry."

How the fuck could she joke at a time like this? My vampire was riding shotgun about to reach over and take the wheel. She needed to leave. I finished the bag in less than a minute, ripping the empty plastic away from my teeth and tossing it into the still open cooler.

"You need to go," I growled, reaching for a second bag.

"Yeah, not going to happen." She rolled her eyes and crossed her arms as she leaned back against the opposite door, watching me curiously. "I'm going to sit right here and make sure you don't do anything to hurt anyone."

I looked around with the bag pressed to my teeth and when I was done with the second one, I spoke. "There's no one around but you. Leave. I could hurt you."

She laughed, withdrawing one of the daggers I'd given back to her and flipped it around in her grip until the handle was in her palm. "Good luck with that. You try to hurt me and I'll have you stabbed and bagged before you know what hit you."

"Stabbed and bagged?" The blood I'd drunk sloshed in my stomach and the deeply rooted hunger began to recede, but just to make sure, I reached for a third bag.

She shrugged, laying the dagger at her side. Barbie's eyes centered on the bag between my teeth for several seconds. She sat forward, her lips tightening as she stared. "So, what … um … what does it taste like?"

I blinked as I finished it off and tossed it into the cooler, snapping the lid closed with a sigh. "Like cold water flavored with copper and rust. What else?"

"Oh." She frowned. "I just thought that it would taste, I don't know, I guess different to your kind."

"I think when it's from the vein, it does," I said. "But I've never taken blood from the vein before."

"You haven't?" She retrieved her dagger, emitting a slight wince that had her looking down at her hand before she sighed and slid it back into its hiding place at the small of her back. "Why?"

I arched a brow her way. "I'm surprised you're not overjoyed."

"What does that mean?" she asked.

"You're a hunter," I said.

An awkward beat of quiet passed. "Right, sorry, dumb question." She shook her head. "I was just curious. Come on, we should get back to the game."

Her hand went to the door handle and I snapped out to stop her. It was as if my limb moved on its own. I hadn't actively wanted to stop her until I was already doing it. My chest pressed against her side, my fingers over hers on the handle.

"What is it with guys not letting me out of fucking cars?" she muttered beneath her breath.

"Wha—" I stopped, the scent of something delectable entering my nostrils. My mouth watered and though they'd just receded, my fangs descended once more. I glanced down where my fingers covered hers and pulled back. Blood—fresh and red—marred her skin and now mine.

"Shit, I'm sorry, Torin, I didn't think you'd notice. It was just a small cut." A small cut. Yes. It was tiny, barely discernible. There was no real wound. Just a few droplets of rich red lifeblood. I had just drunk my fill. I wasn't hungry. I had seen people hurt before. I had seen her covered in blood and it hadn't affected me as much as it was then. She'd been dying then, though. I hadn't been focused on anything other than healing her—saving her life. Now, though, we were in an enclosed space and the soft scent of her was wrapped around me. "Torin, let me go." She pulled against my hold, but I couldn't force myself to let go.

Instead, I pulled her closer, lowering my head until my lips touched the curve of her throat and neck—just above where the collar of her shirt rested. She stiffened in my arms. I didn't bite her. I wasn't going to. I wouldn't ever do that to her. But my cock strained in my jeans, pulsing with a hard throb. I rubbed against her, licking at her skin.

Wait for it … my vampire urged. *Wait for what?* I wondered. I didn't—*there it is*, he said. Triumph. Smugness. Desire. It lanced through me when I scented something new that rose from her skin. Lust. Attraction. She was aroused.

"Barbie." Her name was a whispered plea against her skin as I groaned. Her head turned and I took her lips in a rush of movement, sucking first her bottom lip into my mouth and nipping gently as I reached up and cupped the back of her head, sliding my fingers through the blonde strands, holding her steady.

I devoured her mouth. She arched against me, and a small whimper escaping her throat was all of the encouragement I needed. I turned her and had her in my arms in a split second. Her hands came down over my shoulders as her pussy pressed between the fabric of her jeans and mine down against my raging hard on. I ground upward, pushing against her as I kissed her like a mad man.

I had lost all control. I gathered the strands of her hair and yanked it back, baring her throat to my attention, licking straight up the center and over her jawline as she gasped. I could hear how fucking wet she was as she returned my attention. Her hips swiveled against me, more of those luscious sounds emanating from her throat with fervor.

Mate. Mine. Mate. Mine.

My vampire was howling in my mind—a veritable monster clawing to get free. My eyes were pure red, I knew, but when Barbie's lids lifted and she glanced at my face, she didn't appear afraid. No, I smelled a shocking wave of her arousal as it filtered in the air around us. She liked it. I hissed through my teeth as she yanked me back, her mouth descended with a ferocity I hadn't expected.

She stole the very breath from my lungs with her kiss. Her tongue played with mine as she moved against me. Impatient. I closed my eyes and reached for the hem of her shirt, pushing it upward as my fingers skimmed low on her belly. She sucked in a breath, her stomach hollowing out. Electricity danced between us as she stared at me. Both of our chests pumped, but all of the oxygen had been chased out of the space.

She pulled back, blinking to clear away the arousal in her expression. Her cheeks flushed a gorgeous pink even though I knew the moment was over. It was ruined and she would leave, but I couldn't help but think about how fucking stunning she was.

"This shouldn't have happened," she whispered. I didn't say anything as she scrambled off my lap. "I'm sorry," she said. "I shouldn't have..." She trailed off, looking back at me. Still, I kept my lips shut. I wouldn't apologize for it. I wasn't sorry. Barbie cursed and reached for the handle once more. I watched her leave, slamming the SUV door behind her as she took off across the parking lot. This time, I let her go.

FORTY

BARBIE

I SWALLOWED DOWN MY NERVOUSNESS AS BEST I COULD
while Olivia and I dressed for the Homecoming dance
later that night. The game—what I'd caught of it—had
ended in a win for St. Marion, 17-10. Olivia chattered
away as she brushed my hair, pulling it to the side to
braid it around the front, leaving a few strands hanging
in my face.

"Ryan is so cute, you have no idea. And he absolutely adores me. I can't believe I never noticed him
before," she said. "He's in art class. Won't show me any
of his stuff, but I bet it's good. His mom's a big art
collector."

"He's coming to pick you up, right?" I asked
absently, trying to keep the conversation going with as
minimal input as possible while I worked through what
had happened in the parking lot with Torin not but a
few hours ago.

"Yeah," she answered brightly, finishing with my
hair and moving onto her own as she reached for the

curl taming solution on her vanity. I stood up and moved out of her way, heading for the dress bag I'd laid on her bed earlier. I opened it and pulled it out, shedding my clothes as I went, turning my back towards the wall as I discreetly removed my daggers.

I pulled the dress up and zipped it, sliding my daggers under the fabric of my skirts and securing them with special garters I'd ordered online.

"I was right," Olivia announced as she stood up and turned towards me, her sleek curls bouncing around her face. "That dress looks hot on you."

"Thanks," I said, but this time instead of any sort of smartass comment, I meant it.

Olivia beamed at me as she moved to her closet and came back a few minutes later, zipping up a floor length emerald green gown. "Alright, the guys should be showing up any minute."

As if the universe had heard her, a knock sounded on the door at the tail end of her statement. "Girls?" Olivia's mom—a rounded woman with a short crop of the same cherry red hair—popped her head into the room. "The guys are here."

"Thanks, Mom!" Olivia reached for my arm and pulled me towards the hallway. She stopped when she looked down. "Wait, what the hell is on your feet?" I looked down at the scuffed combat boots and shrugged. "Are you serious?" Her clear eyes glared at me. I couldn't tell her that fighting in heels was a no go for me.

"It's just a dance," I said lamely.

"You're going with *Torin Priest*," she hissed.

I'd made out with Torin Priest. I'd let his vampire go down on me—sure it had been in a dream, but it wasn't like he'd been a figment of my imagination. I swallowed as I remembered.

"It's fine," I said, moving past her for the stairs.

"I can't fucking believe this," I heard her say at my back.

"Olivia!" her mom snapped. "Language."

I resisted the urge to smile as we descended the stairs, my black boots next to her silver heels. I stopped at the third step from the bottom as Torin turned from the front door. A flush rose to my face, but I pressed down the feelings they brought forth and kept moving.

"Ready?" he asked, looking me over.

I nodded, watching him closely. His eyes had faded from the red back to his normal green orbs.

"No, no, no, wait!" Olivia's mom called as Olivia went to a tall, broad shouldered guy with a small diamond in his left earlobe. I frowned. Was he really an artist? "Pictures!"

I groaned lightly, bringing a grin to Torin's lips. I glared up at him as he put his arm around my waist and pulled me close so that the older woman could snap a few shots. I shivered when he leaned down and pressed his lips close to my ear. "Smile," he ordered.

I let my teeth show as I spoke through them. "Careful," I hissed. "You might want me to think you enjoy this."

"Tormenting you?" he asked, his eyes flaring wide as his own smile broadened. "I do enjoy it."

"Alright, time to go," I announced. "Thanks so

much for letting me come over and get ready, Olivia," I said turning to her as she looked up at her date with gooey eyes. "I'll see you there."

"See ya!" she said, waving me away as her date reached for her hand.

I fled outside and stopped when I didn't see the SUV he'd been driving earlier. Torin's smirk as he bypassed me and circled Olivia's white Porsche should have been warning enough. I followed him and stopped when I saw what he'd brought.

"You're fucking joking."

"What?" He picked up a helmet and handed it to me.

"I'm wearing a fucking dress," I hissed, gesturing down as if he couldn't fucking see it. "I can't ride a fucking motorcycle in this thing."

"Yes you can, just tuck the fabric between your legs." I growled as he swung his leg over the side of the bike and looked at me expectantly.

"You're such a fucking asshole," I muttered as I moved forward. I tried valiantly to clamber onto the hulking behemoth of a bike and tuck my skirts firmly under my ass all while his body shook with laughter. "I hate you."

"You didn't seem to hate me a few hours ago."

My whole body went rigid at that reminder. "We don't talk about that, Torin," I said, serious. He looked back over his shoulder at me, an eyebrow raised. "I'm serious. It was an error in judgment. It won't happen again. It can't." I kept my gaze trained straight ahead.

Quietly, almost too quiet for me to hear, he spoke.

"Don't make promises I have no intention of letting you keep, Barbie."

Before I could ask what the fuck that meant, however, he kicked up the stand and roared out of the driveway as Olivia and her date were leaving the front steps, forcing me to snap my arms around him to keep from falling off.

BULBS FLASHED. GLITTER RAINED DOWN OVER THE DANCE floor. Music pumped a rhythmic beat through the room. High heels clicked and clacked on the hardwood floor as girls and their dates bumped and grinded to the pulse of the speakers. I stood to the side with Torin, our eyes trained on the crowd. Searching.

"I can feel them here," he said. "But with so many people, it's hard to get a bead on them."

I ground my teeth together, tightening my jaw until it ached. My foot tapped repetitively as I tried to think of what to do. A dark figure emerged from the dancing crowd and made its way towards us.

"Maverick." He stopped in front of me, looking from me to Torin.

"Anything?" he asked.

We both shook our heads. He cursed.

"I vote we split up and look for anything that might seem suspicious," I said. Both of them frowned at me. "What?"

"I don't like that idea," Maverick admitted.

"Neither do I," Torin agreed.

I frowned. "I'll be fine," I said with a roll of my eyes. "But if it makes you big babies feel better, if any of us see anything, we'll call the others."

Maverick stared me down. "You swear?" he demanded.

I lifted my hand and curled all my fingers down, leaving nothing but my pinky free. "Pinky promise," I said.

He waited a beat and nodded. "Okay, I'll take the back side of the room, closer to the entrances and see if I can catch anyone slipping away." With that, he disappeared back into the crowd.

"I'll cover the crowd," Torin said. "Try to sniff him out."

"Alright, I guess I'll get"—I trailed off as Torin turned and walked away, leaving me to finish my sentence to nothing and no one—"the rest," I grumbled.

Shoving down my irritation, I spun on my booted feet and headed for the side of the dance floor, moving through the crowd of bodies jumping and gyrating.

Half an hour passed as I searched the edges of the room, watching people as they laughed and spiked the punch and danced wildly. By all accounts, this was a normal dance—or so I assumed since I'd never been to one before. There was nothing out of the ordinary at all. Maybe we'd been wrong. Maybe the connection between victims hadn't been the parties, but something else. I pulled my phone out of my bra and checked for any messages from the guys. Nothing.

With a sigh, I took off for the double doors leading

into the hallway and headed for the bathroom. This was as good a time as any for a break.

I was finishing up washing my hands when the door to the women's bathroom slammed open. Stalking in on her high heels was none other than Rachel Harris. I rolled my eyes when she stopped as she saw me. Dressed in a skin tight dress that plunged deep between her plumped breasts, with an emerald amulet dangling between them, she looked like a high class hooker. I turned off the sink and reached for a hand towel.

Leaning back against the door, she crossed her arms and watched me. "You gonna stand there all night, or you got something to say?" I prompted as I turned and faced her.

She tilted her chin to the side, her eyes eerily sharp. I frowned as a light slithered through her irises. What the fuck?

"I'm hungry," she said, her voice sounding deeper than it ever had before.

"Okay?" With forced casualness, I walked to the trashcan against the wall and dropped my used towel into the bin and faced her. "What do you want me to do about it?"

"I'm not into women," she said.

I blinked. I hadn't expected that. "Okay…" I waited for something more. Seconds crawled by and I grew more uneasy. I watched her with careful consideration. Her hair was pulled back, revealing her long slender neck. Her skin appeared tighter and it was practically translucent. Despite the fact that it looked like she'd tried to hide it with makeup, dark circles were visible in deep creases below her eyes.

"I can't stop it," she said, taking a step forward. I tensed, taking a step to the side, keeping the door in my sights. "I'm so fucking hungry and you,"—she cut herself off as she gritted her teeth and put a perfectly manicured hand to her temple, pressing down. There was something off with her hand. Her nails. I looked closer. They weren't perfectly manicured as I originally thought. The nails were longer, sharper. Like they'd been filed into razor tipped points.

"You came in and destroyed everything with Maverick. He won't even fucking talk to me anymore. We were going to date. We were going to get married and he was going to realize how perfect I was. But then you came here and,"—she broke off again, shaking her head—"you *ruined* everything."

Her whole body trembled as she seemed to struggle with herself. I moved along the wall, keeping the exit in my peripheral vision even as I reached down, ever so discreetly and unlatched one of my daggers from under my skirt. The loose strap on my arm pulled tight and I cursed.

"Maybe if I kill you, the voice will go away," I heard Rachel whisper to herself. "It didn't start until you came here. That's it, it wants you gone. I'll kill you and it'll be over. It can all stop."

"Rachel." I put my empty hand out towards her as I edged closer to the door. "I think there's something wrong with you. You need to—"

"No!" she shrieked, the sound sharp and piercing. I

winced as it lanced through the room and a crack formed across one of the mirrors. I stood there and stared at it, slowly turning my head back towards the girl before me. Her eyes were wild, glowing brightly as she opened her mouth and unleashed a demonic growl, her teeth sharpening right before my eyes.

"Holy shit," I whispered. "It's you."

FORTY-ONE

MAVERICK

"Find anything?" Torin's question echoed in my ear through the phone as I strode down the hallway. Other than the gymnasium, the rest of the school was a ghost town.

"Not a damn thing," I cursed. "Maybe we fucked up. Maybe it's not—" At that moment, my phone beeped. I looked down. Barbie. "Hold on, Tor." I switched lines, putting the phone back to my ear. "Hey, did you—"

"Courtyard." The sound of Barbie's pants were loud in my ear. "Now." The line went dead and automatically my phone switched back to Torin's call.

"What—"

"Courtyard," I snapped. "Barbie's in trouble."

I hung up and took off, my feet pounding against the floor as I headed through the hallways, cutting across the cafeteria. Through the glass wall of windows, I saw a flash of pink and then gold. Two girls. I frowned, turning and hitting the double doors leading outside. As soon as my feet slapped concrete, a loud shriek echoed up the walls of the outdoor courtyard. I watched as Barbie dodged the girl's attack.

My mouth popped open. "Rachel?" But it wasn't Rachel. Her face had changed. Her eyes were wild— glowing as if a golden light was pouring out of her. She slashed at Barbie with nails sharper than needles.

Panting and bleeding, Barbie jumped away and brought her dagger down, slicing across Rachel's wrist. Blood sprayed the ground and Rachel howled in pain— the sound deeper than anything I'd ever heard from her, rumbling like an injured animal.

"Maverick!" Barbie yelled. "It's her. She's the demon."

The creature that had once been Rachel whirled on me. "Maverick?" Her voice calmed, settled—sounding more human and less … something else. "Maverick, you came for me?"

"What?" I stared in shock as Barbie launched herself onto Rachel's back and took her down to the ground, her legs kicking at the back of the other girl's knees. Within seconds though, Rachel roared and lifted up with more strength than she should've had and flung her back. I watched as Barbie sailed through the air, her back slamming into one of the concrete pillars circling the small outdoor alcove. She fell, hitting the dirt with a pained grunt.

I darted off the sidewalk and down into the main part of the courtyard, withdrawing my gun as I went. Rachel's gaze fell on me and she smiled. "Maverick you came for me," she cried, lifting her arms. I leveled the barrel of my gun on her, stopping in my tracks.

Behind me, the glass doors to the courtyard shattered as Torin shot through them. His gaze fell on Barbie's body and then trailed to where I stood, aiming at Rachel's chest. With a snarl, he launched across the remainder of the space, slamming into Rachel. I lowered my gun and stared in shock. His whole face was changed. Darkened. The skin pulled tight. His eyes were filled with a raw fury I'd never seen in him before. He moved with the speed and grace of something inhuman.

"Maverick!" he yelled. "Barbie."

I jerked, realizing that I'd been stunned into a frozen state like a fucking idiot. I cursed and dove for Barbie while Torin fought the creature.

"Barbie." I turned her over, frowning as my hands came away wet with blood. Red dripped down the side of her forehead, over her temple and eyebrow only to curve back into her hairline. "Barbie, can you hear me?" I shook her lightly. No response. I peeled one eye open and then the other. Her pupils responded at least. I hunched over her form as something went flying over my head. When I was sure we were clear, I lifted up and gaped. It had been Torin. He hit the ground and rolled, popping back to his feet with a snarl.

I had known what he was when he'd told me, but seeing it in person was different than simply hearing about it. His eyes were red, twin points of red hot rage. His muscles were drawn taut, his entire body was bigger —lethal. I turned my head as a responding deep feminine scream sounded.

"Is she okay?" Torin barked.

"She's out," I called back, leveraging her into my arms.

"Get her the fuck out of here," Torin snapped.

"Can you handle this on your own?" I asked.

"Go!"

I booked it, my feet crunching under broken glass as I hefted Barbie's body in my grip. But nothing was as simple as all that. Rachel's head turned, she spotted me, and let loose an unholy cry that would haunt me until my dying days. I didn't have a second—not even a millisecond before she was on me. Her long nails ripped Barbie from my grip and tossed her to the ground. Torin's shout was at the back of my mind. Her hand latched onto my arm as I reached back.

"You're mine!" she screamed, spittle flying in my face as her golden eyes leveled on me with furious anger. "Not hers! I want your heart."

Her other hand pulled back, nails sharpening together—elongating. Somehow, in the moments before she struck, the pieces of the puzzling murders all came together. All of the victims hearts had been ripped out and she was planning on taking mine as well.

"Not. Fucking. Likely. Bitch." My eyes settled over Rachel's shoulder as a familiar blonde head appeared— blood matted the golden strands to the side of her face as she withdrew one of her remaining daggers. The creature before me didn't even seem to hear.

"Don't—" I couldn't stop her. Barbie wasn't listening. She attacked, her arms threading over Rachel's shoulders as she jerked the other girl back. One hand in her hair, the other gripping her dagger. Barbie yanked Rachel's head back and pressed her blade to her throat.

Metal swiped across my vision. Blood spurted against my face. Rachel's necklace crashed to the ground. A roar erupted. I couldn't tell whose it was—Torin's, Rachel's, Barbie's, or something else.

The gem that had been attached to the necklace hit the ground at my feet. Rachel's gaze darted to it and with a mighty shriek—the sound of someone who had truly lost their fucking mind—she reared up and smashed the heel of her shoe down upon the thing.

A white light blinded me, washing the whole scene in an illuminating glow that was there and then gone. In the span of a few heartbeats, Rachel's body crashed to the ground at my feet, and behind her, Barbie went down as well. I reached for her, trying to stop her downward descent, but it was too late.

Her hands went out to the ground, her ashen face looking up at me as she hit. I dropped to my knees. Pain dulled blue eyes met mine.

"Worst fucking Homecoming ever," she whispered.

It was such an outrageous thing to say that I couldn't help but laugh. I gathered her into my arms as Torin ambled closer, favoring one side of his body. "Homecoming from Hell," I assured her, gently brushing back some of her hair. She didn't respond. Her eyes closed. "Barbie?" No response. "Barbie!" I shook her. "Fuck. No." Torin stopped behind me. I felt the heat of his body, but my whole world zeroed in on the woman in my arms.

FORTY-TWO

BARBIE

I CAME AWAKE SLOWLY, FLOATING ON THE FEELING OF *nothingness. My eyes lifted and almost immediately, I knew it wasn't the real world. Clouds drifted past my head, white and fluffy. That wasn't the abnormal part. It was the deep red sky beyond—like burned wine had been spilled across the vast expanse —that told me this wasn't reality.*

"You're an interesting one, I'll give you that." The raspy, sexual voice startled me, jerking me up from the ground as I darted a glance around. My mouth dropped.

If I had ever before wondered what beauty incarnate would look like, this would be it. She *would be it.*

One eye the color of a gorgeous summer sunset, the other as crystal as the ocean waves. Her skin was a roadmap of patches, some brown, some white. And yet, somehow, they seemed to be stitched together to create the most lustrous of figures. Her lips were full, pouty. Her hair, long and untamed. Wild, curled, a tangled web that fell to her waist. It wasn't the kind of beauty that one saw on magazines, it was a beauty that stole the breath from some- one's chest or made them stop and stare. The kind that wouldn't be forgotten years following even if all I'd ever glanced at was an imitation.

But I didn't just get the imitation. I got the full frontal effect as she hopped off of a large boulder and strode right up to me, bending low and offering me a hand. I stared at it.

"Well, are you gonna take it or what?" She tilted her head.

I did the same. "Thanks, but I think I can get up on my own steam," *I said, rolling to the side and moving first up to my knees and then my shaking legs.*

She watched, the smile never leaving her lips. In fact, it widened. "Suit yourself." She rocked back on her heels—or rather her bare feet.

"Where am I?" I demanded.

She looked away, out over the grassy field that we were in. "Nowhere special," she said lightly. "Just your soul."

"My what?" I blinked at her.

With a grin, she turned back to me. "Your soul, silly. You broke my amulet."

"I'm sorry?" What the hell did that have anything to do with where we were? *I shook my head, weakly lifting my hand to my face. Just as I was about to shove a chunk of my hair back, I spotted it—the marking on my palm. "What the fuck is this?" I shoved my hand towards the woman, glaring at her as I showed her the crescent moon and cross combination that was etched into my hand.*

She laughed, a sound like wind chimes rising in the distance. I started and looked around. What the—"That's my mark," *she answered.*

I waited a beat, but she said nothing more. "Okay, how the hell do I get rid of it?" She laughed again. "You're starting to piss me off. I'd suggest you stop fucking laughing."

Her eyes flashed, the gold one dilating as she leaned forward. "You're different from the other one," she said. "Much more ... brash, I think. There's a core of strength in you. Perhaps you can actually make life a little fun around here."

"What are you talking about?"

The woman flipped around, tossing one heavy mass of curls over her shoulder as she walked away, heading straight back to her boulder. I stared with a mixture of awe and confused irritation as she climbed up on the mossy mound and turned to look at me.

"Alright kiddo, listen up. That mark isn't going away; it's mine and so are you for the foreseeable future." I clenched my fists, but she powered on. "My name's Satrina and that amulet you destroyed was my eternal resting place. My last hurrah, if you will. Whoever possessed my amulet allowed me to see through their eyes, to use their body as my own. Those with less than adequate resistance turned over almost all willpower to me. The last girl was rather..." The woman, Satrina, tapped one delicate nail against her lip. "I don't know how to say this nicely, so I won't." She lowered her finger. "She was weak and as I exert a lot of effort to possess someone, possessing her made me hungry."

"The hearts—" I started. If Rachel had been possessed by this creature, this demon, then she had made her take the victims' hearts. What had she done with—

"The hearts of man are willful and easy to consume," Satrina said, answering my unspoken question.

"Consume. You ate them?" I gaped at her.

She shrugged. "Elizabeth Bathory bathed in the blood of virgins. I eat the hearts of men."

"I'm not going to let you do that," I warned her.

Her smile, when she turned it back on me, was vicious. Beneath her full lips were razor sharp teeth. I blinked. They hadn't been that sharp a moment ago … had they? If she was a demon, perhaps she could change her appearance.

"That is yet to be seen, darling," she said. "As it stands, in breaking my amulet and stabbing yourself with the shard—"

"I didn't stab myself with…" I stopped, trailing off. I had felt a sharp pain in my hand as I'd blacked out. Thinking nothing of it, I'd put both palms up to stop my downward fall. I must have accidentally put one over a broken piece of the amulet.

"You did," Satrina continued. "And as such, you've kind of taken away any opportunity to get rid of me."

"What?" No. That couldn't be right. There had to be a way to get rid of a demon. Exorcism. Something.

"To keep me from possessing something before, all one had to do was remove the amulet. When you shattered my amulet to pieces, I jumped ship and the only available lifeboat was you." She pointed at me with one long nail.

My mind worked through that. Remove the amulet, stop being possessed. "Rachel only wore it at parties," I realized. Even though I hadn't gone to them, that must have been the reason why she was mostly normal at school but had attacked me in the bathroom and then tried to kill Maverick.

Maverick. My head jerked up to the sky as if, instinctively, I knew that was the way out. Was he out there? Had I made it in time? Was he alive? What about Torin?

"Hmmmmm." Satrina's hum jerked my attention back to her. She watched me with big eyes, her lashes fanning across her unwrinkled cheeks. "I think I know exactly what you're feeling, darling…" Her eyes lit up as she licked her lips, a small pink tongue darting out to swipe across the lower one. "And I like it."

"I don't know what you're talking about," I lied.

"Sex," she said simply. I sucked in a breath. "Arousal. Attraction. I'm not just any demon, darling. I'm a succubus. The best of the best. Strongest of the strong. What you desire is not unknown to me."

"I don't desire anything except vengeance," I defended.

"That too." She waved a hand absently through the air and from the air a glass of wine appeared. Putting the rim of the glass to her lips, she drank from it. Once she had downed half of the contents, she released it, letting the glass fall from her grasp. Before it hit the ground, however, it disappeared—as if it had never been there in the first place. My eyes were rooted to the spot where it should have landed for a moment and then she spoke, once again demanding my focus.

"I have nowhere else to go and it appears you're stuck with me. I don't want my human body to die and leave me without any sort of portal to enjoy myself—"

"Portal to enjoy yourself?" I repeated. "What do you mean?"

She huffed, crossing her legs as she folded her arms over her abundant chest. "I am a demon," she reiterated slowly. "Demons are relegated to the lands of Hell. The underworld. Purgatory. Whatever you wish to call it, it's home." She growled, her hands clenching on her arms as she continued. "And because of a stupid little treaty with those white-feathered fuckers from up above, I'm not allowed to travel outside the realm of my home. At least, not in body."

"So … what are you doing here then?"

"I'm a mimicry," she answered. "An impression left behind by my last jaunt on Earth. And for hundreds of years, that amulet has remained safe—passed from person to person. But oh, no, as soon as you show up—it's destroyed." She threw her hands into the air and leveled me with a glare. "So, like it or not, we're going to have to make a deal."

"I don't make deals with demons," I said stiffly.

The world changed. The ground fell out from beneath my feet and I found myself descending down into a long dark pit. It was so fast, I didn't even have a split second to scream. As soon as I realized I was falling, I was already landing. Hard.

I grunted as my back slammed onto hardwood floor. With a fall like that, I should've shattered every single bone in my body, but this wasn't reality. I rolled over onto my side as a door opened in the distance and Satrina came striding in on blood red heels, clicking sharply—the sound piercing my ears like daggers. I struggled to my feet, feeling woozy and off balance as I tried to gather my bearings once more.

This was an ... office? A large mahogany desk spanned several feet in front of me. As I looked out past it through a glimmering window, out over several buildings far beyond, I blinked in confusion. Satrina strode around me and the desk, taking a seat in the plush leather chair and swinging her gaze my way as she waved her nails and a thick pile of papers fell from nowhere, landing right in front of her, a black-feathered pen in her hand.

"Here's the dealio, kiddo," she said sharply. "You need me. I need you."

"I don't need you," I snapped.

She sighed, laying her pen down across the papers and steepling her fingers beneath her chin. "You're in a lot of trouble, Barbara Steele." I started at my full name. "You just don't realize it yet. I'm a demon, but more than that, I am the spirit of a demon. I know a lot. When I go through the spirit channels to get to my portal—previously my amulet, now your body—I pick up information, and I've heard about you."

"What have you heard?" I demanded, narrowing my eyes as I stepped up to the desk. "From who?"

She tsked and shook her head. "That's not how this works,"
she said lightly. "The fact of the matter is, I know you—I know
what you've done. Who you've killed and who you've…" She
trailed off looking to the side. Unintentionally, I followed her gaze,
my mouth falling open at the sight of a wall of mirrors emerging
from the blurry edges of the office.

It was me—or rather, my body. Maverick was covered in
splatters of blood as he tried to wake me. Torin was behind him,
staring down—his eyes glowing red as his hands clenched.
"Come on, Barbie. Wake up. Wake the fuck up!" Maverick
shook me, his face etched in panic. His eyes were wide, darting all
over me, his grip on my arms tightening and loosening as he lost
his cool.

"She can't die," Torin said quietly as he bent next to Maver-
ick. "She can't…" He reached for a lock of my hair. An unnamed
emotion squeezed my chest as he sifted the strand between his
fingers, his head bowed in defeat. "Please…"

"We have to get her to a hospital," Maverick said, lifting me
up in his arms, my body hanging limply—devoid of life.

Torin nodded. "Go, I'll take care of things here." Maverick
didn't even look back.

The image faded, leaving me feeling hollow. "As I was
saying," Satrina started again. "I know a lot. You're in danger.
You've killed vampires and there's a new power among the blood-
sucking crew that won't take too kindly to that. He's got big plans.
So, here's the proposal I'd like to make." I turned to her, giving her
my full attention. "I will act as your protection. If and when—
because let's be honest with each other, it'll happen—I feel that
your life is being threatened, I will possess you. Your weakness will
be my opening. I don't want to be stuck in here completely, so you
will allow for conversation."

"Conversation?" I repeated with a lifted brow. "What are you a teenage girl at a slumber party?"

She shrugged, a grin rising to her lips. "I get bored," she said. "But essentially, the deal is, I protect you, you let me possess you."

"Nothing is ever as simple as that," I replied, shaking my head. "No. I won't just let you possess me whenever you want." I reached out and clamped my hands down on the edges of the desk. Bowing my face forward, I sucked in a breath and spoke. "I want power," I said. "I want the ability to defeat my enemies. I'll take your protection, but it's a no on the possession."

"You can't have something without giving anything in return, Barbie," Satrina said, her smile widening as she reached for the stack of papers, turning them towards her. She plucked the top one off and scribbled a few lines before turning it to me. "I am allowed full possession only in cases of emergencies," she stated, tapping the end of the pen against the paper. "You will keep a channel open —you should anyway since it'll allow you to pick up some of my own abilities—for conversation. At any point, if I feel your soul has weakened, however, you forfeit all of the restrictions I've put on myself." She lifted her eyes to mine, the different colors shining with challenge. "Grow weak and I will take over. Utterly. Completely."

"I won't grow weak," I stated, reading the paper before me.

She gestured to the paper and set her pen down in front of me. "Then sign."

Did I dare? A deal with a demon? Protection. The power to find and kill the one responsible for my family's murder. As much as I hated to admit it, she was right. You didn't get something for nothing.

I slapped the paper down on the desk and plucked up the pen, scribbling my signature across the dotted line before I flung it back in her face. Her hands lifted, fingers snapping and the whole orchestrated room dispersed.

"And so the deed is done," Satrina said. "I hope you know what you're in for, kiddo."

I swallowed and lifted my gaze, meeting hers head on. "Underestimate me," I challenged. "That'll be fun."

She laughed. "I think I'm going to like you."

"I think you're tolerable."

Her laughter dimmed into a wicked grin. "Oh, and just in case it wasn't clear, you'll need sex." She paused, letting the announcement linger on the air. "Soon."

I choked. "What?"

Shrugging lightly, she kept her eyes on me. "I'm a sex demon, what did you expect? My powers will grow within you, but the more you take on, the harder it'll be for you to control. You need to relieve the tension—ergo—sex."

"Fuck me," I muttered.

Satrina's smile was the last thing I saw as she faded from existence, but of course she had to have the last word. "That's the point, darling."

FORTY-THREE

TORIN

NEVER BEFORE HAD I FELT SUCH BLOODLUST. THIS TIME, however, it wasn't due to hunger. No. I wanted retribution. Anger pulsed in my veins as I stalked through the front doors of my home. Katalin lounged in the living room. In the back of my mind, I recognized that seeing her do something so mundane as painting her nails was out of the ordinary. When I entered, she looked up, stopping.

I didn't pause.

I didn't hesitate.

In a flash, I had my hand around her throat and her back pinned against the opposite wall. My fangs were on full display.

"You knew there was a fucking demon in that amulet!" I yelled.

Katalin blinked at me. "Did you defeat it?" She could have been asking if I had passed my last History exam for all the concern she showed.

"It's been dealt with," I growled out, clenching my hand around her neck. Barbie had been rushed to the fucking hospital. The authorities had been called. Rachel likely wouldn't remember a thing when she came to, but I'd used what little mind control capabilities that I had to convince the officers who'd arrived on the scene first that she'd lost her mind. Sweat beaded on my upper lip with the strength I was exerting. I'd already used too much to push my suggestions into the officers' heads. As it was, Rachel would likely be sent to an institution for the criminally insane. The demon had likely ripped through the girl's mental defenses and she'd nearly fucking killed Barbie in the process. I couldn't find it in myself to feel pity.

Mate! My vampire prowled in my mind, a caged panther—hungry and wrathful. I ignored him. Focusing, instead, on my sister.

"I trusted you," I gritted out.

Katalin sighed, reaching up. Her delicate looking fingers closed over my wrist. What started out as a light touch soon became a crushing grip as she pried my hand from her throat. I didn't cry out or flinch even when the bones in my wrist cracked and broke. "Trust is for children, Torin," she said coldly. "You are a pawn. Never forget that."

She dropped my mangled arm and strode around me, picking up her nail polish and disappeared up the stairs. I turned and pressed my spine against the space she had once occupied. Black spots dotted my vision as I slid down the wall.

Tonight, my fears had been realized. Barbie was weak. Maybe not in mind or spirit, but her body was fragile. Breakable. The further down the path of vengeance she went, the lower her chances of survival. I didn't know if I could live with that.

EPILOGUE

BARBIE

Harsh fluorescent lighting and even more aggressive scents intruded before I even realized I was awake. An annoyingly repetitive beeping sound rose in volume and then lowered again a moment before my eyes opened. Turning my cheek, I spotted the source of the noise at my bedside. A small square flat screen on a pole. A heart monitor. Which left me with one crucial piece of knowledge, at least. I was in a hospital. I groaned lightly.

"Oh my goodness, Jon!" Beth's cry made me flinch. The noise was too much. "She's awake, come quick!"

There was a flurry of movement and then Beth was standing over me, a tissue clutched in her hand, tears in her eyes. A moment later, Jon was at her side, his arm going around her waist. "Oh honey." Beth sniffed, reaching for my hand and squeezing it in one of hers.

I looked down. "How'd I get here?" What was the story the others had fabricated?

"You were attacked," Jon answered as Beth sniffed

again, pressing her tissue to her mouth and nose as if that would keep the sound of her choked crying quiet. It didn't. Without much else to do as tears leaked from the corners of her eyes, I squeezed her hand back, hoping that would make her stop. Again, it didn't, but she seemed to take some comfort in it at least, smiling down at me.

I awkwardly turned my attention to Jon. "What?" I played dumb.

Jon sighed, his free hand coming up as if he wanted to touch me. He hesitated, unsure, before dropping it back to his side. "One of your classmates attacked you at the dance," he said. "Torin and Maverick found you. The girl's been taken into custody. Apparently, she's claiming she doesn't remember any of it. They suspect she's behind the murders, but um..." He paused, looking away.

Beth picked up where he had left off. "She's been diagnosed with some sort of personality disorder," she said. "She claimed that there was a voice in her head telling her to do bad things. The only attack she doesn't completely remember seems to be the one on you."

"Oh." *A voice in her head?* I thought. *There probably had been if she was possessed.* "Where are Mav and Torin?" I looked at both of them.

They exchanged a look. "Torin stayed back to deal with the cops, but you'll have to give a statement," Jon said. "He's probably at home right now. Maverick's in the cafeteria grabbing something to eat."

I looked at the bottom of my bed and wiggled my toes. They felt all right. "How long was I out?"

"Just last night," Beth said.

"When can I leave?" I asked. There was that look again. I frowned. "What?"

Beth closed her eyes, her lips straining. "Social services is coming by to interview you. They'd rather you remain at the hospital until they could get someone here," Jon said quietly.

"What?" I gaped at them. "Why?"

"We want to adopt you," Beth blurted.

Shock startled me into silence. I stared at them. They stared at me. Jon was the first one to break the tension. It was the most I'd ever heard him speak before. "Only if you want," he said. "When they heard about what happened, though, they wanted to send someone familiar. Someone you'd feel comfortable with. Terra is going to stop by and have a talk with you about everything that's happened. Think of it as counseling. If you want to see a therapist after this, though, we'd completely understand and we're footing the bill. You don't have to worry about—"

"Why the hell would you want to adopt me?" I said, interrupting him. "I'm almost eighteen. When I hit that, you don't have to take care of me anymore."

Beth released my hand and pulled back, letting her back rest more firmly against her husband. "You're ours, Barbie," she said solemnly. "We worry for you as we worry for our own son. When we got the call that you'd been hurt"—she stopped, sucking in a sharp breath, her lips whitening—"I thought my heart would fall right out of my chest. We can't wait any longer. We don't want to be your foster parents. We want to be your real parents."

No. Panic shot through me. My hands grew slick with sweat. I absently wiped them on the bed covers, clutching the white fabric to keep them from shaking. I only had one family and they were dead. I shook my head, but the words never came. My chest hurt. Being my parents wasn't safe. It wasn't good. And then what did that make Maverick? My brother? Their eyes darted to my heart monitor as the beeping increased.

"Why don't we give you some time to think about it?" Jon suggested gently as he urged Beth back. "There's no need to put so much thought into it right now. We understand it's a lot to take in, especially after last night. We're gonna run down and have lunch with Maverick. You don't have to make a decision right away."

I didn't say anything, but that didn't seem to matter. They both seemed to take that as their cue to leave, quietly slipping out into the hallway and shutting the door behind them. Almost as soon as they were out of sight, I reached down and tugged the electrodes on my skin away, wincing at they ripped out little baby hairs when I finally pried them off.

Flinging the covers to the side, I reached for the IV stand and tenderly felt for the floor with my toes before stepping onto the cold tiles with a sharp breath. I moved slowly in regard for how I looked. Like a wounded patient, like a fragile flower trying to find her way home. Except I had no home. I'd burned mine down, and I'd been the reason my parents were killed. I didn't deserve a second chance.

I had no clue where I was going. All I knew was that

I needed to get outside. I needed to see the sun. Not through glass windows, but with my own eyes. I needed to feel air that wasn't recycled on my skin.

I took an elevator down to the bottom floors, thankful that it seemed my hospital gown wasn't one of those cheap ones that billowed—but remained tightly closed all the way down the back. I didn't feel a breeze at all. It was like wearing a big mumu. No one stopped me as I made my way past several nurse stations and to a garden area. Apparently, this wasn't just a normal hospital, but a high class one. It was probably due to all of the wealthy families that lived in the area. That didn't matter.

I found a path in the garden and took it, wheeling my IV stand along with irritation. I wanted nothing more than to rip it out, but honestly, I felt like my legs might collapse without it. I was panting and out of breath by the time I found a small secluded bench under the shade of a long limbed tree. I sat down, putting my head between my legs and just breathed.

I don't know how long I sat like that, letting air infuse my lungs only to escape and refill them. It helped calm my racing heart. After a while, however, a niggling sensation at the back of my neck alerted me to the arrival of someone else. I lifted my gaze and met a pair of rich fiery brown eyes. Maverick met my gaze and held it.

"I thought you were with your parents," I said quietly, shifting on the cold bench.

"I thought you were supposed to be in your hospital bed," he replied.

I grimaced. "I thought I told you no hospitals."

His gaze narrowed. "When you keep passing the fuck out after fighting supernatural creatures, you forfeit a choice." He turned and sat. I sucked in a breath. He smelled like spring breeze shampoo. Heat skittered down my spine, making my back arch. He shot me a look but didn't say anything and I tried to scoot just a hair's breadth away because whatever was causing the sensation seemed to be directly tied to how close he sat to me.

"You showered?" I asked, that spring breeze scent still clogging my nose. It was all I could fucking smell. I pressed my thighs together and tilted my head to look at him out of the corner of my eyes.

"I went home and picked up some things for you," he said. "Thought I should probably wash the blood off."

I winced. "Yeah…" I swallowed, turning my hand over in my lap. "Probably a good idea." A light marking drew my eyes and I sucked in a breath when I realized what it was—the mark of my new demon friend. I curled my fingers together and crossed my arms over my chest to hide it as I sat up straighter.

"You okay?" he asked.

"What? Yeah, of course, why?" I said a bit too quickly.

He eyed me. "You almost died."

I shrugged. "Wasn't the first time."

He stared at me, his expression enigmatic before he finally looked away, facing forward. "I don't like this," he admitted after a beat.

I sighed. "Yeah, I don't blame you," I said, looking up into the branches of the tree as birds flitted overhead. "And for what it's worth, I'm sorry—"

"I mean I don't like *me* like this," he said, interrupting me. Startled, I returned my attention to his face. Maverick's head bowed forward. His hands clenched in his lap, fists taut and knuckles white. "I hate feeling so fucking weak. I can't do shit to protect you. Torin and you … you're both leagues ahead of me in terms of skill."

I frowned. "Maverick, it's not a competition and you just—"

"No, it's not," he agreed, cutting me off again. "It's more important than a fucking competition. It's life or death, and in this arena, I'm fucked."

"So, you'll train more," I said, already hating myself for saying it. But there was no going back for him. I couldn't erase what he'd learned. With knowledge came a certain responsibility. I fucking hated that I'd done this to him. "You can't expect to be perfect off the bat," I continued anyway. "I wasn't. We all lose and this? This wasn't a loss." We had all managed to get out with our lives. It was a fucking win.

Maverick was quiet for a moment before his head turned my way. Without thought, my gaze fell to his lips. A slow burning heat started in my belly and built, growing outward. Awareness. Need. Desire. My lips twitched. I bit down hard on the lower one. His gaze went to where my teeth sank in.

No! I wanted to scream at him. *Look away. Don't look there, you fucking idiot.*

"Barbie…" I unfolded my arms and shifted uncomfortably as I lifted my gaze to Maverick's face. Why did my name on his lips sound so good?

Because you want it to, a familiar voice taunted. Realization echoed through me. Satrina. The demon. Was she doing this to me? *Oh, no, dear, this isn't me. This is all you,* she said. *But I might have forgotten to mention that having a succubus inside you heightens your emotions a bit. All of your emotions. Lust especially.*

Maverick's head moved closer. I couldn't back away. My body was frozen. My eyes widened. He paused, his gaze running over my face. When he pulled back, his eyes closed with disappointment darkening his face, I should have felt relieved but I didn't. I felt like I was burning alive and he was the only source of water that could save me. My chest rose and fell in quick pants.

"I should let you rest before you go back inside," he said quietly. "You don't need…" He darted a look back at me when my hand found the sleeve of his shirt. My fingers clenched in the fabric. *When the hell had I decided to touch him?* I wondered.

My movements were my own and yet, they weren't. Fingers snagged on the collar of his t-shirt and drew him closer. He didn't resist. *Why the fuck wasn't he resisting?* I cupped the back of his skull and drew his head down. His breath fanned across my lips milliseconds before his mouth was on mine.

I closed my eyes and sank into the kiss with a groan. My tongue rolled out to play with his. Sparks shot through my system, flaming a dark path through my body that lit me up inside. I clenched my hands into fists against him as the weight of one of his heavy palms settled on my waist.

More. I wanted more.

That's it, Satrina said. *Take what you want, dear. Feel him against you. Let him ravish you.*

Madness. Kissing Maverick was pure madness. And in it, I fell. His mouth consumed me, ravaged my mind and destroyed all of my reservations. When he moved his hand up from my waist, strong, sure fingers, gripping my chin and holding tight, a gush of wetness slid between my legs, slicking against my thighs. This really wasn't the time. And this certainly wasn't the fucking place. *What the fuck was I doing?* I demanded of myself. But still, I couldn't stop. It felt too fucking good.

I arched against his chest, my nipples pebbling beneath the fabric of the hospital gown. Air was no longer important. Having Maverick's mouth on mine, though? That was priority number one.

A soft groan broke free of my lips as his jaw tensed. Maverick broke first, pulling back. My eyes opened. His stared at me in shock, his eyebrows raised, his mouth slightly gaped. I licked the taste of him off my lips. "Why would you do that?" he asked roughly.

It took longer than I cared to admit for my senses to return, but when they did, my cheeks heated and I could feel a blush crawling down my neck as well. "I-I..." I shook my head. "I don't ... know."

His eyes narrowed on me suspiciously. "What are you trying to pull?" he demanded, pulling away from me even more.

As if I had any clue, I thought. When I remained

quiet, he stood and took a step back, staring at me as if I were dangerous. Who fucking knew now? Maybe I was.

I didn't reach for him, but still Maverick watched me, and slowly, his brows lowered, and a crease began to form between them. His lips—still wet from my kiss—parted as if he might say something, but then he stopped and shook his head. He took another step back and another and another. I forced myself to let him go, to keep my hands right where they were. To not stand up and go after him. What could I say? What could I tell him? *I'm sorry the fucking sex demon I made a deal with made me do it?*

Made you do it? Satrina's laughter flitted inside my head. *Oh dear, you're going to be one of those humans, aren't you?*

I gritted my teeth. I didn't know what she meant by that, but I couldn't respond.

"This didn't happen," Maverick suddenly announced.

"What?" I blinked up at him, sure I had heard wrong.

"This," he repeated on a growl. "Didn't. Fucking. Happen." With that, he turned on his heel and strode away, his wide broad shoulders tight as he stormed down the path.

Sinking my head into my hands the second he was gone, I cursed myself.

"What the fuck have I done?"

More laughter echoed and if I wasn't sure I would've broken my knuckles on the concrete bench, I would've punched it to at least have something to take my frustrations out on.

Oh, I can tell you something you can use to take away your frustrations, Satrina offered.

"No fucking thank you," I hissed aloud. It was as Maverick had said. Never again. It didn't fucking happen.

I felt the ghostly sensation of a finger trailing up my spine and then a hand delving into my hair. I felt the mental tug from my new demon. It wasn't her presence that bothered me, but the next words she whispered into my ear as if she were a dangerous lover come to impart dark wisdom.

Never say never, dear.

ABOUT THE AUTHOR

Lucinda Dark, also known as Lucy Smoke for her contemporary novels, has a master's degree in English and is a self-proclaimed creative chihuahua. She enjoys feeding her wanderlust, cover addiction, as well as her face, and truly hopes people will stop giving her bath bombs as gifts. Bath's get cold too fast and it's just not as wonderful as the commercials make it out to be when the tub isn't a jacuzzi.

When she's not on a never-ending quest to find the perfect milkshake, she lives and works in the southern United States with her beloved fur-baby, Hiro, and her family and friends.

Want to be kept up to date? Think about joining the author's group or signing up for their newsletter below.

Facebook Group
Newsletter

ALSO BY LUCINDA DARK / LUCY SMOKE

Fantasy Series:

Barbie: The Vampire Hunter Series

Rest in Pieces

Dead Girl Walking (Coming Soon)

Ashes to Ashes (Coming Soon)

Dark Maji Series

Fortune Favors the Cruel

Blessed Be the Wicked

Twisted is the Crown

For King and Corruption (Coming Soon)

Nerys Newblood Series

Daimon

Necrosis

Resurrection (Coming Soon)

Dystopian Series:

Sky Cities Series

Heart of Tartarus

Shadow of Deception

Sword of Damage

Dogs of War (Coming Soon)

Contemporary Series:

Iris Boys Series (completed)

Now or Never

Power & Choice

Leap of Faith

Cross my Heart

The *Break* Series (completed)

Study Break

Tough Break

Spring Break

Break Series Collection

Standalones:

Expressionate

Wildest Dreams

Made in the USA
Columbia, SC
16 May 2021

37505175R00221